CONNIE BRUMMEL CROOK

Connie B. Crook was born near Belleville, Ontario, during the Depression. As a child she had to walk more than a mile no matter the weather to her one-room primary school, and later three miles to her high school. When she grew up she taught English in several secondary schools across the province.

Although Ms. Crook has always loved writing, she didn't get a chance to pursue it until her recent retirement. Now living in Peterborough, Ontario, she spends her time writing, visiting schools, walking, swimming, reading, and babysitting her twin grandsons, who play the part of Daniel King in the popular television series *Road to Avonlea*.

PRAISE FOR FLIGHT
"A gripping fictional treatment of the true-life experiences of one of Canada's foremost families . . ."
— *Roy Bonisteel*

Meyers' Creek

CONNIE BRUMMEL CROOK

*We acknowledge the Canada Council for the Arts and the
Ontario Arts Council for their support of our publishing program.*

A GEMINI BOOK

First published in 1995 by Stoddart Publishing Co. Limited

Published in Canada in 1998 by
Stoddart Kids,
a division of Stoddart Publishing Co. Ltd.
34 Lesmill Road
Toronto, Canada M3B 2T6
Tel (416) 445-3333 Fax (416) 445-5967
Email Customer.Service@ccmailgw.genpub.com

Published in the United States in 1998 by
Stoddart Kids,
a division of Stoddart Publishing Co. Ltd.
180 Varick Street, 9th Floor
New York, New York 14207
Toll free 1-800-805-1083
Email gdsinc@genpub.com

Distributed in Canada by
General Distribution Services
30 Lesmill Road
Toronto, Canada M3B 2T6
Tel (416) 445-3333 Fax (416) 445-5967
Email Customer.Service@ccmailgw.genpub.com

Distributed in the United States by
General Distribution Services
85 River Rock Drive, Suite 202
Buffalo, New York 14207
Toll free 1-800-805-1083
Email gdsinc@genpub.com

Canadian Cataloguing in Publication Data

Crook, Connie Brummel
Meyers' Creek

ISBN: 0-7736-7436-5

1. United Empire loyalists — Juvenile fiction.
I. Title.

PS8555.R6113M4 1995   jC813'.54   C95-93-0887-3
PZ7.C76Me 1995

Cover Design: Bill Douglas/The Bang
Cover Illustration: David Craig
Computer Graphics: Tannice Goddard

Printed and bound in Canada

To my daughter,
Beth Ann,
who is always willing to help
those around her,
and who by her words
and deeds makes this world
a more beautiful place

Contents

ACKNOWLEDGEMENTS

I would like to thank Belleville Public Library for allowing me to read their files, preserved by the library and the Historical Society. Thanks also to Gerald Boyce of Belleville for answering my questions and sending me a Sidney Township map with marked sites of the original Meyers' family lands, based on the Land Registry Office records.

Thanks also to Gavin Watt of King City, Ontario, for answering questions about muskets, pistols, and clothing; Robert Bruce, the O.P.P. officer, who shot a rabid bear at Madoc, for his help in the bear chapters; Joan Lucas, a United Empire Loyalist genealogist, who was a nurse in Peterborough Civic Hospital maternity ward for many years, for her help with the birthing chapters and historical references; and Cynthia Rankin, a teacher with the Peterborough County Board of Education, for preparing a study guide.

A special thanks to my cousins, Thornton and Doris Brummel of Napanee, Ontario, for their research and answers to questions about the Napanee and Kingston areas.

A special appreciation goes to my editor,

Kathryn Dean. Thank you for all your questions, helpful suggestions, and detailed editing. And thanks to Donald G. Bastian, Managing Editor of Stoddart Publishing, and Elsha Leventis for their support and encouragement.

Part One

Into a New Country

One

"I don't see why I can't go, too!" Mary stepped briskly off the back stoop, tossing back her thick auburn hair. She hadn't liked the colour until her father told her it looked like the flowing mane of a great racehorse they'd seen in Montreal. But today she wasn't thinking about her hair. She was thinking about her father's unfairness. He was letting two of her brothers, George and Tobias, go with him to Albany while she had to stay behind to wash dishes and scrub floors.

It was the first of July 1786, and the early morning sun shone fresh on the patch of wild roses that grew by the stoop just outside the back door of the four-room cabin that was now the Meyers' home. Only two hundred feet to the south, the waters of the Bay of Quinte lapped against the pebbly shoreline. Just to the east, a bubbling stream ran into the bay. The family had named it Meyers' Creek. Mary's father planned to build a mill there eventually.

Mary headed towards the southeast corner of the yard, where her brothers were loading the wagon for their trip. "Better get out of the way,

Mary," George said. He flung a bag of oats over the side of the wagon, barely missing her shoulder. "We don't have much time to lose."

"You've got lots of time," she shot back. "Father said you wouldn't be leaving for another hour."

"That may be true, but one thing's for sure — you're not coming with us. This is no pleasure trip. It's a raid! And we don't need any girls slowin' us down."

"It's not that we don't want you, Mary," Tobias said. He was always the diplomat. "It's just too dangerous for you."

Mary was not afraid. She loved adventure and she knew the route to New York State as well as any of them. But there was no point in arguing with her brothers. She must persuade her father to change his mind.

Mary looked at her father emerging from the kitchen doorway. His dark auburn hair had grey streaks in it now, and his majestic military uniform from the days of the American Revolution had been replaced with homespun trousers and an old red shirt that always seemed to have bits of straw sticking out of it. "What do you expect me to wear?" Father had said once when Mary objected to the loss of his military look. "That uniform was appropriate at the time, but not now, with the hay to harvest and more land to clear."

"Hans, I wish you wouldn't go," Mary's mother said. She always addressed her husband by this name given to him by his Dutch ancestors. He had been christened Johannes but had changed his name to John, the English version. "It's almost time for the wheat harvest and it's just plain dangerous going back there," she said.

"I know you have missed our oak cupboard and mahogany staircase, Polly," her husband replied.

"But Hans, what you're planning is a raid," Polly Meyers protested. "After six years of running for your life in the Revolutionary War, do you really want to go back and put yourself in danger?"

"We are not planning a raid," he replied. "We are just going in at night to take what is ours. It's bad enough that those thieves took our farm; they don't have to keep everything else, too."

"Well heaven knows I can't stop you," Mother sighed.

Father stepped around Mary and put a hand on Mother's shoulder. "We'll be fine. We all lived through a war didn't we? . . . There's really nothing now to be worried about. I'm more concerned about that bear here in the woods. Don't let Leonard and Jacob go chasing after it. We'll get it when we come back."

Leonard was almost seventeen now and was sharing the work with his older brothers. He wanted to go to Albany, too, but he took some pride in the fact that he was being left behind to take care of the farm. He would have to manage most of the work with his sisters, since Jacob was only nine years old.

"And you know right well I have to see my parents," Father added. "They haven't seen any of the children since the third year of the war — they may not even know we're still alive."

Mary could hold herself back no longer. "I'm

going, too! You'll need someone to prepare meals on the road."

"You want to cook?" Anna said. "Catharine's the one who should go if they need a cook!" Anna at fourteen was Mary's youngest sister. Catharine was almost eighteen, only a year younger than Mary, and would not enjoy a risky trip like this one. During the war, she had almost died of bronchial pneumonia. She still had bouts of bronchitis.

Father stared at Mary. "No, you can't go. There are rumours that Loyalists are still being tarred and feathered."

"I know that, but the boys are going." Mary stared defiantly at her father. "Is it just because I'm a girl that you're being so mean?"

"Mary, you are going to stay and help your mother."

Mary bit her lip and looked down so quickly her mob cap fell to the ground and her thick hair tumbled down over her shoulders. It wasn't fair. After all, Mother had married at nineteen. In fact, quite a few girls married much younger.

"C'mon! We're ready to go!" George yelled. "Tobias and John have gone over all the supplies and we're all set!" George, his face almost as red as his hair, leaped up on to the wagon and grabbed the horses' reins. George's friend, John Bleecker, jumped over the other side.

"Just wait a minute, George," Tobias said, running up to the wagon. "We forgot the extra food the women packed!" He laughed and shook his deep brown hair till it shimmered. He was a year younger than George and John, who were almost twenty-one, but he was calmer than either of them and always remembered the details.

"Yeah, George. Wait up. I just remembered I have to get another bag of oats, too." John jumped back down and headed for the feed shed at the back of the house. John was Dutch, too, a stocky fellow, a little under six feet, not like Tobias and George, who were almost six-feet-four now like their father. But no one could beat John in a wrestling match. He had changed a lot since the day he was tarred and feathered by a mob at Wallkill in New York State. George had found him at his aunt and uncle's home, the skin on all but his face and neck burnt red by the hot tar. The scars had dimmed with time.

"Don't feel so bad, Mary," John said as he brushed past her. "It might not be as much fun as you think — cooking for the lot of us."

"Who says I'd just be cooking? I can do other things, too, like driving the team. I'm a skilled waggoner. And I can shoot a musket straighter than any of you! You know that, too, George. I beat you last year at the turkey shoot in King's Town."

"I just let you win because you were the only girl in the competition."

"Like heck, you did!"

"You are not going, Mary. And that's final," her father said.

Mary turned and started for the back door of the house, but she ran straight into John, who was coming from the storage shed with the bag of oats over his right shoulder. To her surprise, he put his free arm around her shoulders. "I am sorry you can't come," he whispered. Mary gazed up into his deep blue eyes. She had never met anyone as handsome as John.

Mary pushed away and darted to the door. She had always liked John and talked with him more than her brothers. In fact, sometimes when George had refused to let her do things with them, John had persuaded George to let her tag along. John could make any trip fun with his joking and laughing. But even his kind words did not soothe her this time. It was so humiliating to be ordered around by her father — and right in front of John.

Mary ran through the doorway into the kitchen-sitting room. It was a large room, almost twenty-five feet by twenty, and ran the full length of the house from north to south. A huge fieldstone fireplace built in the west wall heated the whole cabin, including the three small bedrooms just off the kitchen on the east side.

She barely missed bumping into her sister Catharine, who was coming to the back door carrying a huge basket covered with a large red-checked cloth. Catharine's long, blonde, wavy hair curled out from under her cap and streamed down her back. Her freshly ironed short-gown hung loosely over the waist of her stiff petticoat and matched her large bright-blue eyes.

"I heard what Father said, Mary," Catharine said. "I'm sorry. I know how much you were counting on this trip."

Mary grinned. "Oh, I'm still going, Catharine.

But I'll need your help. Please get them all to come in here, so I can slip outside and get into the wagon."

"Sneak into the wagon? That won't help. When Father finds you, he'll just bring you back."

"No, I'll hide under the canvas till they're too far from home to turn around."

Mary didn't wait for a reply. She hurried into the boys' bedroom and pulled Leonard's baggy breeches and shirt off the bedpost. She grabbed his straw hat from a nail on the wall, then dashed through the adjacent doorway into the girls' room. She threw off her heavy petticoats and stepped into her brother's light homespun knee breeches and full linen shirt. It would be easier to travel in boy's clothes. And they might be good for a camouflage.

She reached under her bed, an army cot the British authorities had provided. There she grabbed a small cloth bag and stuffed inside two dark-striped petticoats and a short-gown, along with a couple of white shifts and a change of stockings.

Then she peeked out the door into the kitchen and, seeing the way clear, dashed across the room and out the back door. She quickly turned left, so she could sneak around the the bedroom side of the house, which was farthest from the kitchen and the front yard, where George and the rest of the family were now waiting to leave. It all depended on whether Catharine could convince the men to come in to eat.

At that moment, Catharine was putting the plan into action. Smiling pleasantly at John, who was at the front door now, chatting with Mother and Father, she handed him the food basket and said, "There's more. Why don't you come inside for a bite before you go?"

John smiled back at Catharine and took the basket. His blue eyes softened and lingered on her. "I'd like that," he said. Then he lifted the cloth. "Hmmm. Does this smell good!"

"C'mon, John," George yelled from the wagon seat, facing out towards the trail that led east along the north shore of Lake Ontario. On his left, just beyond the large garden, a field of green wheat rippled gently in the morning breeze.

John rolled his eyes, stepped over to the wagon, and set the food basket down.

Catharine glanced uneasily at George and then at John. "Did you know that George is planning a side trip to New York to get his dog, Boots? I guess that's why he can't wait." Boots was the dog they had been forced to leave behind when they had been shipped out of New York Harbour, headed for Canada. And Curly, their old dog, had died a year ago.

"Well, he's had to wait three years now, so I can't see that another few minutes is going to hurt. . . . Hey, George, come in for a cup of tea before we leave."

Mary stood peering around the northeast corner of the house, waiting impatiently for her chance to make a run for the wagon. Why did George have to be so stubborn?

"Where's Mary?" Tobias asked.

"I guess she's gone inside," Catharine said. "You

know she's had her heart set on going back to see Grandma and Grandpa Waltermyer. I wish Father would let her go."

"No point in arguing with him," Tobias said. "You know what he's like when he's made up his mind!"

"Did I hear something about a fresh pot of tea brewing?" Father beamed as he strode towards John and Catharine.

"Yes, I just set it to steep," Catharine said.

"C'mon, boys. Let's have a bite before we go on the trail."

George finally came down from his perch and joined the rest of the family crowding their way into the kitchen.

When the last member of her family had disappeared into the house, Mary sprinted lightly across the open space to the wagon. She jumped on to the back of the load and dove underneath the canvas. Quickly she found a hiding place between a bag of oats and a barrel of food supplies. It wasn't too bad so far, though it might get too warm later. One thing was certain — the canvas made an excellent camouflage. From outside, she probably looked like just another bag of grain.

The July sun sparkled on the canvas the way it had three years ago when the family had come to Canada from New York City to join Father. John W. Meyers — as her father was called by people outside the family — had joined the British side of the American Revolution in 1777 and had become one of the most famous Loyalist couriers. He had spent the entire war running messages from New York City to Quebec through the woods of upstate New York.

Then the British had lost, and Loyalists were forced off their land in the new United States. Like many others who were unwanted in their homeland, the Meyers family had received land in Canada from the British authorities. Her father had come north first while in service for the British, the rest of the family later. Mary still remembered how impressive her father had looked waiting for them by the dock in full military uniform.

Footsteps interrupted her thoughts.

"We'd better put the rest of the food in here," Father said. Mary held her breath. Fortunately, her father lifted the canvas only a crack, letting in a thin shaft of sunlight. He wedged the food basket in and tied the canvas down again. Mary gave a sigh of relief. Then she heard Father walk around the wagon and jump up beside George on the front bench.

"Where's Mary?" John's voice came from just behind George.

"Probably sulking in the house," George said gleefully. "Goodbye, Mother! Bye, Catharine!" the men called out as the horses began to move.

"Bye, Mary," John shouted out louder than the others.

Well, they hadn't missed her much, Mary thought bitterly. They hadn't even waited to say goodbye to her. Only John had asked where she was. Wouldn't they be surprised when she came out from under the canvas dressed in Leonard's breeches and baggy shirt!

Two

George slapped the reins on the horses' backs and started them into a trot. Then he clicked his tongue to coax them along.

It would be a long trip to King's Town, where Lake Ontario met the St. Lawrence River. Once they got there, Father would apply to the government for land they still owed him. None of the land he'd been given was fertile enough to grow adequate crops, so Father had staked out some good land and built their house on it. But they didn't own it. They were just squatters.

George drove the horses along the trail that clung to the bay. The shoreline was covered with reeds, but as the way became marshy, the trail veered north into the wooded area, thick with maple, poplar, spruce, and pine. Through the trees, the bright light from the sun and glistening water of the bay dappled the occupants of the wagon.

"Haw!" George pulled the horses' reins tightly to the left. "This trail sure is miserable in places." The wagon had barely missed a stump that was too large to straddle.

"It's a fine trail, son. I've seen far worse in my day. At least the large trees have been cleared. And look up ahead — another clearing just like our meadow. Who could ask for more?"

"Well, it's not like around Albany," Tobias said.

Father laughed. "Someday, it will be."

Knowing that the men would all be looking ahead, Mary lifted the canvas a crack and peered out at the receding trail. She knew the route, for she had listened carefully when Father had gone over his plans at mealtimes.

They would travel east along the shore of the Bay of Quinte, past the mouth of the Moira River, where Captain George Singleton had set up a trading post two years before, then on to Deseronto, and north along the Napanee River to Napanee. A millwright named Robert Clark was building a new mill there, using government supplies and local Loyalist labour. Farmers like her father were overjoyed that a mill was finally being built this close, since the drive to the King's Town Mill took a full three days. The Napanee mill was near completion, and they would leave the wheat, two bags left over from the spring seeding, to be ground into flour. That was one reason they hadn't gone by bateau straight along Lake Ontario. Besides, the land route was safer. They all knew how high those waves could be even if they paddled close to shore.

After Napanee, they would go south past Hay Bay — then along the shore of Lake Ontario to King's Town, where they would leave their horses and wagon with John's stepfather, William MacKenzie. From there, they would cross by bateau to Oswego in the United States, then head on foot to Albany, where they would rent a team and wagon that would take them to their old farm at Cooeyman's Landing.

Mary's mind began to wander as she listened to the dull chucking of the wagon wheels.

Sometimes when work on the farm got too tedious, Mary would dream about living back in King's Town and having John Bleecker coming to call on her. He certainly had an exciting life. After he had finished working with the crews that surveyed the land west of King's Town, he had taken his wages and set up his own trading post, where he did business with the Mississaugas and other travellers. He also traded with a few settlers across the bay. "John's going to be a prosperous business man just like his father was," George said — always loyal to his best friend.

There was some truth in what George said, however. John's father had run the general store in Albany until that fateful day when the rebels had ordered his store closed. Mr. Bleecker was a Loyalist, so he was a natural target. When the rebels accused him of spying for the British, however, his heart — overworked and weak — had given out completely, and he had died on the spot, on the front steps of his store. No longer feeling safe in Albany, Mrs. Bleecker moved with the children to New York City, where she met and married Mr. MacKenzie, a rough waggoner, who made John work very hard in his business. Now the whole family but John lived in King's Town.

Mary laid her head back on a bag of oats and

tried to forget the horrible scene of Mr. Bleecker's death. Mother had taken all the children into Albany that day to make some trades with Mr. Bleecker — so Mary had seen the whole ugly incident. She brushed away her sad thoughts and congratulated herself on her clever plan. Who said girls had to stay at home and bake pies?

* * * *

Mary was jolted out of her sleep as she hit a sack of oats. The wagon was jerking from side to side, throwing her about, too.

"Whoa," George yelled.

Mary was thrown forward against the sharp iron rim of a wooden bucket.

"Ouch!" Mary yelped, the sound echoing loudly in her ears. Mary hoped they hadn't heard her. Clinging to a floor board, she peeked out from under the canvas. Behind the wagon was a forest, thick with maple, birch, spruce, and pine. On the other side of the trail, a few cedars and willows overhung the shore of a lake.

"Whoa! Whoa!" George shouted again as he pulled on the reins.

The horses were running off the trail. Heavy branches whipped the sides of the wagon. Mary threw back the canvas and sat up to get a better look at what was going on. Tobias and John were hanging on to the opposite side of the wagon and looking back along the trail. Tobias, usually so quiet and reassuring to Mary, looked as though he had seen a ghost.

Three

Mary ducked back under the canvas, but it was too late. The stuffy air became clear and the sun shone hard and bright on her head as her father peeled away the canvas.

"What on earth? Mary! How did you get here?" Father looked too surprised to be angry.

Mary sat up slowly and tucked a stray piece of hair inside Leonard's cap.

"Well, account for yourself, young lady." Anger had replaced the surprise in Father's voice.

"I have to see Grandma and our old home and all the other special places," Mary said. "And I can handle the horses and shoot as well as any of the boys."

"Mary, that's not the point. We can't take you on this trip." His face was red with anger. "We'll drop you at Adolphustown." That was a small settlement on the north shore of Lake Ontario where Peter Van Alstine, a friend of Father's, had led a group of Loyalists in 1784.

Mary watched Father walk back to the front of the wagon in long strides.

Tobias smiled. "Well, since you're here, Mary, you might as well come up with us."

Mary crawled unsteadily towards Tobias and John, who were sitting cross-legged on canvas just behind Father and George, who were seated on the front bench. She plumped herself down on the hard wagon floor between them.

John turned towards her with a smirk. "You sure do look fetchin' in those clothes, Mary!"

"What if I do? This outfit is a whole lot better than a dress. It would make work easier if women could wear breeches." Last year when Father had tried to farm that barren land near King's Town, she had actually seen neighbouring women hoeing the land with their petticoats trailing in the dirt. At times like that, she realized how lucky the Meyers girls were to have grown brothers to help Father with the hard farm labour. Of course, there would be less of a problem if women were allowed to wear men's clothes.

"You may be right, Mary," John said.

Four hours later, the heat of the day was subsiding. Waves slapped against the shoreline and crickets chirped in a sleepy rhythm.

Three sharp hoots broke through the lulling sounds. Branches seemed to snap beneath the weight of some heavy creature — or creatures — moving about just beyond the edge of the trail.

"That's just an owl, Mary," Tobias said. "You don't need to be afraid of an old owl."

"Well, you never know," John said as he reached around and nudged Tobias behind Mary. "It might be the Mohawks from Deseronto getting ready to tomahawk us. They may be lying in wait . . . "

"Yeah," Tobias said, "they've heard all about Mother's raspberry pies and fruit cake and they're gonna raid our wagon and leave us to starve — or worse — eat frogs all the way to Albany."

Mary knew they were just trying to frighten her. But if she had any hope of persuading her father to change his mind, she couldn't show the tiniest trace of fear. "Well, I'm certainly not afraid to travel in these woods," she said, checking for John's reaction out of the corner of her eye.

John turned and smiled at her. "I travelled by canoe all the time when I was surveying the government lots from King's Town to the bay. I liked that better than travelling by land."

"So you canoed along Lake Ontario? That can be quite dangerous, can't it?"

"Yup. I used to paddle from King's Town to Adolphustown. The lake was great when it was calm, but when there were waves, it was lots of fun — cutting them."

"You sure have had some exciting times, John. Not like us. It's been a steady grind — farming! Who would have thought we'd live on three farms the first three years in Canada — at Missisquoi, King's Town, and now the meadow near the Trent River."

"I still can't understand whatever possessed the government to make you move from Missisquoi Bay to King's Town."

"That was a good farm at Missisquoi Bay," Mary said. "And we had lots of neighbours, too — all the soldiers from Father's company."

"But we were right next to the border," Tobias

said, "and the American farmers on the other side petitioned their government to get Father moved inland. They were afraid of him."

"Governor Haldimand should have stood his ground and defended your father's right to stay there," John replied. "After all, your father risked his neck for Haldimand all through the war, carrying his messages to New York City."

"Yes, that's true," Mary said. "It's hard to understand why he was so easily persuaded. But Father says that other officers were moved, too. It's almost as though Haldimand was trying to build up an English settlement farther inland and away from the French seigneuries."

"But he claims it was the complaints from the Americans," Tobias said. "And maybe it was. The war's over and Governor Haldimand wants to live in peace. He's an old man now."

"How daft can the Americans be to start all that fuss with no cause?" John asked.

"Oh, they had a crazy notion about Father," Tobias said with a smile. "They thought he had supernatural powers to escape being caught when he was spying during the war. At least that's the rumour Father heard from the old neighbours who gave him shelter on his trips."

John laughed. "Well, I think the real reason was they were afraid of him and his sons — afraid he'd do just what he's doing now — plan a raid over the border."

"Why, John! However would they get an idea like that?" Mary asked. "He's never taken anything but what's his. And now, we're going back only for our own things. I plan to look in my bedroom and see if my old bear is there."

"A toy bear!" John laughed. "I can't believe you would want to look for that old thing. Even Jacob's too old for a toy bear."

"But it was no ordinary bear! Mother made it from an old bearskin stuffed with wood wool. It seemed like a real bear cub. It was big enough — a good three feet long and really fat. We all loved it."

The moonlight showed a clearing down by the Napanee River. Thick patches of cedar loomed on this side and a huge willow tree and several smaller ones hung over the other bank. George turned the horses in that direction. "Father says we'll camp here for the night," he called back.

About twenty minutes later, Mary was bending over a small fire in the clearing, stirring dried venison and baked beans in an open iron-spider frying pan. She'd filled a kettle full of water for tea, but it was still not boiling. The horses, tied about twenty-five feet away, switched their tails at the mosquitoes and munched at the grass.

Mary's brothers and John had gone for a swim, but Father was sitting on the other side of the fire, his long legs stretched out in front of him.

Any moment now Father would start his interrogation. Mary looked down at the ground to avoid his eyes and spotted two arrowheads. Maybe she could distract him with them. "Oh, look," she said, "these must be from the Mohawks. Are we near Deseronto?"

"Yes. And we're not far from Napanee. But let me see them. They don't look like Mohawk arrowheads." He looked closely at the chipped stone. "They're from the Mississaugas, a Huron tribe. The British have purchased all this land from them. In fact, the British now own land as far back from shore as a man can walk in a day."

Mary started to giggle.

"What's so funny?" Father asked.

"I can just imagine George testing how far he owned. He'd be running all the way."

Father smiled — and Mary breathed a sigh of relief. He seemed to have forgotten that she wasn't supposed to be there.

Father ran his fingers through his red hair. His sunburned face looked darker than usual in the light of the fire, and the lines around his mouth looked deeper in the shadows cast by the flames.

"We should take you back," Father said, "but I hate the delay. I've been thinking on it and I've decided to drop you off at King's Town with John's sister Lucy and her mother. We'll pick you up on the way home.

"But, Father — "

"No 'buts' about it, young lady. This trip's a risky business, and I don't want you in danger. Things haven't settled down yet for Loyalists in the States. Land is still being taken away and there's talk of tarring and feathering."

Father stared into the burning fire, and Mary knew he was remembering his friends back at Albany, especially John's dead father.

"But I wanted to see Grandma," Mary said.

Father seemed to hesitate. "It's just too risky. And you could endanger our whole mission." He reached over and stoked the fire.

Mary splashed spoonfuls of beans and dried venison on a plate and slapped it down beside her father. Her cheeks were red with fury. How could he take the boys so blithely into the danger but consider her a problem? Then she turned back to the fire and served herself. They ate in silence.

In a few minutes, George came walking briskly into the light, swinging his wet towel. Tobias and John were close behind.

"Stop that, George. You're getting water all over me!" Mary screamed.

George smiled and gave his wet towel a hard squeeeze right over Mary's head.

"Eek!" Mary jumped up, water dripping down her face. She clenched her fist and gave George a hard punch in the side, but he just laughed and jumped away.

"How much longer are we going to have to put up with her?" George asked, but there was a twinkle in his eye.

"Till King's Town," Father said.

"King's Town! I thought we were dropping her at Adolphustown. Now it's King's Town. Seems like next thing, it'll be Oswego and after that Albany."

"Mind your own business, George!" Mary snapped. She grabbed the towel he'd thrown on the ground and slapped the dripping thing over his head.

"My head's wet already," he laughed. "You can't do me any harm."

"Is that grub ready, Mary?" Tobias asked, coming up beside her.

"Yes. Now sit right down. I'll serve you the best meal ever." Mary began filling three tin plates.

The boys sat down cross-legged on the ground and waited to be served. "She's acting like Mother or Catharine — serving us like this . . . trying to get on the right side of Father," George said with a smirk.

"Oh, c'mon George," Tobias laughed. Then he turned to John. "Who's managing your trading post while you're away?"

"I closed it up. We'll be back in a fortnight."

"It'll be longer than that, John," Father said.

"Aren't you afraid your customers will get mighty thirsty while you're gone?" George laughed, looking knowingly at his friend.

John stared straight into the fire and frowned slightly. "There aren't many furs to trade just now. It's a good time to leave."

"What furs do you get?" Geeorge asked.

"Well the marshes on both sides of the Bay of Quinte are full of muskrat and some beaver, too. I do a bit of trapping, but the Mississaugas supply me with most of my furs — beaver, fox, muskrat . . ."

"Where do you sell your furs, John?" Mary interrupted.

"Oh, I take them to Montreal sometimes. But more often to my stepfather in King's Town. He takes them to Oswego, and they sell as far away as Albany."

"How much do you make for — a — well a muskrat fur?" Mary asked.

John stared at Mary and a slow smile spread across his face. "Well, now . . . it all depends on who's buying."

"Mary, you don't ask a man such questions," interrupted Father, who had been watching John closely.

"For you, Mary, the price would be venison stew and that strawberry pie you and Catharine sent me in the spring."

"How many muskrats would I need to make a fur cape?"

"Oh, I'm not the expert on that. They make the capes in Albany or Montreal. I just collect the furs."

"John, would you like to eat strawberry pie all winter long, made from the best wild strawberry preserves in the entire Bay of Quinte area?"

"I sure would, Mary," John said, smiling. "It's a deal. I could get the best tanner in Montreal . . . "

"Wait a minute, Mary. What about us? Whose preserves do you think you're trading?"

Mary gave George a sharp poke with her elbow and winked at John. "Think how warm I'll be this winter!"

"Mary!" Father said. Mary looked up, then lowered her eyes. She knew Father didn't like the talk of her trading for a coat whether she was serious or not.

"Tell me, John, do you have any advice about trapping?" Tobias said. "I'd like to try a little myself."

As John turned to her brother, Mary strolled away from the campfire. Their voices became fainter and fainter as she walked the couple of hundred feet to the water's edge.

Four

Mary really needed to cool off, and now was the perfect time. She took off Leonard's heavy twill pants and loose shirt and threw them on the ground. Her soft moccasins landed on top of the pile. Then she walked a couple of steps in her white shift, which hung straight and loose from the shoulders to the knees. In her rush, she had left it on under Leonard's clothes.

Mary hoped Father had not noticed her leave. She didn't want him down here telling her it was too dangerous to swim alone. After all, she was within calling distance.

She stepped slowly into the water. It wasn't even cold. Soft waves washed over her bare feet and legs, but she could feel small, sharp stones on the bottom, so she hurried out a little farther. She slipped into the water and leaned backwards to wet her long, thick hair. Finally, feeling a bit cooler, she started to swim out. She took long strokes and gained more energy as she moved ahead. Although she was not far from shore, she knew that the water was deep because it held her without difficulty.

The moon shone before her on the low, rippling waves. She knew not to go too far in these unknown depths. With her head in the water, she stretched out and again took long, firm strokes, this time back to shore. The water felt so smooth against her body that she turned over to float. Her shift billowed up around her on the surface of the water.

It seemed that only minutes had passed when she finally turned over — but to her surprise, she saw that she had drifted a long way. The river was narrower here and the current swifter. Mary swam towards two large rocks that jutted out along the shoreline. When she finally reached ground, a stone cut into her right foot. The whole riverbank was covered with small, sharp stones. Her linen shift clung to her breasts, slender waist, and hips as she emerged from the water, and even though it had been a hot day, she started to shiver.

There was grass just steps away, which would have been easier to walk on, but she stayed near the shoreline. She didn't want to cut through the trees and be surprised by a bear. She saw a clump of cedars about thirty feet to the north that she had not noticed as she'd drifted down the river. Obviously she had come farther than she thought. Suddenly she stepped on an even sharper stone.

"Owww!" she yelled. Then she gasped with fright, for branches were cracking and moving just ahead. Could bears swim? Should she jump into the water? She stood frozen, unable to move or even scream. Then the shadowy figure of a man came out from under the branches, still half hidden by the cedars.

Mary turned and rushed over the stones, not even feeling them cutting into her feet. She plunged into the water and flung herself headlong into the current, slashing at the water helplessly with her arms as she tried to swim upstream.

As she lifted her head for a gulp of air, she glanced back to see if the man was still there. At that moment, a streak of moonlight fell across blonde-white hair, and Mary began to laugh with relief as she recognized John waving to her. She waved and headed back to shore.

As she walked out of the water and stepped carefully onto the sharp-stoned shore, she saw that he was staring at her, a huge smile spreading across his face. In an instant Mary realized what a sight she must be. Her white cotton shift, clinging to her, barely covered her knees. She turned and raced back to the water in embarrassment and plunged below the surface.

"I knew you'd gone for a swim, but I didn't know you were headed back to Deseronto," John said. "Do you realize you're almost half a mile from camp?"

Mary winced as her foot hit another rock. She was winded and did not want to go back to the deep water again. Still, she could hardly walk out in front of John in only her undershift.

John pulled off his long cotton shirt. "Come on out, Mary. You can wrap my shirt around you. It'll keep you warm."

"Maybe I could swim as soon as I get my breath."

"It's a lot harder to swim upstream."

Mary nodded and headed towards John. Her teeth were chattering, and she was starting to shake as she reached him. Suddenly she felt tired. But as John wrapped his thick cotton shirt around her shoulders, Mary felt a resurgence of warmth and energy. The shirt was wide and went around her slim body almost twice, for John was stockily built. He was only an inch under six feet and even Mary, the tallest of the Meyers girls, had to look up at him from her height of five feet eight inches. Mary stumbled ahead a few steps before John put his arm around her and led her in silence to the grassy field beside the shore. The ground felt smooth now beneath her feet.

"Are they looking for me?" she asked.

"Probably by now," John said. "But they weren't when I left."

"You didn't need to follow. I'm a good swimmer."

"Still, it's never wise to swim alone. And I know these waters. I travelled them when I was surveying along here."

"I didn't know you surveyed up here! I thought you just worked south of here — on the north shore of Lake Ontario."

"That's where I did most of my work, but I did a bit up here. Do you know there's an inland tide in this river? It only causes the river to rise a few inches, but it is a tide."

"I thought tides were only in the ocean." Mary was going more slowly now, even though they were walking on the soft grass.

"Would you like to sit for a bit to catch your breath?" John said, pointing to a greyish granite stone just ahead of them.

"Yes . . . please . . . but for just a minute. They'll probably be looking for me soon." Mary sat on the stone with John standing beside her, facing the water.

John bent over, picked a piece of wild rye, and started to chew the end of it. Then he spit it out and said, "Do you really want to go back to Albany, Mary, to see your grandparents?"

"Yes, I do. And you, John? Do you have any family in Albany now to see?"

"No. And it'll be too far to travel to Uncle Peter's at Wallkill, though I'd sure like to see him and Aunt Jane again. But I'm not going to risk it." Even in the moonlight, Mary could see the scars left across his broad bare back from the tarring and feathering he had received when he had visited his aunt and uncle at Wallkill right after the war. Their neigbours had still been feeling the loss of their sons and were in a vengeful spirit when John had gone back to see them. They did not care that John was their neighbours' nephew; they just saw him as a Loyalist traitor who deserved to be punished.

"I'd not be here today if George hadn't rescued me," he said softly. Mary knew that her brother and John would stay fast friends forever.

"John," Mary said wistfully, "do you ever wonder what it would have been like if there hadn't been a war? You'd have been back in Albany running your own store, and you would probably have ended up being mayor, like your father and grandfather."

"I wish Father were still alive. I'll always remember him, Mary. He was such a kind father. Working for him . . . learning about the store . . . it was all fun. But working for my stepfather . . . was just plain hard work, and not at all like the kind of work I did in Father's store."

"I'd love to see your trading post sometime. Is it anything like your father's store?"

"It isn't much to see yet, but I have plans, and you shall see it, just as soon as I get back. . . . You could come over with George. I'd go for you, but I can't leave the place much once I get back. I'm building a stockade around my house."

"Why do you need a stockade, John? There's no danger in the area, is there?"

"I hope not, but the Mississaugas I trade with could become angry sometime."

"Why should they be angry?"

"Well . . . sometimes . . . oh, never mind." John's response made Mary even more curious.

"I can't imagine they would have any hostility towards you! When we first settled in the Bay of Quinte area, the Mississauga women came with woven baskets that they exchanged for bread. And Father and the boys traded fishing spears with the men for a few furs. We thought they were very good neighbours."

"I'm sure they will be. But I like to be cautious. No one is going to move into my place and take over the way the Rebels took over Father's store in Albany. So I'm building a stockade and I'll keep what's mine, even if I have to fight for it."

"The fighting is behind us now, John. We're

in a new land now."

"I hope you're right, Mary. I try to live peacefully, but I won't back down from a fight either. Still, my trade is growing in spite of problems."

"What problems?"

John turned to answer but hesitated as he stared down into Mary's upturned face and questioning green eyes. Even in the moonlight, her wet hair was glistening, and her shapely body was not completely hidden by his shirt.

"Mary . . . I think we'd better start back before your father and brothers get worried. They may already be out looking for us."

Mary took the hand John extended to her. It felt warm and strong, and her spirits lifted a little. She did feel a bit embarrassed, though — wearing John's baggy shirt, and her hair clinging in heavy wet clumps to her back with no mob cap to cover it.

When they reached the spot near the camp where she had left her clothes, John let go of her hand. "Now you can get out of that wet shift and put on your dry clothes," he said, smiling. Then he turned his back to her.

Mary took off John's shirt and dropped it lightly to the ground. Then she slipped out of her shift and into Leonard's baggy pants and loose shirt.

"I'm ready now . . . and thanks," she said, handing him his damp shirt.

John pulled it on as Mary watched. In spite of their farm work, her brothers did not have John's broad, muscular shoulders and arms. As he turned around, the moon cast a ray of light across his rugged features, and his blue eyes seemed to shine.

****

"Just where have you two been?" John Meyers barked.

"I went for a swim and got lost," Mary said, trying to look remorseful.

"How on earth could you get lost?" Father was talking to Mary, but he was eyeing John out of the corner of his eye. As John noticed the grim stare directed his way, his lips tightened and his eyes narrowed a little.

"I floated down the river. It was so peaceful, I almost fell asleep in the moonlight."

"Almost drowned is more like it!" Father shouted. Then he paused and cleared his throat. "Well, I'm glad John found you, but I never thought you'd go off like that, Mary. I thought you were just washing up . . . that is, until a few minutes ago. Then Tobias got worried and we all spread out to look for you — which reminds me — the boys are still in the woods." Father gave three hoots like an owl — the signal that all was well and Mary had been found.

Mary's face flushed red now as she marched over and sat down cross-legged on the ground by the campfire. John strolled over and stood beside her. Why did Father always have to be so bossy? And right in front of John. She sat looking at the low coals and turned away from the men. She was warm now, for it was not a cold night, but she was glad of a little smoke from the fire because it kept away the mosquitoes that were coming out. One thing was for sure — she wasn't planning to rub on any of that horrible-smelling bear fat Mother had packed. It would scare the bugs away all right, but everyone else, too.

Tobias and George stepped inside the circle of campfire light. "You sure gave us a scare, Mary," George said.

"Well, I noticed she was gone, and went looking for her before any of the rest of you!" John said.

Tobias laughed. "Don't let George fool you, Mary. He said he knew that you and John had sneaked off together. He wasn't worried at all."

"John and I did *not* sneak off together. . . . I sneaked off, er, went for a swim and John came to look for me."

"Oh, yeah, sure," George snorted.

"Don't tease her, George," Tobias said kindly.

"Why not? She's always getting me into trouble."

"Oh, yeah? Since when?"

"Ever since we were children. Like the time she told Father that you and I were sawing the doll's carriage in half."

"Oh, c'mon, George," Mary interrupted. "You were already building a wagon out of it right in the barnyard. Father couldn't have missed it even if he'd been blind. He would have tripped over it on the way to milk the cows."

Father had been gazing quietly into the fire, but now he interrupted: "Sun-up comes early, and I want to be in King's Town by tomorrow night. Mary, see that you put on your own clothes in the morning."

Five

A t dusk the following day, their wagon
creaked its way past the large, grey lime-
stone bastions of Fort Frontenac that
loomed at the mouth of the Cataraqui River. After
the war, the ruined fort had been rebuilt and
soldiers had returned there from Fort Haldimand,
for Carleton Island was now south of the Canadian
boundary established by the peace treaty of 1783
in Paris.

The small settlement of King's Town was busier
than Mary remembered it. A whole field of tents
had sprung up, reminding her of Long Island
before the end of the war. Many Loyalists had lived
there in tents until they could be evacuated to
Canada. Now more Loyalists were waiting for the
government to assign them land.

At least thirty homes — mostly small cabins —
were spread out just beyond the tents and north of
the Fort along this west bank of the river, where a
few bateaux were tied to a jetty. George drew the
horses to a halt in front of a dooryard about a
quarter of a mile from the shoreline. A tall, thick
clump of cedars sheltered an ample-sized log

cabin that belonged to John's stepfather. A rail
fence made of freshly cut logs circled around the
back of the house and over to the long barn-shed
to the northeast.

It had been a hot day, but a refreshing breeze
blew up from the lakeshore, and the crickets were
creaking in the hayfield behind the house as they
came to a stop at the edge of the dooryard. Even
in the darkening shadows, the house appeared
larger than most log cabins, for it had a founda-
tion and a loft.

John Bleecker gripped the edge of the wagon
with his right hand, sprang over the side, and
stomped along the grassy path leading up to the
front door.

Mary wondered what her friend Lucy would be
like now. During the war, her mother had kept her
home to work and she had become less talkative
and not at all like the bubbling girl she had been
back in Albany. Mary did not have long to think.
Out came the real Lucy, letting the front door slam
behind her. Well, that much hadn't changed. Lucy
had always been impulsive and noisy. Her thick
blonde hair was flying out around her shoulders
and she had hitched the front of her dress up to
the middle of her shins so she could run faster. In
her left hand she was holding a bucket.

"Hey, Lucy," John yelled. "It's me, John!"

Lucy dropped the bucket and broke into a grin.
Then, smiling, ran past her brother, up to the
wagon where Mary was sitting. Lucy and John were
not going to change. Always yelling and never listening to each other.

"Mary? Is that you, Mary? What are you doing here?"

"I stowed away in the back of the wagon," Mary said in a low voice, "and they had no choice but to let me come!"

"Oh, you — always getting into trouble, even at your age!" Lucy then dashed round to the front of the wagon where she had spotted George and Tobias. George dropped the reins on the seat and jumped down beside Lucy. Father grabbed the loose reins to keep the horses from bolting away while George grabbed Lucy and gave her a big hug. He looked as if he'd just found hidden treasure. "Wow, you sure have grown up!"

"I've been grown up for a long time, George," Lucy snapped.

"It's the same Lucy!" George laughed. "Always has an answer."

Lucy always did put on airs just because she's a year older than me, Mary thought. Mary was remembering the Albany days less wistfully now. Lucy used to boast about her fancy party gowns.

Tobias came around from the other side of the wagon and stood quietly beside George. He looked at Lucy with admiration and said, "Nice to see you again." Lucy turned and stared up at Tobias. His dark brown hair and deep blue eyes held her gaze, as she forgot all about George.

"You'd better help Father with the horses, Tobias," George said. "After all, *I* drove all the way here. It's your turn to work now." George wrapped an arm around Lucy's shoulders, turned her swiftly about, and propelled her towards the house.

Mary stepped into the cool kitchen-sitting room. They must have an outdoor bake-oven to be this cool in July, she thought.

"Why, Mary Meyers, it's so nice to see you, dear," Lucy's mother said, giving Mary a big hug and a kiss on the cheek. She was still thin, but she had colour in her cheeks now. She smiled a welcome with the sweet smile that Mary remembered from when she had visited the Bleeckers in Albany.

Mr. MacKenzie rose from a straight wooden chair by the back door and stepped across the floor. He wore his waggoner's baggy trousers and long shirt. He was a big, muscular man with a thick mop of dark hair and bushy eyebrows. He held out a hand to Mary and smiled. The old, gruff stepfather that John had feared seemed to have gone.

"Welcome, Mary," he said with a twinkle in his eyes. "I'll get myself right out to take care of the horses." He turned and strode out the back door.

"Now, just come over here by the candlelight. You must be dead tired. I do declare you have become such a fine-looking young lady," Mrs. MacKenzie exclaimed. "And I see you haven't lost your freckles. I always think freckles give a person such a healthy look."

Mary squirmed. Why did she have to mention those childish freckles? She had tried so hard to get rid of them. She nearly always wore a straw hat in the summer to protect her face from the sun and wind, and she used to bathe her face in milk, but she still had freckles. Then she'd tried a mud pack that got so hard Mother and Catharine could hardly get the pieces off. But the freckles had stayed. Finally, she was convinced that they were a punishment for her temper. So they would never go away, for with four brothers, how could she ever learn to control her temper? Especially when one of those brothers was George.

"Lucy," Mrs. MacKenzie said, "take Mary and her things up to your room. She may want to wash for supper."

Lucy gave George a long goodbye look and then led Mary up a steep, narrow stairway. The loft of the cabin had been divided into two rooms. Lucy opened the door on their left.

"It's all mine," Lucy said. "Isn't it huge?"

The bed was covered with a bright patch quilt of many colours. Two pink cushions with blue trim lay on top of the quilt. Muslin curtains of the same pink shade billowed out in a breeze coming through the window.

Lucy motioned Mary to the small washstand beside the bed. Mary poured water out of a china pitcher into a basin decorated with pink flowers and started washing her face.

As she felt the cool water on her skin and the breeze wafting in, she was reminded of the girls' bedroom back on their first farm at Cooeyman's Landing, and a wave of homesickness came over her. She hadn't been in such a comfortable room since they'd moved to Canada. The family had slept on the cold ground, on floors, on piles of straw, and now on little army cots that Father had bought when the army had disbanded.

"What do you think? Should I?" Lucy asked.

Mary suddenly came back to the present. Lucy

had apparently been talking. "What were you saying, Lucy?"

"I was saying that I think Tobias is handsome. How *can* you have such handsome brothers? And I was saying that I want to ask Tobias to take me to a dance tonight, but that I don't want to hurt George's feelings 'cause I know he likes me, too. But I'm not sure if Tobias really, really likes me . . . A girl can always tell, don't you think, Mary?"

"Well, I . . ."

"George definitely likes me, I mean *really* likes me. But it's hard to tell with Tobias. I know he likes me, but does he *really* like me? . . . Mary, why aren't you saying anything?"

"I haven't had a chance."

"Yes, I know!" Lucy said in despair, flinging herself on the feather mattress inside the oak bedstead. "I talk too much. John says so. But he's not around a lot anymore to tell me. I miss him, even if he does pester me." Lucy looked sad for a moment, then brightened. "Well, Mary. Would you like to go to this dance at my friends' tonight? You could keep George away from me, and I'll dance with Tobias. I had no idea that Tobias was so handsome."

"Lucy, I don't have much influence over George, but I can distract him. He's always trying to boss me around."

"Oh, good! Oh, wonderful! You can wear one of my gowns. We're almost the same size. Oh, Mary, it'll be so much fun. And then we'll come back and talk all night long. I've so many things to tell you."

"I have a lot to tell you, too."

* * * *

The proud owner of the cabin, where the dance was held, was newly married and an employee of Mr. MacKenzie. It was not a large dance, for the small cabin would only have two rooms even after the partition went up.

Three young men turned and looked at the girls as they entered the house with their brothers. They were all wearing cotton homespun breeches and loose-fitting beige overshirts, much the same as Mary's brothers and John. But across the room, there were soldiers in bright red coats, white breeches, and high leather boots, helping themselves to maple-sugar candy.

Lucy gave Mary a nudge with her elbow. "Look . . . soldiers from Fort Frontenac. Aren't they handsome?"

Mary turned and stared. "With their backs to us . . . how can you tell? And how can they stand wearing those wool uniforms in July?"

Mary felt flushed, too, but quite elegant in the yellow linen gown that Lucy had lent her. It fit a little tightly, but she could still turn easily in it, and she loved the ivory lace trimming at the throat and wrists. She looked down and smoothed out its folds, to avoid the glances of the men. The soldiers had turned now, too, and were staring at the two of them.

Mary looked over at her brother and grabbed his arm. "George, you have to dance with me. You know I can't dance well enough to dance with anyone here."

"You must be daft, Mary. I'm not going to dance with my *sister*!" George brushed her aside and walked around to Lucy. "May I have this dance, Miss Bleecker?" he said in a soft tone of voice that was completely new to Mary.

Lucy smiled and took George's arm. Mary felt a moment of panic as she stood there alone in a room almost full of strangers. Then Tobias nudged her. "Mary, there's nothing to dancing. Come on, I'll show you." She had forgotten he was there. He held out his arm and gracefully led her onto the dance floor. For the moment, Mary felt rescued.

There had been so little opportunity for Mary to learn to dance. Only a few shanties had been built in their area, and these were a long distance away. There had been no real house-warmings like this. Tobias and George, though, had been in the military for a short time after they had come to Canada. So, of course, they were quite good at dancing. Everyone knew that the forts gave the best dances. Lucy had become a real expert at parties she had attended at Fort Frontenac.

Mary was fast becoming more comfortable under Tobias's leading. She even smiled as she saw George and Lucy sailing by. Then she remembered that Lucy wanted to dance with Tobias.

"Tobias," Mary said, looking intently at his face, "do you like Lucy?"

"Of course! Who wouldn't?"

"I mean do you really, really like her?" Mary hoped that she wasn't starting to sound like Lucy, but she didn't know how else to ask the question.

"Well, Mary, I would really like to get to know Lucy. She's always been friendly, and now she's a real beauty. She's the most beautiful girl here tonight. Look, there, a soldier's cut in on George." Mary looked over in time to see the scowl on George's face.

"Yes, she's a beautiful girl, but I couldn't say that I really, really like her," Tobias continued. "I don't even know her anymore. She was still a child back in Albany."

"Well, Tobias. I want to rest a while. Why don't you cut in on Lucy's dancing partner and start to get to know her."

Tobias led Mary to the side of the room and hurried over to tap Lucy's partner on the back. Mary watched him take Lucy into his arms on the dance floor and smiled slyly as she looked over at George, who was still staring at Lucy. As Mary was wondering what might happen next, John came up and asked her for a dance and led her around the dance floor. Then a young man tapped John on the back and tried to cut in, but John said, "Mary has come with me tonight. She's promised me all the rest of her dances."

Mary almost burst with joy.

Six

The wagon was like many that travelled through the countryside around Albany. The horses, too, had a familiar look — they were the type with large heavy feet that farmers used to draw ploughs. On the front seat of the wagon sat a young woman with a short-gown hanging loosely over the waist of a dark brown petticoat. Her hair was all tucked under her mob cap, as was the fashion, and a large straw hat, obviously a man's, shaded her head and eyes. This was a common sight, too. Women often borrowed the hats of their menfolk to protect them from the sun.

Beside the woman sat a young man, probably her husband, for he looked slightly older. He had brown hair and deep blue eyes and wore homespun breeches and a loose-fitting shirt tucked in at the waist. Occasionally, he slapped the horses to hurry them along. No farmer would have time to dawdle at this season of the year. There were crops to tend, and the harvest would soon be upon them. The couple had obviously been to Albany to get supplies; the back of the wagon was full of produce covered with heavy canvas.

It was a week since the dance, and Mary, sitting on the wagon, was thinking again about the time in King's Town. She had danced the rest of the evening with John and loved every minute of it. The next morning, she had raved about the dance to her father and said what a great time she would have while they were gone. She and Lucy planned to go to all the dances at Fort Frontenac. After that, Father had suddenly decided to let Mary travel on with them to Albany. He seemed to realize that having a woman in the group would make them look more normal. After all, an all-male group might look more menacing to the local town and countryfolk.

"It's not far. We're at the back part of Grandpa's farm now," Tobias said. "George, do you remember the creek we fell into on the way home from hunting one night? That's where we are."

"How could I forget? How was I supposed to know the tree bridge wasn't there anymore?" George grumbled.

"The crops look good, Father," Tobias said, changing the subject. "The corn's higher than you."

"It's always been an earlier harvest here, son."

"Hurry up, Tobias," Mary said. "Can't you trot the horses now? There's no one in sight but the farm hands in the fields. . . . Looks as if Grandpa has bought more slaves since we left." Most of Grandpa's original young slaves had gone to war. They had fought on the side of the Loyalists and the British because they had been promised their freedom in return for fighting against the Rebels. Though slavery was still practised in some places in Canada, Father would not own slaves and paid his Black workers. Back here in the new States, however, slavery was not only legal but also considered moral.

The horses trotted over a knoll, and the driveway to Mary's grandparents' house appeared before them. A long line of fresh washing was blowing on the shed side of the old grey clapboard house. "Grandma's as spotless as ever," Mary said. "Look at the size of that wash!"

"Maybe the servants do it all now," Tobias said.

"I hope so," Mary said as she remembered the hours she had helped her grandmother. The family had stayed there for a year during the war, after Father had left them to join the Loyalist troops.

Father was mumbling something under the canvas. "Drive right up to the house and you two go in alone. Find out how the folks feel. If they want to see us, drive into the barn and close the doors. Then they can come out to the barn and not be seen by servants or anyone else who might drop by unexpectedly."

A great yearning for her childhood days came over Mary as she looked at the front of the house. Large, bright red roses were blooming all along the flowerbed in front of the verandah. A green vine with thick wide leaves filled the space from the top of the verandah railing to its roof. Mary could remember her grandmother pointing out the little green pipes growing along the vine. Just to the left of the front door was a large wooden table covered with Grandma's pink and white geraniums. Mary remembered coming out here to talk to Boots and George when she was tired of all Grandma's housework. Boots used to sit on the front step of the verandah and wait for her to bring out his food. She hoped that George's trip to Long Island would be successful and he'd bring Boots back.

Then she remembered that horrible day after they had been put off their farm. When they had finally reached the house with their two wagons full of belongings, Grandma had stood in the open light of the doorway, a candle in hand, and waved them inside. How glad they had been to see her sweet smile through her tears as she welcomed them.

Mary's heart was pounding with joy as she saw her grandmother come out the front door down the steps to the path that led to the barn. Long forgotten was her resentment of Grandma's clean ways that kept her scrubbing and cleaning the whole time the family had stayed during the war.

Grandma was holding a bucket in one hand and shaded her eyes against the sun with the other. "Can I help you?" she called out, coming down the pathway towards the small gate at the foot of the yard. Her voice sounded a little shaky. Grandma was bent over now, with a hump on her back that even her loose-fitting brown over-gown could not hide. Her worn striped petticoats dragged on the ground as she shuffled towards the visitors. It was not surprising that she had aged. Nearly eight years had passed since the family had left to join Father in New York City.

Mary jumped off the wagon, swung open the narrow gate, and brushed past a ferny asparagus bush as she ran along the pathway to the house. "Grandma!" she cried in a whisper. "It's me, Mary — but don't let on that you know me."

Grandma stared at Mary in disbelief. "Mary? John's daughter Mary? My granddaughter? I didn't think I would ever see you again." Grandma went to give Mary a hug and then stopped herself. "Ah, you took a big risk coming here. And how did you get through?"

Mary pointed over at the wagon where Tobias was sitting.

"Oh, somebody brought you . . . of course." Grandma squinted in the direction that Mary was pointing. Mary realized then that Grandma could not see as well as she used to.

"It's Tobias."

"Little Tobias? That man on the wagon? Well, I'll be!"

"You came alone?"

"No, there's also Father and George and John Bleecker — all hiding under the canvas."

"You're all here?" Grandma laughed. "Well, we have to do something to get you hidden before the servants see you — or worse, our neighbours. There's still no tolerance for Loyalists around here. They aren't looked upon kindly. I think you should drive the wagon into the barn at least," Grandma said. "Then we can figure out what to do with you. It surely is good to see you again." A smile lit up her crinkly face, and her pale blue eyes sparkled like a sixteen-year-old's.

Mary ran back to the wagon and motioned to Tobias to drive the horses into the barn.

The barn was hot. Beams of sunlight filtered in through the cracks between the barn boards, and dust danced in the air. There was a pile of fresh-mown hay in the loft, and loose hay lying around on the dirt floor.

Father, George, and John got out from under the canvas, and George began pacing around the wagon. Just then the little barn door opened and in walked Grandma.

"Mother!" In one long stride, Father reached her, but George was already wrapping both arms around her.

Grandma's wrinkled face showed no emotion for a moment. Then tears formed in her eyes and one escaped down her cheek. She turned to kiss her son. "I thought I'd never see you again." After a minute, she looked around to the others, her eyes adjusting to the darker light in the barn. Before Tobias could reach her, there was the sound of footsteps outside the barn. Father motioned them all through the narrow granary door near the back of the barn. As the men stepped inside, Mary could see the empty bins waiting for another harvest. Only Mary stayed behind with Grandma.

The little door inside the big barn door swung open, and in stepped Grandpa.

"Oh, Hans, it's you," Grandma said with relief. "I thought it might be. . . . You'll never guess who's here."

"No, I don't think I will. But what I want to

know is what those horses are doing in our barn. I was washing up at the back pump and saw them going in!"

"If you knew whose horses they were, you wouldn't be talking that way!"

"Well, I must say, I *don't* recognize the team. Whose horses *are* they?"

"This is Mary, Hans — your granddaughter Mary."

"Mary? Little Mary? Well, I don't believe my eyes. What are you doing here?" Grandpa looked at her in shock. Then he leaned over as Mary came up close and threw her arms around him. His white hair didn't have even a tinge of red now, and like Grandma, he was bent and not as tall as he used to be. He held Mary back a little now. "So you're a grown-up lady now. But how did you ever get here?" His face darkened again. "You didn't drive that team alone, I'll bet."

"She didn't come all by herself, Hans," Grandma said. "There are a few other surprises here for you. . . . They're in the granary." Grandma and Mary led Grandpa into the granary, where the men were hiding.

At first, Grandpa and Father just stared at each other as though they couldn't believe their eyes. Then they clapped their arms around each other. Grandpa gave a deep sigh that sounded almost like a sob.

Then they both started to talk at once. "Are you well?" Father was clutching Grandfather's hand.

"How are you, son?" Grandfather asked.

"Fine . . . just fine," Father said. "Look at these two. You'll see." Father turned with pride to

George and Tobias, who were standing on either side of him.

"We're doing all right," Father said. "We've set up farming three times since we reached Canada, but I think we'll stay where we are now. It's in a pleasant meadow off the northern shore of the Bay of Quinte. As soon as it's surveyed, I'll apply for ownership. The government owes me."

"Yes, they do, I'm sorry to say. I'll never understand your choices, John. I'll never understand."

"You must be hungry," Grandma interrupted with a tremor in her voice. "Come with me, Mary. We'll go to the house and fetch some sandwiches and pie."

"Oh, boy! Grandma's apple pie!" George grinned as if he was a little boy again.

Then Grandpa stared over at the sturdy, fair-haired young man beside Mary. "I don't believe I know you, son. You aren't Leonard, are you?"

"No, I'm John Bleecker."

Father extended his hand. "So you're Janse's son. A son of Janse will always be welcome in my home. Your father was wrongly accused. They never did prove he wasn't loyal to the Rebel cause."

John's eyes darkened. "But I became a Loyalist. I joined DeLancey's battalions in New York City and I have never been sorry. The Rebels killed my father as surely as if they'd put a gun to his head. They were a bunch of bloody —"

"John!" Father placed a hand on his shoulder. John flushed red and became silent. They could all hear his deep sigh in the silence of the granary. The musky air was stifling.

"We'll get that food now. Come, Mary."

It was not long before Grandma and Mary had made up the sandwiches. Grandma had always been a hard worker and a tough taskmaster — and she had not changed. When they reached the barn, food in hand, they could hear loud guffaws of laughter coming from the granary. Mary smiled at Grandma as she tapped on the door. At first it opened just a crack and then Grandpa swung it wide open.

"We must be going, now," Father said, his hand resting gently on Grandpa's shoulder as they walked to side of the wagon. The boys shuffled along behind. Grandma and Mary still carried the food.

"Be careful," Grandpa sighed. "I know it's a serious undertaking you're planning. I'm worried for you and wish I could change your mind."

Mary looked up at Father with surprise. She did not think that Father had meant to tell his father about his plans. Grandma looked worried now, too. Father broke the silence by walking straight over to his mother and wrapping both of his big arms around her thin frame. "I'm sorry we can't stay longer, Mother, but it seems too dangerous. I'm surprised that hostilities aren't cooling down now that it's a full three years since the end of the war."

"It's partly the times," Grandpa said. "The farmers are finding it difficult to pay their taxes and make ends meet. So some are using any excuse to grab and steal in order to get funds for expenses. Former Loyalists are a prime target."

"I see. Well, we'll be on our way. But first, do you think my brother would welcome us . . .

just for a fast stopover?"

"No, Hans, no. Jacob still resents you for going to the other side. And I think he's a bit jealous. After all, he didn't become famous like you."

"You mean infamous, around here," Father said sadly.

"I'm afraid you're right, son."

"Well, I guess we'd best be off. We'll go out the way we came in, with Mary and Tobias up front."

As Tobias backed the snorting horses out of the barn, Mary waved to Grandma, who was holding a handkerchief up to her eyes.

They were out of the barn now, and Tobias turned the horses towards the laneway. Just then a figure appeared over the crest of the knoll ahead.

"It's Uncle Jacob," Tobias gasped. The canvas moved a little as Father peered out.

"Get down," Grandpa grumbled as he pushed hard on the canvas. "I sure hope he didn't see you."

"I'm sorry," Father mumbled. "I wasn't thinking for a moment. . . . It's been so long. I wish I could just —"

"You can't see him, Hans. You can't. He's too bitter yet," Grandpa mumbled, peering around from the far side of the wagon. "He's heading for the house, now, but he'll be out here soon when he doesn't find us there. Hurry along, Tobias."

Grandpa moved around the back of the wagon and headed for the path to the back kitchen.

The wagon creaked along the laneway past the house at a leisurely pace. Mary looked away so no one could see her face.

Fifteen minutes along the road, Mary broke

the silence. "Why am I still here? I thought I was supposed to stay at Grandma's."

"Father thinks it would cause too much suspicion to leave you there," Tobias explained in a low voice. "With feelings the way they are in these parts, people would start asking the wrong kinds of questions."

"You mean, I'll have a part in the raid after all? I can even —"

"Wait a minute, Mary. Give me a chance to explain," Tobias cut in. "We're going to leave Father and the boys by the cave at Cooeyman's Landing until dark. But you and I are going to have a picnic by the Hudson River not far from our old home. Would you like another swim?"

"I understand now," she said. "Then at nightfall, we'll circle back for the others."

"That's it. And leave *you* in the cave, out of danger ."

"No, you're not! I'm not staying in any cave with the bears!"

"Don't be silly, Mary. They're not holed up at this time of year."

"I'm going with the rest of you, Tobias," Mary said with fire in her eye. Then in a loud voice, she said, "Father, I've been a great camouflage for you on this trip. Don't you think we might get right up to the door without suspicion if I were with you?"

"She'll just mess things up for us," George grumbled.

Even through the canvas, Mary could hear Father's heavy sigh.

Seven

"Keep your voice down, Mary. This is not a picnic!" Tobias hissed as Mary shouted in in excitement at seeing the old apple orchard again.

The canvas moved as the men loaded their muskets — the ramrods steadily packing the powder, the wad, and the ball in each one.

Mary wasn't feeling the best about this visit after all, but it was too late to change her mind now. It had been decided that she would stay outside and hold the horses while the men raided the house. The apple orchard was now behind them, and they had reached the edge of the yard. The swing was still there. She couldn't believe it . . . the same swing in the same place. As the moon shone right across it, she remembered Catharine swinging little Anna high in the sky the first day that Father had run for his life from the Rebel mob. Everything had changed since then. They had lost track of Father and moved from place to place. Mary doubted that they would ever have a real home like this one again.

All was quiet as they approached the short

laneway that led to the front door of the two-storey house. At the entrance to the lane was a hollow and a clump of cedars where Mary was supposed to stay with the horses — out of sight of the house and road.

"Now, remember, Mary. After we have control of the house, we'll signal for you to come with the horses."

"Don't forget that toy bear!" Mary said.

"At a time like this, she thinks about a toy," George said with disgust. He was trying to sound calm, but his voice betrayed his excitement and fear. "Are you ready, John?"

John crawled out from under the canvas carrying a musket. "I sure am," he said. The moonlight shone on John's face and cast shadows on his craggy features.

"What are you waiting for, Tobias?" George whispered. He threw Tobias's musket over the edge of the wagon and Tobias caught it by the butt. Then George jumped down beside Tobias and John.

"Just a minute," Father said. "I'm going to tie the horses to one of these cedars, just in case gunfire spooks them. I don't want them running away."

The boys paced impatiently. There was still no sound from the house, and no lights were burning. "There'll be a dog," Father said, fishing a piece of pork out of the food basket.

Father stashed the pork in his shirt pocket, then reached beneath the canvas and handed Mary his only pistol. "It's loaded. Don't use it unless it's absolutely necessary. If you're in danger, fire it into the air." Then he turned to the boys. Now take it easy, boys. Follow me. There will be no shooting, I hope."

Mary got down off the seat of the wagon, the pistol in hand, and crouched in the hollow. The ground was damp. She looked across the yard to the old home. In the moonlight, it didn't really look so different. The same stone chimney across the south side of the house stood straight and firm. Lilac bushes still grew along the left side of the house, right up to the front steps and along the little verandah. The elderberry bush was there, too, by the other side of the steps. Even the old rocking chair was still beside the front door, rocking a bit in the breeze.

Suddenly Mary felt panic at being alone with no one to protect her. A dog started barking sharply. After what seemed like hours, the barking stopped. The dog must have liked Grandma's pork! Mary watched for the light of a candle to appear in one of the windows, but none came.

Clutching the pistol a little more tightly, Mary turned to the left and saw a horrible sight. Six men were stepping out of the shadows the orchard was casting on the side dooryard. They raced the short distance to the lilac bushes. Would her father and the boys see them? Probably not. They might all be inside the house already, not even thinking about danger coming from the outside.

How could anyone have learned that Father had planned an attack here tonight? No one but Grandma and Grandpa knew, and they would never have betrayed them. Maybe Uncle Jacob had seen them? Or perhaps someone had recognized them as they were travelling during the day. Suspicion would then be aroused and all kinds of rumours started.

Mary's mind raced, thinking of ways to warn Father. If she entered the house from the front, she might reveal her father's presence to the owners inside. But she dared not go in by the back door as these men were headed that way and would reach Father first. Now she could see the dark shadows moving behind the lilac bushes.

Mary scrambled up from the ground and untied the horses. Steadying the pistol with her left hand, she cocked it with her right thumb. Then she grabbed the horses' reins, pointed the loaded pistol into the air, and fired. When she saw the men come back around the side of the house, Mary jumped onto the wagon, slapped the horses' backs with the reins, and headed down the road in the direction they had come. Tall trees with thick waving branches cast deep and flickering shadows across the road as she sped ahead into the darkness.

* * * *

Father waved George and John inside and left Tobias to watch by the door. He posted the other two inside the kitchen. Striking a match, he saw that the shelves held supplies of seasonings, flour, and sugar. A wooden bowl stood on a table, half full of melted butter. He crept into the dining room and parlour. Moonlight streamed in through the front window of the parlour making shadows play across the old horse-hair couch. From outside the window came the sharp sound of breaking twigs. He tiptoed over to the glass, straining to hear the sound again. There was none. Perhaps he had only imagined it.

George and John grew impatient waiting in the kitchen and lightly mounted the narrow, creaking back stairs while Father finished checking the front rooms.

No one appeared to be home. Were they away visiting at this busy time? It was possible, since the crops were not ready for harvest just yet. This may be easier than I thought, Father said to himself.

As he went up the stairs, he ran his hand along the smooth wood of the banister. He would use this staircase in the fine house he would build in Canada. Many years ago, he had carved it out of hard maple; it was one of the best pieces of his own handiwork.

Soft footsteps from above jolted him out of his reverie. He pulled his musket down from his shoulder and crept up the stairs with the barrel in front of him. He would not shoot — but he was equally determined not to see his family hurt or taken prisoner. He pushed ahead cautiously. It was much darker in the upstairs hallway. The windows must be covered, he decided, for light had always streamed across the hallway on a night such as this. Then he heard the footsteps again.

"Father! It's me, George!" The voice sounded so shaky that Father chuckled as he pulled back his musket and placed it across his left shoulder.

"Did you find anyone, son?" he whispered back.

"Not a sign of anyone. The beds haven't been slept in," George said.

John peered over his friend's shoulder and added, "But they are all made up — as if someone lives here."

"Did you check the attic?"

"No."

"Stay here, then." Father moved past them towards the attic door, but it was bolted. "No one can be up there when it's bolted on this side."

George moved swiftly to the door. "I have a few things to get for Mary."

Father smiled. In spite of their constant bickering, George was going to get Mary's toy bear. And there were other family treasures — maybe still there. He turned to follow George.

They heard a sharp crack. The smell of gunpowder wafted on the breeze into the hallway through an open window in one of the front bedrooms.

"Follow me," Father yelled to the boys as he raced down the stairs and out the front door. He was just in time to see Mary going down the road with the wagon in a whirlwind of dust. Six men were racing after her on foot.

Just as the men were turning back, Father stepped into the shadows of the cedar bushes. George and John moved over to the right side of the road, and Tobias circled behind to the left.

Father stepped out onto the road with his musket aimed. "We have you covered on all sides," he said calmly.

Tobias's musket poked out between the trees,

glistening in the moonlight.

"Lay down your arms!" Father said. The six gave up without a shot. The men threw down their muskets, and George checked each person for hidden weapons and found none. The men scowled and shuffled, awaiting their fate.

"To the house," Father growled and the men marched ahead.

There was no sign of Mary. Only a thin cloud of dust could be seen on the road where she had been.

"Where's Mary gone? Do you think the horses ran away with her?" George asked anxiously.

"She knows what she's doing. She'll be back," Father said. "Now we have a night's work ahead of us."

The bedraggled group of prisoners sat down around the kitchen table. "You have some rope?" Father asked.

"In the cupboard," one of the men said. Father found the rope and a few candles, which he lit and set down in the middle of the table. He recognized one of the men as his second cousin and the new owner of their house. Then he noticed that his cousin and friends were visibly shaken. No doubt his reputation had preceded him. And a good thing, too, he thought, doing all he could to make sure the illusion would not be broken.

"Put your hands behind the back of the chairs," he barked. He handed the boys the rope and motioned to them to tie up the prisoners.

"You don't plan . . . to shoot us?" the new owner asked in a shaky voice.

"Maybe I should. You couldn't wait to move in here once the Rebels drove us out of the only home we'd ever known. You must have had your eye on this place even before the war."

"Take what you like," the man said. "And we'll not come after you, I promise. Only leave us alone."

"Your word means nothing to me. I'd never believe a man who'd take from his own kin and leave seven young children homeless."

"Well, they found a home, didn't they?"

"My father took them in, but it wasn't their home. You had that!"

George moved over beside his father. "The lot of you came on my twelfth birthday to drive us out! Some birthday party! Some relative!" In the candlelight, it looked as though two Hans Meyers were standing there. The men, now with feet and arms tied firmly to the chairs, shrank down as low as possible. "Don't shoot the rest of us," pleaded one of the men. "*We* didn't take your farm."

Father recognized the speaker. It was Peter Sager. Father's eyes blazed. "No, you didn't take my farm, but you killed my neighbour. You were one of the mob who killed Vandervoot. Then you came by the next morning and tried to trick my wife into telling you where I was."

Tobias watched his father and brother growing angrier and angrier. He shook his head and said, "Father! I'm going out to look for Mary." He could not stand watching their anger any longer — especially when Mary was out there, possibly in great danger.

Father shouted after him, "Tobias, go out to the

road and show Mary in when she comes back. I'm sure she can't have gone far."

Then Father looked silently at the prisoners. He really didn't want to fire any shots. He knew these men had wives and families. In fact, he had never killed a man, for he'd never been in the heat of the battle.

With the men securely tied, and George and John left to guard them, Father went to the dining room. Against the wall stood the cupboard he had made with his own hands and given to Polly for a wedding gift.

Father strode back into the kitchen. "Ready for some hard work, boys? George, let's start in the attic. John, you keep standing guard."

* * * *

Mary drew the horses to a stop and looked to the left and the right. Her pursuers were nowhere in sight, and she had passed the Sagers' farm a long time ago. She knew now that she must have a plan. A girl should not ride wildly through the countryside in the middle of the night alone. It was just not safe. She could see no one, but there was a high-pitched whistling sound in the dense growth of trees. Was it the wind? Then she heard footsteps — heavy footsteps — and the crackling of twigs breaking beneath a heavy weight. That was no scampering of light animals. What was it?

Mary shivered. She must not waste further time listening. She pulled her bag of clothes out from under the seat, and pushed off her heavy petticoats and short-gown. Then she slipped into Leonard's breeches and baggy shirt. Last of all, she pulled off her mob cap, knotted her hair into a thick, heavy roll, and pushed it all up under Leonard's straw hat. She hoped she would pass for a boy now and not cause suspicion. Young men travelled home from courting at all hours. She was tall enough to be taken for one of them. She sat back down in the driver's seat, leaning forward with her knees apart and her wrists resting on them, the reins held firmly in her hands — just the way her brothers drove the team when they were in a hurry.

Mary circled around the Sager farm to another country road that cut across the back of the Vandervoot place. She would approach their old farm from the other side.

As Mary passed the Vandervoots' farm, she shuddered. She could still remember that awful night when she and George had discovered Mr. Vandervoot's tar-covered body hanging lifelessly from an apple tree. Mary flipped the switch across the horses' backs to make them go faster.

A few minutes later, she slowed the horses to a crawl as she got closer to the clump of cedars. No one seemed to be in sight, but there were candles flickering in the hallway. That could mean any number of things. She wished they'd decided on a code so she could know what was happening inside the house.

Mary drew up beside the cedars. They'd be bound to come back and look for her here — as long as they weren't all captured, or worse. Maybe they were lying dead in the yard of their old farm-house. Maybe the six men had taken the bodies inside. After all, if those men were armed, it was six against four, and Father had not wanted to shoot anyone. Had they waited too long and been killed instantly — all of them?

A figure flitted behind the clump of cedars. Mary froze in her seat. She was not going to take off back down that lonely road again. This time she would stand her ground. Keeping her eyes glued to the slowly moving figure, she cocked the hammer of her pistol and pointed it towards the trees.

The figure came around the cedars.

"Mary!" Tobias shouted. "Is that you, Mary?"

With relief, Mary uncocked the pistol and laid it on the seat. Then she jumped over the side of the wagon, into Tobias's arms.

Eight

"I don't know why I let you come," George grumbled as he and Mary jumped out of the bateau that had taken them from New York City to Long Island. "You do seem to make a habit of getting your own way."

"Boots was my dog, too, you know, George. In fact, John gave him to me — back at their store in Albany. Remember?"

George was trying to catch the boatman's attention. "Sir, when does the last bateau leave tonight?"

"Ten-fifteen sharp. It's better to be here a bit ahead to get a good seat. The last trip over is sometimes crowded."

"We'll be here," George said with a smile. Then he and Mary stepped off the wharf onto the dirt road that led to the Lloyds' farm, where they had lived the last three years of the war.

After the raid, the wagon was so full of goods and furniture from the old homestead that there was barely enough room for everyone to ride. But they had all piled in anyway. There was no time to waste.

For some reason, Father had asked Mary to go

with George. Perhaps to stop the attention that John was showing her. Father gave George money to buy horses to take them to Poughkeepsie. From there, George and Mary took a bateau down the Hudson River to New York City — the same route the family had taken during the war.

George took long, firm strides along the narrow roadway leading from the wharf to the Lloyds'. Mary followed, half running. Cedar trees still grew in heavy clumps along the way, but there were some bare patches where they could see across the farmland for miles. Fields of wheat, oats, barley, and corn seemed to be thriving, and new young trees were sprouting up in the bare spaces at the roadside. Mary knew these were there because trees had been cut down for firewood during the war. Mary remembered, too, that this road had been filled with marching soldiers and a steady stream of refugees.

Only when Mary and George rounded a bend did they see a slow-moving wagon approaching them. George pulled his cap down to shade his face, and Mary tucked a few loose strands of hair under Leonard's straw hat.

"Slow up, George," Mary said. "I can't keep on running."

"We have to keep moving. It will soon be night-fall."

"I know, but I look more like a child than a man — hopping along like this!"

George reluctantly slowed his pace, and Mary took slower, longer strides, which made her look much more like a young man. The wagon, only about a hundred feet away now, was moving into the middle of the road.

As the team drew up beside them, George nodded, and with one hand on his cap, pulled it even lower on his forehead. Mary did the same. The man was dressed in the familiar homespun trousers and shirt of a local farmer. He smiled in such a friendly way that George felt compelled to stop.

"Hello, there," the farmer said. "Are you two new around here?"

George lifted his head a little and nodded. Mary continued to look at the ground.

"Well, this is your lucky day. I'd be glad to hire you for farm hands. The meals are good, though the pay's not high. How would you like the work?"

"Well, we'll think on it, Mister," George drawled. "Thank you."

"Well, hop aboard. I just have to leave this load at the wharf, and then I'll be travelling right back to my farm."

"We have business to attend to first . . . but thanks. Anyway, how do you know we're good workers?"

"We've been so short-handed since the war, and with the slaves being gone, farmers around here have been taking most any help they can get. I must say, though, you look like a strong fellow, but your friend looks too slight for the heavy work. What do you say for yourself, young man?"

Mary looked over helplessly at George.

"My kid brother is just getting over the fever, Mister. He's not spoken a word since it hit our

whole family a month ago." Mary coughed violently while George continued. "We lost our parents.
God rest their souls. And I've brought my brother
here to the Island to get away from the city."

The man's eyes widened and his mouth closed
firmly for a second before he spoke again. "I guess
I won't be needin' you after all. Good day." He hit
the horses across their backs and went on down
the road.

They hurried along for another twenty minutes,
then rounded a corner, and came upon the Lloyd
estate. Beyond the rail fence, the weeds and grass
were clipped back from the circular driveway and
the four pillars at the front of the house shone
white against the soft light of the setting sun. Even
the red brick had a new clean look. The flapping
shutters had been repaired and painted as white
as the pillars. Pink geraniums beside the front
steps were in full bloom, and the rose bushes were
trimmed. Mary remembered her mother planting
those rose bushes.

George was studying the yard intently. "I think
we'll just scout around," he said.

"Do you think Boots will recognize us?" Mary
asked as she looked sideways at George.

"Of course he will." George was peering into
every corner.

"Well, let's go knock at the door," Mary said.

"Wait. We don't even know if Mrs. Lloyd still
lives here. And besides . . ."

"You don't have to convince me, George. You
may be recognized. So I think I should be the one
to get Boots while you wait in that hedge of lilac

bushes over there by the barn."

"Ha! Ha! With your manly voice?"

"I can talk gruff," Mary said in a deep voice.

George laughed again and said, "Look, Mary. I let you come along because Father suggested it, but don't you think you're going to take over. For once, you'll do what I say. We could be in real danger. Mrs. Lloyd's son was a Rebel, you know, and if he's back home, there could be trouble. You hide behind that lilac hedge while I sneak inside the barn and try to find Sam. He'll be able to advise us." Sam was Mrs. Lloyd's elderly slave, who had been kind to the family during the war days on that farm.

George jumped the rail fence with a single leap. Mary crawled between the rails and ran to the thick hedge of lilacs just east of the barn. Through the branches she could see George walking briskly towards the barn. Would Sam be there? Mary wondered.

George opened the small barn door inside the large one. From the other side of the barnyard, Mary heard a low growl and the sound of an animal's feet running along the ground.

The dog was within fifteen feet of George when it took a flying leap and knocked him right over. It was Boots all right. Even in the dusk, Mary could see the white star on his forehead and the four white feet. George sat up and drew the large collie onto his lap. Boots was a great golden mass of wagging body and tail as he happily lapped at George's face.

George kept saying, "Boots! Oh, Boots! You knew

I'd come back for you." Finally, he stood up and Boots glued himself to his side, his tail wagging still.

"Well, Mrs. Lloyd must be here," he said. "I know she wouldn't leave you behind." He started walking slowly towards the lilac bushes.

Mary could contain herself no longer. "Boots!" she shouted, running towards George and the pile of fur. She knelt and grabbed the dog in her arms. Boots was still wagging his tail, but in a minute, he nosed his way over to George again. "Come back, Boots," Mary grumbled. "You were my dog first."

"Your dog?" George grimaced. "I think it's clear whose dog he is . . . And would you lower your voice? I don't want to be recognized. I just want to see Mrs. Lloyd to thank her and tell her we're taking Boots home."

"Well, let's go and knock on the door!"

"All right, all right. I was just going to suggest that," George grumbled, picking himself up off the ground and brushing off his trousers.

As they walked up the one step to the back kitchen door with Boots close behind, a tall, thin man in his mid-thirties opened the door, nearly bumping into George as he stepped forward.

"What are you doing slinking around behind my house?" he growled.

"We've come to see Mrs. Lloyd," George said. "I thought we'd be less bother, coming to the back door. May I see her?"

"Why do you want to see my mother? I don't even know you." The burly man looked down at the dog wagging his tail beside George. "Boots seems to know you, though." His jaw tightened and his grey-green eyes narrowed into slits. "You must be one of those . . . those Loyalists billeted here during the war . . . the one who left this mutt behind."

Mary shifted her weight and hitched up her trousers, trying to look tough.

"The war is over," George said calmly. "We've come to see a kind lady . . . just for a few minutes . . . please."

"No traitor is going to see my mother. Leave now, and leave quietly or I'll send for the authorities. You and your kind are not welcome here! Not now and not ever! Good day." The man reached down beside George, grabbed a handful of Boots's long golden mane, and pulled him towards the open doorway.

Boots gave a low growl and snapped at the man's hand.

"Come back here, you miserable cur," the man shouted, lunging for the dog and grabbing his mane again. George grabbed the man's wrist, and the man loosened his hold on the dog.

"Get your hands off me!" the man shouted. "I'll send for the authorities."

"We don't mean any harm, Mister," George said. "We'll go quietly. But may I pay you for the dog?" A glint showed in the man's eyes. George knew he was interested.

"How much?"

"Ten pence?" George offered. That would be a soldier's wages for two weeks and more than he could afford.

The man shook his head as he eyed the

strangers. Their clothes were not expensive, but neither were they dressed in rags, as some who wandered about since the war, begging for a bite to eat.

George sighed. Fifteen pence was all the money he had in his pocket and if he offered it all, they'd have to earn passage money back to New York City and then sell one of their horses they'd boarded there.

The man was still staring at George, Mary, and the shaggy dog standing between them. In an instant, George knew that he could not leave Boots behind. "Fifteen pence and that's final," he said. He thrust his hand in his pocket.

"Sold. Give me the money, take the dog, and get off this property."

Just as George put his hand into his pocket, Mrs. Lloyd's voice came from behind the man. "Bill," she said. "Who is it?"

"It's me — George Meyers!"

"George!" Mrs Lloyd appeared from behind her son. "Come in, come in. And bring Boots with you."

George still held the money in his hand. "I was just paying this man fifteen pence for Boots."

"You'll do no such thing," Mrs. Lloyd said as she motioned George to put the money back in his pocket. "Why would you offer to pay for what is yours already?" Then she turned to her son. "Bill, this is the oldest son of the family who took care of me when you were off to battle." Bill stepped back to make way for his mother and nodded at George, but he was still scowling.

Mrs. Lloyd then saw Mary standing behind George and frowned. "But I don't recognize this young man."

"Oh, this is a friend of mine from Albany," George said. "He was down on his luck, so I let him tag along." Mary gave George a sharp fist jab in the middle of his back as Mrs. Lloyd led them down the hallway towards her parlour.

When they reached the velvet carpeting, George bent over and said, "Stay, Boots!" The dog lay down on the floor just outside the parlour while George and Mary followed Mrs. Lloyd inside.

Once Mrs. Lloyd had closed the door and the three of them were alone, George smiled and said, "This is really Mary in disguise. We felt she'd be safer travelling like this."

"Little Mary!" Mrs. Lloyd exclaimed, gathering Mary into her arms. "But you're not little anymore!" She stood back and looked up at the tall girl, who had pulled off her straw hat and let her long, thick roll of auburn hair fall down her back.

George shifted from one foot to the other. He was obviously uncomfortable in the parlour in his homespun. Mary couldn't blame him, as she felt the same. After all, Mother hadn't let them come into this room at all when they lived here.

Mrs. Lloyd went over to the door, opened it, and called her servant. "Bring us tea, please, Bessie," she said as the middle-aged woman appeared. "And bring lots of rolls and cheese, too . . . and those fritters and the apple pie you made this morning." As George and Mary ate, Mrs.

Lloyd followed the servant girl to the door and whispered, "Pack a large basket of food with lots of ham sandwiches and cheese slabs, and apple pie and fruit cake. Hurry. Do not tell anyone."

"May I see Sam before I go?" George asked.

"I'm sorry to have to tell you. . . . Sam passed away shortly after you folks left, and his wife fell sick a month later and died. I was in desperate straits when my son came home and took over the estate. And he's been good to me, he has. But he still holds a hatred for the Loyalists — even his own brother. So you must not stay long. And take your dog — though, I shall miss him."

George wolfed down a last chunk of cheese and stood up from his chair. "Mrs. Lloyd, I wish we could stay, but we must catch the bateau back to New York at ten-fifteen."

"Yes, you must go, I know, but just wait a moment. Bessie!" Mrs. Lloyd called down the hall. "Oh, here she comes."

Bessie walked in with a basket full of bread, cheese, and apple pie.

"Put these in your knapsack, George. . . . Now remember me to your mother. I dearly wish I could see her again."

As Mrs. Lloyd was leaning over to give Boots a last pat, they could hear the sound of a carriage coming up the front driveway.

"Someone's coming," she gasped. "It looks like the town watchmen. I'll hold them off a while, but get to the dock as fast as you can. I'll direct them inland to the old barracks. They might expect you would go there."

George, Mary, and Boots slipped silently out the back door and raced across the yard. When they got to the road, they kept back in the fields, so they would be hidden by the cedars along the way. They dashed past the open spaces.

"Well, it's not the first time we've been running away together, is it Boots? Remember how you caught up with me when I left Grandpa's farm?" George ran his fingers through the dog's heavy coat.

"It's not the first time you've had me along either," Mary said, remembering how they'd got lost in the snowstorm in New York City.

"I guess you're right, but it's the first time all three of us have been running away together."

Then they heard the sound of fast-trotting horses and slunk down behind a clump of cedars with Boots panting between them. It was going to be a long, hard night.

Nine

George pulled the reins tightly and brought the horses to a halt in front of the Meyers' cabin. A shaft of light fell across the thatched roof of the house and onto the walls of the storage shed with its poled lean-to just east of the house. In the fall, Father and the men would build a proper barn for the animals, but at the moment Duke and Bonnie would be happy to be housed again under the Meyers' former tent.

A candle flickered inside the front kitchen window, which faced north to the main trail. Mary sat bolt upright now on the back of the wagon with Lucy, who had accompanied the family from King's Town to visit her brother John. "Wake up," she whispered, nudging Lucy. "We're home!"

Father, walking behind the wagon with the other men, smiled at the sight of the inviting light in the window. It was a full month and five days since they had left.

Jacob burst out of the front door in his nightshirt, obviously straight out of bed. "You're back! You're back!" he yelled, running up to the wagon. Then his eyes fell on Boots. He lunged forward and hugged Boots so tightly that the dog could barely wiggle away to greet the others. But Boots did pull himself free and ran to Mother and Catharine, who had come out onto the front stoop with their aprons still on. "Ho, there," Father said. He came around from behind the wagon, the tired look leaving his eyes. He embraced Mother first and then gave Catharine and Anna each a hug.

"Thanks for taking care of things here, Leonard," he said to his son, who was looking quietly over his mother's shoulder.

"I'm glad you're all home, I can tell you." Leonard brushed back his light brown hair and wiped the sweat off his brow. "I have been going early and late to keep ahead of the weeds, and I had to start cutting the wheat. It's been difficult work alone — no one even to sharpen the scythes."

"In the moonlight, it's hard to see, but it looks like a good crop, son."

"It is," Leonard said with restrained pride in his voice.

Lucy nudged Mary and giggled, "Let's head for the bay."

Mary smiled and turned to her sister. "Catharine, would you bring us some soft soap and fresh shifts?" Remembering her departure, Mary was hoping to avoid Mother as long as possible. But her mother said in a firm voice, "I'm glad you're home safe, Mary, but we'll *certainly* talk later."

Turning back to Lucy, Mary said "Let's go!" They ran to the bay, and stripping to their shifts, they jumped into the low, rippling waves.

"Does this water feel good!" Lucy said. "It's so beautiful here and the water's so calm. Is it always like this?"

"Not at all. The waves are sometimes as high as me. It can be very rough."

"It was a good trip, Polly," Father said later as they sat to eat. "And you'll love all the things we brought. Remember your good oak cupboard?"

"Yes, of course, I remember it. Don't tell me you brought it back with you!"

Father nodded and smiled.

"Oh, Hans, I can't believe it, but I'm so pleased."

"Yes, and we brought the staircase and all the wallboard trim." He scooped out a huge helping of potatoes. "And, Polly, do you remember the little cradle I made for George — the one we used for all our children?"

"How could I forget!"

"Well, I brought it, too."

"I don't think we'll be needing it, Hans," Mother said, raising one eyebrow.

Father smiled. "It's for the grandchildren, of course, along with the toy bear."

Mother laughed.

"We all loved that bear," Catharine said. "I'm glad you brought it, Mary. Some day our children can play with it." Catharine always had a way of making people feel better just when they were feeling a little foolish about something. And for Mary, that happened often when George was around. John was like Catharine. He had made her feel important on the trip. He hadn't kept as close to her on the way home, however, and she was wondering if the evening at the dance in King's Town was all a dream. Still, John had been busy helping drive the team and keeping the load from coming loose. And they had all had to walk much of the way in order to save the horses. Often John had walked along beside Mary while Lucy entertained George and Tobias. He mentioned his business only once, but Mary felt quite certain that it was never far from his thoughts. In fact, he had said that very thing one time when she had asked him the reason for his silence. He hadn't expected to be away so long. And Singleton's trading post at the mouth of the Moira River did a good business with the Mississaugas, too.

"Have you seen any more of that black bear?" Father said, looking around the table.

"No, not sight nor sound of him," said Leonard. "I even went out with a gun to hunt for him one day last week. I caught a few squirrels and saw a deer, but no bear."

"You went hunting for that bear?" Father thundered.

Leonard looked down at his plate and mumbled, "Well, the crops were all weeded and the wheat wasn't quite ready then."

"It's far too dangerous to go bear hunting — especially alone. Don't try that again!" Father paused and caught his breath. "You're a very good hunter, Leonard, I'm sure. But bears are very unpredictable. I don't want to lose you."

George laughed. "Sounds like something I'd try, Leonard. Only you beat me to it. Maybe we can go hunting together."

"You'll do no such thing," Father shouted, giving George a shocked stare for defying him. George didn't seem to notice.

Catharine came to the rescue again, carrying in two huge pieces of raspberry pie. The first piece went to John and the next to George before she went back to the side cupboard for more. Both men smiled up at her as she served them. George's eyes were on the piece of pie, but John was looking straight at the server.

Father thanked John for his help on the trip.

"Any time, sir. I like a bit of adventure."

"Which reminds me about that other matter," Father said. "When do you think you can bring me the livestock?" Before John could reply, Father turned to Mother to explain. "I bought a few livestock and left them at Oswego. John's going to bring them up by bateau."

"I'll be so glad to have milk," Mother said. The British government had provided only one cow for every two families, and since the other family had small children, Mother had insisted that they keep the cow when the Meyers had left Missisquoi.

"You and Lucy must stay the night, John," Mother said. "It may not be safe to travel now through the woods. And you must be tired."

"Do you really have room, Mrs. Meyers?"

"Of course we do. The boys can double up, and Lucy can sleep with the girls. We have extra cots we can set up in no time."

"Well, if it's not too much bother, we'd like to," John said, following Catharine around the room with his eyes. She was clearing the table now, and

John had suddenly developed an interest in every knife, fork, and spoon that had to be lifted from the table.

"Of course we'll stay." Lucy smiled. "I'm not wanting to travel through that wilderness at this time of night."

"A fine pioneer wife she'll make some day," John laughed, temporarily snapping out of his daydream. He turned to George and Tobias, looking for a reaction, but they were paying no attention. They were both smiling at Lucy.

As John's eyes returned to linger on Catharine's face, Mary felt an invisible fist in the pit of her stomach.

Ten

"I'm going to visit John this week, and I don't care what you say." George cut an extra wide swath of fall wheat. Father kept on scything the crop at a steady pace. The early morning sun glinted off the brim of his straw hat. Boots was sitting in the shade of a willow tree at the edge of the meadow, with his tongue hanging out.

"John might need me, you know. He's building a palisade around his home to make sure he's safe if hostilities break out."

"There are no hostilities in this area, George," Father said evenly. "And I need you to help on the farm. I just hope we can get this wheat harvested before the corn's ready. And then there's the new barn to finish." Father sighed.

"We're always doing something — and it's just not fair," George said, giving his red hair a shake. "John invited Mary and Catharine along with Tobias and me *two weeks* ago. Everyone agreed to go, and here we are still working. Feels like we've been home a month already."

"You may have agreed to go," Father said, "but farm work is farm work. It waits for no man, and I need your help. You're my right hand, you know."

"I am not your right-hand man. I'm your son. If you wanted a farm hand, why didn't you hire one when you were in the States?"

"That's just about enough, George."

"One of these days, I'm starting my own farm. Then I can hire my own help instead of *being* the help all the time. Then I can go away whenever I want to."

"That's where you're dead wrong, George. That's when you'll really be tied to the land."

"I doubt that," George grumbled, raising his scythe even higher and cutting another wide swathe.

"Don't think that I don't miss that other life — the excitement of crossing enemy lines and outwitting Rebel trackers," Father sighed. "Tilling soil and scything hay and grain doesn't appeal to me *all* the time either. But life's not all excitement, George. There's lots of plain, gut-sweating work to be done — especially around here before winter sets in."

"Then why are you letting Tobias go? Why are you favouring him?"

"Listen, George. Remember last spring — that two-week trip you took to King's Town to buy more seed grain just after we got here and things were really rough? We didn't have the house built yet. We were just living in a canvas shelter. And remember how it took you three weeks to get back because you ran into John, and you waited to come back with him while *we* sweated it out here, clearing and tilling the land?"

George's freckled face flushed as red as his hair now, and he knew he'd lost the argument. A small bright-blue Finch chirped shrilly from the branch of a nearby maple, "Cheerup, cheerup."

"Ah, shut up," George grumbled, wiping the sweat dripping from his brow and glaring up at the innocent bird.

"What did you say, George?"

"Oh, nothing." He slashed into the wheat again. Before long a stretch of wheat was lying behind him, and he was a good ten feet ahead of his father. At this rate, the field would soon be cut and they could rake it into windrows, ready to be tied and stooked.

"I can see that both you and Tobias like Lucy a lot," Father shouted to his son. "I can't say that I blame you, but before you get any serious ideas in your head, you and Tobias had better realize you'll need a home to take a young wife to. Settling the land is hard enough when your family is the age of mine, but starting with a new wife and babies in this wilderness could be downright dangerous."

George looked his father straight in the eye. "So is that what you said when you were younger than me and married Mother?"

"It was far different in Albany. We had a fine home and a midwife nearby and helpful neighbour women in the area — even a doctor in Albany."

"Well, you'd better talk to Tobias. He's planning to take the girls over to Bleecker's Castle this evening."

"Bleecker's Castle? Where did you pick up that

name? Bleecker's Castle! That rough shack of a trading post?" Father took a handkerchief out of his pocket and wiped his eyes. Then he let out another chortle and put the handkerchief away.

"That's not the name of the post. It's what John calls his log cabin. But I think the Mississaugas called it that first. John liked the name so well that he insists on everyone using it. The point is, though, that Tobias and Mary are heading over there today, and Tobias is going just to see Lucy."

"Well, I guess it's time I had a little talk with Tobias, too. And I'm thinking . . . Leonard's the one who needs a break. He can take the girls over for a little visit and give John a hand. After all, he's a sturdy lad and he didn't go with us to Albany, so it's his turn. Besides, he won't be noticing Lucy."

"I wouldn't count on it," George mumbled. But he had to admit it was some compensation to know that Tobias wouldn't be going either. Still, he had wanted to go for reasons that had nothing to do with Lucy. He'd wanted to get away from Father and all his orders. He would help just this one more year on the farm, he thought, as the sun shone hard and hot on his back. Then next year he'd set up his own place.

Father kept saying he should wait until the land was surveyed. Then he would be given a proper lot, signed and sealed by the government, as they had promised the Loyalists and the children of Loyalists. But it was taking the government a long time, it seemed to George, to pay their debts. If *farmers* took that long, they'd be jailed!

Eleven

"The Lord had said unto Abram, 'Get thee out of thy country, and from thy kindred, and from thy father's house, unto a land that I will show thee: And I will make of thee a great nation, and I will bless thee, and make thy name great; and thou shalt be a blessing' . . ."

Mary gazed out the front window as Father read his favourite passage from Genesis. It was a crisp morning in late September. An early frost had hit the night before, and the meadow between the cabin and the bay was still touched with white.

It was all she could do to sit still on the bench beside Tobias. She and George had finally convinced Father to let them go to Bleecker's Castle today. The barn had been built and the wheat had been harvested and stored, so there was actually a bit of spare time before they made their final preparations for winter. Manure would be banked up around the base of the house and barn. It would not blow away as straw would and, when frozen, would make a good insulation. A large supply of wood must be cut and dried nearby, as there had not been time in the spring to prepare it ahead. This winter they would cut for next year. That way they would be sure of drier wood in the future.

So Sunday was the only day that Father would let them go because that was the only day on which extra work was never done. Although the Meyers never went to church because there were none closer than King's Town, Father and Mother kept a strict Sabbath, and Father always did a Bible reading and prayer. The story today was familiar to Mary, since Father had read it so many times — all about how Abram changed his name when he went into a new country and became Abraham, the father of a great nation. Mary knew that Father was thinking about how he had changed his name from the Dutch "Waltermyer" to the English translation of Meyers, and how they had left all their family to come to this new land. "Our lives are much like Abram's," he had said. "Like him, we've come to a new country, and some day, we'll be the beginning of a great, new nation. It's not winning or losing a war, but building a new nation that's the real challenge. We're here and here we'll stay, God willing. We're building for the future now — in a land we can be proud to call our home."

Mary looked around the table at her family and wondered how God was possibly going to make a great nation out of them. Then Father said, "Of course, we can never be great like Abraham, through whom the world was blessed, but we do have a responsibility like his. God has blessed us with this wonderful land and this bountiful harvest. And we must be ready to help those who come after us."

As Father bent his head over the Bible, Mary noticed grey streaks lightening his auburn hair and began to remember the hardships in the last three years. The British government still hadn't paid Father any compensation for his losses in the States as they had promised, even though he had carefully tabulated it all. But they did pay him his half pay because he had been an officer, a captain, in their service. It amounted to five shillings and three pence a day, or 92 pounds a year. But his savings had been spent on supplies and cattle, and he was now in debt to John's stepfather for the use of the bateaux in transporting them.

"Help others?" George burst out. "And how can we do that? Seems like it's hard enough just looking out for ourselves these days." For once, Mary had a feeling that George was right. Life was certainly much harder than it would have been back in Albany.

Father stared silently at George. Then he said, "To begin with, we can build a mill on Meyers' Creek east of our cabin. One day, newcomers won't have to travel so far to Napanee. You pointed out this site, George, but I made the decision to stay here for two reasons — the meadow *and* the stream."

"A mill! That's no small task!" George exclaimed.

Tobias groaned and looked sympathetically at George. Mary knew they were both overwhelmed by all the work Father had planned. She didn't mind so much, though. She knew that more

Loyalist settlers might come in the spring, and then there would be more shanties built and more parties. She could hardly wait.

* * * *

"Phew! I thought Father would never stop talking," George said as he guided the horses along the Bay trail to Bleecker's Castle. "I like that bit about Abram coming and taking over a new land, but we've heard it already . . . "

"Yes," Mary sighed, "when Father gives us a day away, it's after we've done the chores and listened to him talk for hours."

"That's not fair, Mary," Catharine said. She was sitting just the other side of George on the front bench of the wagon. "We only have a Bible reading once a week and it's for Sundays."

Their conversation was shattered by the distinct loud howl of an animal in the woods — and not far away.

George tensed and reached for the loaded rifle at his feet. Boots bristled and stared into the woods.

"Isn't it silly to have that musket loaded, George?" Mary asked.

"I like to be ready, just in case." George sounded as if he was hoping for danger. "It sounded a lot like a wolf."

"The horses will run away if they're frightened, and then we'll be in more danger from runaway horses than from wolves," Mary said.

"Well, I can handle them, so why are you worrying?"

"I'm not worrying. But I think the more immediate danger is from runaway horses," Mary shot back.

"You two are both crazy," Tobias shouted from his bed of hay. "The wind's from the south, and it's carrying our scent north into the woods. The bears are our main worry — more than wolves — and no bear will hang around the road to greet us. If there are bears in the woods, they'll be headed north as fast as they can go to get away from us."

"I didn't know that, Tobias," Catharine said with relief.

"It's when there's no breeze and you startle them — that's when they fight," Tobias continued.

"Except when they have young," said George. "They're more aggressive then."

"But it was a wolf's cry. What will a wolf do?" Catharine asked.

"The small animals in the woods better watch out," Tobias said. "Besides, it's probably just a lone one. We haven't seen any packs around. Anyway they go for easier prey unless they're starving. And at this time of year, they have plenty."

"Enough about wolves and bears," Mary interrupted. "Are we anywhere near John's?"

"Almost there," said George, who had visited John in the spring. They had been travelling almost an hour when the horses broke over a rolling hill overlooking a fertile valley below. On the west side of the mouth of the Trent River were two small cabins about three hundred feet from shore, surrounded by at least three acres of meadow. A palisade surrounded one cabin and a small shed. The other cabin stood outside the palisade to the south. Beyond the buildings the wooded hills were aflame with orange, yellow, and red maple leaves interspersed with occasional streaks of evergreen.

"That's the trading post to the left." Still holding the reins, George pointed to the spot.

But Mary was staring at the other building. "And why is the other cabin surrounded by a palisade?"

"He needs to protect himself from attack."

"Attacks from the Mississaugas?" Catharine asked.

"I doubt that. He has an active trade with the Mississaugas and welcomes all who come. And they are happy that he's here. It saves them travelling farther — to Singleton's Trading Post or Napanee to trade their furs and pick up supplies."

"Maybe he's afraid of the wild animals." Mary looked to the north at hills covered thickly with pine trees and undergrowth, just the place for wolves and bears to lurk, and shivered.

Tobias was kneeling now and looking out over the side of the wagon. "There's a good-sized clearing separating John's buildings from the woods, so I can't understand why he needs a spiked fence. After all, animals don't come into a clearing. We're as close to the woods as he is and we have no stockade."

George laughed. "I have never known John to be so wary. Maybe living alone in this wilderness makes even *him* lose his courage."

"Don't be silly, George," Mary snapped. "John is

a lot braver than you, and he has a lot more initiative, too."

"Oh, he has, has he? And how do you figure that?"

"He's set up his own place, hasn't he? And he's farther into this wilderness than even Father dared go."

"What's a couple of miles?"

"Well, it's his own."

"Stop, you two!" Catharine said. "That's crazy talk, Mary. You know George would be settling at his own place now if he wasn't helping the family. And about John . . . I think he's just watchful, since he's living alone. I would want a stockade if I were living alone."

George drew the horses up to the Trent River. Across the three hundred feet of steel blue rippling water, they could see that the palisade was even higher than it appeared at first. The pine spikes were so tightly bound together that no one could see through them. The trading post was in clear sight, however, and so were a canoe and punt drawn up on the far shore. There was no sign of John.

George cupped his hands over his mouth and yelled across the river. "Hello!"

Mary scanned the entire clearing, and around it, but there was still no sign of life. "Hello, John!" she shouted. Her high-pitched voice carried on the morning air better than George's deep voice. "Jo — "

Mary stopped and Catharine gasped.

Two young men, about George's age, came around from the back of the trading post. One jumped onto a lean horse almost hidden from view by a red-leafed maple tree. The other man, carrying a small bag slung over his back, leaped for his horse, too, but as he landed on it, another man fell upon him from the lowest branch of the maple tree. It was John. The two tumbled off the horse and rolled over and over on the ground. By their clothing and their bare-backed horses, Mary knew the two strangers were Mississaugas.

Without a boat to go across, they could not help. George pulled his musket from the wagon.

"Don't be a fool, George," Tobias said. "You don't want to hit either one of them. Anyway, John can take care of himself."

Empty-handed, the Mississauga tore himself free from John and jumped on his horse. He glanced at his companion and they both galloped off to the north. Once again, George raised his gun. Tobias pushed it down with his arm. "Stop, George!"

John put down the bag he had taken from the young Mississauga and ran to the water's edge. He grabbed two oars, jumped into the punt, and began to row across the river. As he came closer, Mary could see that he was a mess of tousled hair and torn shirt.

George tied the horses to a sturdy tree and waited. When John reached the east bank, George grabbed the prow of the punt and pulled it up on the shore. John jumped onto dry land. His bare left knee was sticking out of his brown breeches and his shirt was ripped right down the middle of the front. The dark blond hair on his chest bristled through the gaping hole. His lower left jaw was turning blue, and when he smiled, a bit of blood trickled from his nose.

"I'm fine," he said, staggering up the bank. "I got back the goods. I just couldn't believe it. I have never had any trouble with the Mississaugas before."

"Did you know them?" Mary asked.

"In a way . . . They're youths who came with their fathers to trade a couple of weeks ago. I suspect it was only a prank, but I taught them a lesson they won't soon forget."

Catharine was staring at John with something like fear. "If you had just let them take the things, would their people not have made them return them?"

"Probably not. They might not even find out about it, unless I went there and identified them. And they wouldn't know they didn't trade them for pelts. Anyway, I never mind a good fight."

John strolled over to Mary and Catharine. "I'm so glad you've come. I can hardly wait to show you around."

Mary was not sure whether he was talking to her or Catharine or both, but while she was thinking, Catharine said, "You have been busy, John, but it's been worth it. You've built a beautiful trading post and home." John rubbed the blood and sweat from his mouth and gave Catharine a boyish smile.

Mary wished she had said that first. Now somewhat peeved, she said, "But, John, why do you have a stockade? I thought only forts had stockades."

"That's true, Mary, but I just can't see living this close to the woods without some protection. I don't want to take any risks with wild animals." He looked tenderly at Catharine even as he was answering Mary. Had John built the stockade to protect Catharine? Did he have plans for himself and Catharine? Mary knew that John would never worry about himself, for he'd have a musket nearby to shoot any animal that might stray near the cabin. Mary glanced sideways at John, but his face betrayed nothing.

"Well, now that that's over," he was saying, "we might as well hop in my punt and head over to Bleecker's Grove."

"I thought it was Bleecker's Castle," Mary said sharply. If John was not going to return her affection, she decided she might as well enjoy being angry with him.

"Oh, that's my home," John laughed.

"I'll show you my trading post first," John announced, directing George to steer the punt that way.

"Sure," George said. He was gazing towards the palisade, hoping to see Lucy come running out.

"You go in the front door and I'll go around the side so I can let you into the supply room," John barked, striding towards the post.

Inside the cold, dark building, streaks of sunlight were filtering through chinks in the wall. The sharp smell of freshly cut logs and tanned furs assaulted them. Catharine looked as if she might faint; Mary grinned and breathed in huge gulps of air. "Come on into my supply room," John announced, looking as proud as a barnyard rooster. He pulled a bar behind the counter and it opened like a door. Tobias smiled and whistled at the sight of shelves stacked high with items for trade: cooking pots, beaver and fishing spears, razors, and knives. A pile of pelts lay across a table on the far side of the room.

"Not too many pelts now," John boasted. "I sold all I got in the spring and now I mostly get supplies to trade for winter."

"Do you ever give credit to your customers?" Tobias asked.

"Yes, often. And it's no problem. If misfortune strikes a man who owes me, his clan honours the debt. The other tribes are just as trustworthy. It's a revered custom — to be responsible for their kin."

"Whew, that's better than British law, where they can throw a man in jail for his debts," George offered, still wondering where Lucy was.

"There's not much of that either — not in this new land. Neighbours help each other, you know."

"Well, it's too bad the British government wouldn't honour their own debts. Father said he was to receive three thousand acres for his work as captain, but so far they've given him only two hundred, and all of it barren land around King's Town."

"He had another hundred-acre lot," Mary said, "but it was north of King's Town and miles away from the two-hundred-acre lot. Father didn't even try to find it."

"I can see why," John smiled. "How can you farm a place that's separated by woods and swamps? I don't know what the government thinks it's doing. Governor Haldimand means well, but he's been a soldier all his life and knows nothing about farming and the hardships of clearing the land. Now, I have only around fifteen acres here, but it was a meadow, so I didn't have to clear much of it. I've claimed a few more acres not far from here — across the mouth of the river at Carrying Place. I built a small cabin there when I finished surveying the lots along the shoreline from King's Town. It's a great place to hunt and fish."

"Don't tell me he's boasting about his cabin again." Lucy had just burst into the supply room and was smiling at Tobias and George. They both looked as if they had been struck by a lightning bolt.

"Come *on*, John, I've been waiting and waiting back at the cabin, wondering what had happened to everyone and imagining the *worst*, the *worst*. Now don't let him keep you here any longer. Let's get back to the cabin so you can see around."

John somehow managed to be up front with Catharine again, and when he pushed open the gate in the palisade wall, he took her arm to help her through the opening. As Mary stumbled through last, behind Tobias, her eyes fell on the huge chain and lock on the small gate and on the larger gate that would be used when a team of horses needed to come through.

"What are *they* for?" Mary whispered to Tobias.

"I don't know," he mumbled. "Better not say anything just now, though." Mary didn't know why she shouldn't say anything, but she decided to take his advice.

"Welcome to Bleecker's Castle," John said as he swung open the door of his two-room cabin.

"Bleecker's Castle, eh?" George laughed. "Looks like a log cabin to me!"

The cabin was surprisingly cozy. The brightly coloured chintz curtains were obviously Lucy's handiwork. The first room was large — about twenty feet square. A long table with a bench on either side stood in front of the east window facing the river. On the north side of the room was a mahogany cupboard. A massive horsehair sofa and two wooden and leather chairs stood in front of the fireplace on the south wall.

"Ahem!" Lucy cleared her throat and curtsied. "As hostess of Bleecker's Castle, I welcome you. Just follow me for a grand tour." The boys laughed as Lucy hooked her arm around the smiling Catharine and led her over to the cupboard.

Mary's heart sank and she felt a strong pang of resentment towards Lucy. They were now in Catharine's domain — the household — and thanks to Lucy, she was in full swing.

"Oh, John, how did you ever manage to bring such a fine cupboard here?" Catharine asked.

"Well, my stepfather's shipping business helps," John said. "I bring more than cattle up in his bateaux. Look inside the cupboard, Catharine." John smiled bashfully and opened the cupboard with glee. Catharine gasped. Behind the wooden dishes at the front was a whole set of exquisite china dishes.

"I haven't seen anything this elegant since we left the farm, John!" she smiled.

"Collecting fine china, eh John?" George nudged his friend in the ribs. "I didn't know you were interested in this kind of stuff."

"I'm full of surprises, aren't I?" John smirked. "Now take a look at the bedroom." He pulled aside the blanket he had draped over the open doorway. "It has a fireplace too. It'll be nice and warm." Mary could see a large bed that had been built into the north-west corner of the framework of the room. Then she looked through the little window and out into the backyard. There was a third small shed out there.

"What's that building in the back, John?" she asked. Tobias peered over her shoulder to get a look.

"Just an old shed for storing wood," John said. Then he turned away from the window, and they all went back into the kitchen-sitting room. John kept near Catharine.

Mary couldn't help noticing all the attention John was giving Catharine. Still, her sister was just too frail to consider marriage. Surely Father would put a stop to this romance. Father would *never* allow it. She was certain of that.

Twelve

Mary stared at Tobias in disbelief. There he was, looking at the team of horses he had just brought from the field, apparently unaware that he had just shattered her whole world with the news. "Yes, Father has agreed to the marriage. It seems hard to believe, but he has." Tobias was unhooking the horses' traces from the wagon's whipple trees.

Mary stood and watched, unable to move. Finally she gasped, "Are you sure?"

"Yes, I'm sure, Mary." Tobias looked away as he went around to the front of the horses and removed the neck yoke from Bonnie's collar. "He told me himself, but . . ."

Mary turned and ran towards the barn. She had to get away from Tobias and everyone to a quiet spot where she could think and get rid of the knot in her stomach. She just couldn't go in and face any of them at the supper table.

Mary swung open one of the barn doors, stepped inside, and threw her egg basket down on the floor. As she leaned against the wall and looked at the two cows chomping their feed, her eyes went blurry. She could hear Tobias coming with the horses. She picked up her egg basket, crawled along the landing between the mangers, and started searching for eggs in the hay along the edges. Her brother's sharp steps hit the dirt floor with a thud as he flung Duke's harness onto a nail over the horses' stalls.

"Tobias, I just can't go in to supper now. I just can't."

Tobias sat down beside her. "You know, Mary. This has been awful sudden. I wouldn't be the least bit surprised if it doesn't all fall apart before spring. I think that's the reason Father gave in so easily. I know he's convinced of it. In fact, he told me so. He said, 'John Bleecker has a mighty stubborn streak and it's easier to outwit him than to cross him.' So spruce up."

Mary blew her nose. "You know, Tobias, I've thought the same thing about Catharine and John. They're so different."

"Well, let's go along to supper. It'll be waiting."

Tobias closed both barn doors and dropped the crossbar that held them in place. Mary shivered as she waited. They walked in silence to the new log-rail fence, and Tobias opened the gate for Mary. On the other side, they took the path to the house. At the back kitchen door, Mary hesitated for a minute, then turned to speak to Tobias. Golden rays from the setting sun fell on her auburn hair.

"Thanks," she said. "I'm glad you told me first." She managed a small smile, then steeled herself for the supper ahead. "Guess what!" she said as they walked in. "I found three eggs tonight. We'll soon have enough to bake for a party. Anyone like to have a party?" She was trying to sound happy, but she knew her voice had a hollow tone. John was seated on a straight wooden chair on the far side of the room near the kitchen cupboard. Catharine was smiling at him as she showed him the freshly baked golden-crusted buns she had just taken from the bake-oven beside the fireplace.

John smiled at Catharine, took her free hand, and jumped to his feet. "Well, as a matter of fact, we do have news that calls for a celebration. Now that you're all here, I have an announcement to make."

Father, who was sitting in the big chair by the fireplace, did not turn his head but stared into the glowing wood coals.

John cleared his throat and a slight pink hue crept through the blond stubble on his jaw. "Catharine and I . . . are going to be married!" Everyone but Father stared at John and then at Catharine.

George broke the silence. "Great! You've always been like a brother, John. And now it's official."

Father smiled a little as he came over to shake John's hand and hug Catharine. Mary noticed that he was strangely quiet. Mother also hugged Catharine, but she seemed flustered as she dabbed her eyes with the corner of her apron.

With Mary close beside him, Tobias walked towards the happy couple and said, "We'll miss you, Catharine." And he gave her a hug and a kiss on the cheek.

Mary swallowed, forced a smile, and said, "Yes, we — "

"You won't have to worry about that for some time yet," Mother interrupted in a brisk tone. "We've many things to do to finish Catharine's hope chest. What with moving and all, we just haven't had the time to think about getting ready for a wedding or a new home."

John turned to Mother. "Don't worry about anything. My house has all the necessities. I've been bringing things by bateau for the last several months."

Mother bristled a little. "Well, John, there are some traditions that — "

"We're in a new land. We may not be able to follow the old ways. We must adjust to new ones."

"Well, I'm only talking about a few new quilts, and . . . well . . . a wedding takes time, too."

"Our wedding plans have already been made in King's Town. The minister will be there on Saturday, the seventh of October. My mother has the reception all planned."

Mother turned so pale they all thought she was going to faint. Tobias reached her first and helped her to the horsehair couch.

Father's clear blue eyes darkened as he stood up and glared at John Bleecker, who had taken a position behind the couch. With flushed cheeks and feet apart, John stood silently, staring straight back at him.

* * * *

At King's Town in the Bleeckers' front room, on the seventh of October, Catharine W. Meyers and

John R. Bleecker stood before the Rev. John Langhorn, a Church of England minister. The bride was dressed in a long gown of light blue linen with a wide velvet royal-blue sash. It was not elaborate; it was made out of material from a party gown that Mother had worn back in Albany.

Catharine's radiant hair fell in soft curls around her face and hung waist length below the light-blue velvet hat that her mother had made for her. Now, looking straight up at the minister, Catharine repeated the words that would bind her and John together for life.

Mary sat beside Tobias, straight as an arrow, her eyes fixed on a wall clock to the left of the minister. John spoke his vows in a clear, crisp tone. He was wearing his DeLancey's regiment military uniform. The bright red short coat, with green facing, showed a red vest beneath. The silver edging of his buttonholes and the silver lace along the wings of his coat gave him a rich look that reminded them all of better times before the war. His sturdy figure showed even through his white breeches and stockings, and his short black leggings and black shoes were polished for the occasion.

Even after the minister had finished and everyone was shaking hands, Mary could hardly believe the wedding had actually taken place. A mere three months before she had been dancing and laughing with John right here in King's Town.

"C'mon, Mary. Let's kiss the bride," Tobias said. He took Mary's hand and propelled her over to the couple. Only the two families were present for

the ceremony, but after the evening meal, there
would be a party at the army barracks. It had all
been planned by Mrs. Bleecker, and it seemed that
most of the folks from King's Town and the sur-
rounding area would be coming. John was well
known. As well as surveying that whole area, he
had delivered supplies to many farmers.

Mary reached for Catharine's outstretched
arms and the two sisters held each other quietly
for a long time. Mary had always been able to
count on Catharine for a sympathetic ear. Who
else would ever be so loyal? Mary felt a sharp jab
in her ribs. It was George.

"Move on, Mary. You're holding up the line."

"George!" Catharine said with authority. "Don't
push her!" George shuffled uneasily. "Yeah, yeah . . .
sorry, Mary."

Mary was facing John now and smiling widely.
"You'll make a great brother, John." Then she
whispered just loud enough so George could hear.
"A better-tempered one than George." John
smiled over her head at George, and Mary walked
over to stand beside Tobias, who was already talking to Lucy on the opposite side of the room.

"Oh, Tobias," Lucy said as she rubbed her hand
along his upper vest, "just wait till I show you this
new dance step. We could try it right here so we'll
be ready for the dance later." Lucy looked especially beautiful tonight. Her hair was piled high on
her head and tied there with red velvet ribbons
and bows that hung down on her bare neck and
white shoulders. Her bright red, full linen gown
fell in loose flounces over a full white petticoat.

Lucy took Tobias's arm, put it around her waist, and started showing him the step. "Now you take one step this way, another that way and . . . Tobias, why aren't you dancing? "

"Maybe we should wait," Tobias smiled, taking his hand away from her waist, but doing nothing to prevent her from taking his arm.

"*I'm* ready and available for lessons," George said, pushing up on the other side of Lucy.

She smiled at both brothers but hung onto Tobias's arm and did not move. Mary guessed that George noticed, for when Mary moved away from them, he followed. They sat down together on the horsehair couch near the fireplace in unaccustomed silence. Neither had the strength nor the will to fight.

Mary couldn't stand to watch the newly married couple so she turned to George, who was staring at the long table that servants were setting for the wedding dinner. "Mrs. Bleecker's table looks lovely, doesn't it, George?"

"Yeah, I suppose so," he mumbled. His blue-green eyes had turned dark and glowering.

Part Two

Into the Valley

Thirteen

"Yes, Mother, we'll bring Catharine back," Mary said impatiently.

"Now remember you have the midwife's bag — just in case — and Godspeed."

Mother smiled as she handed the little bag to Mary, who sat on the front seat of the wagon. George had already put the two other bags down behind her — an overnight one for herself and a new layette for Catharine's unborn baby.

The winter of 1787 had gone quickly, and it was already the middle of June and still a whole month ahead of Catharine's time, so Mary couldn't see any reason for Mother's concern. But she smiled back at Mother's beaming face and waved. She knew that Mother could hardly wait to have a new baby in the family.

George led the horses across the dooryard and onto the Bay Trail. This was the name George had given the trail to Catharine and John's. Now they all called it that. The team had just finished a day of hard work pulling tree stumps, so he let the reins hang loosely in his hands and across his knees. It had been a hot day, but a fresh, soothing breeze was blowing up from the bay. Mary wished Tobias had come instead, but George insisted that John was his best friend and had persuaded Father to let him go.

"I hope Catharine comes back with us, but I don't think she'll leave John this far ahead," George said. "So I guess you'll be staying."

Mary really did not want to stay at Bleecker's Castle. She had never had a conversation alone with John since he had announced his intention to marry Catharine. Somehow, she couldn't help feeling a little embarrassed about her feelings last summer. Had he noticed? She thought not, for she had never voiced her emotions. And how did she feel now? She wasn't really sure, but one thing she did know: she would not talk to John or be alone with him.

Mary stared at George, who was still looking at her like a cat eyeing a mouse. "I'll try my best to persuade her to come now," she said. "And I think she'll be willing. But I didn't know you were so lonesome for Catharine, George."

George looked relieved in spite of his best efforts to look superior. "Oh, I'll be glad to have Catharine home all right, but that's not my big worry." He paused for a few seconds. "I . . . I just don't see how Mother and Anna can manage without you." Mary laughed. "Why, George, I do believe it's my *cooking* you'll miss!"

"I must admit that's a part of it, Mary, but it's more than that. It's . . . Oh, boy, I never thought I'd say this, but you *are* strong, Mary, and you never complain. No matter how tough things get,

I always know I can count on you. Yes, Anna's cooking is terrible, and Mother and Catharine are sick so much, it's depressing. Sometimes I think they'll die of consumption one of these days. But you're always the same, so strong all the time and you're always there."

"The willing horse."

"Now, Mary, don't take offence. I'm *trying* to be nice. You know you're stronger than your sisters. I guess that's why you get asked to do so much, but when the harvest is in this fall, you and I are going to King's Town for a great visit."

"Would you really take me?"

"Of course, I would. I'm going to let you in on a secret, Mary. I'm applying for a lot of my own not far from here. Father is hoping to get the deeds to his land, too. Some of his payment from the government came through and he's going to buy the land he's squatting on."

"So you and Father will both be landowners!"

"I hope so . . . but even if I don't get it, I'm going to start my own place next spring. I'll just take this great site I've found. Possession is nine-tenths of the law."

"Really, George? Where is this spot? I'd love to see it."

"It's just west of Father's land. We go past the bottom of it on the Bay Trail all the time, but maybe next Sunday we could look it over."

"I'd love to do that, George. I wish *I* had my own land."

"You can, Mary. The government's working on a new law that says land will be granted to children of Loyalists — not just men. Tobias and I will get bigger lots, though, because we joined up for a while."

Mary laughed. "Yes, after a peace treaty was already signed. It's a wonder they let you do that."

"They were glad of the help at Machiche," George shot back, "with so many refugees to set up and care for."

"I know, I know. And you did a good job, George. But just remember — Mother and I worked like horses helping the refugee women and children, but we didn't get any pay or recognition."

"Next thing, you'll be telling me women should be allowed to join the army," George guffawed.

"Oh, George, we *do* have trouble agreeing, even when we're *trying* to be agreeable."

They rode on in silence. Mary noticed that the moon was coming out full now and there were strange sounds coming from the woods. Boots put his nose in the air and gave a low growl.

"It's only an owl, Mary. They make such an eerie sound for a harmless bird." Mary didn't believe George because she could see that Boots's ears were up and his hair was bristling as he sniffed the air.

Mary peered into the full maple trees and thick cedar undergrowth. Then she flung her arms around Boots, who had moved to the right side of the wagon, between her and the woods. "It's a bear!" she screamed and clung to the dog.

The horses reared and came to a halt. George stood up and peered into the darkness ahead. Mary could not believe what he was doing. He was steering the horses to the right — heading straight for the bear!

"George! The bear!" she gasped out. Then, peering ahead, she could see in the moonlight that the pathway jutted back to the woods at this point, and the space between them and the bay was dangerously narrow. The horses were becoming frantic and refused to move ahead.

"Where?" George asked. "I don't see any bear." With a sharp flip of his wrist, George whipped the horses violently, but they only reared back all the higher.

George was about to whip the horses again when his right hand froze on the whip-handle. "A bear! It's a bear!"

The black beast reared on its hind legs and lunged towards them. George jerked at the horses' heads to turn them around. Their tails brushed against the limbs of a willow, but they scraped through the space. The creaking wagon followed with a sharp twist that almost broke the wooden pole.

The horses, starting back along the trail towards home, were soon going at a frantic speed. The flat wagon was tilting from side to side. Mary hung onto the seat with one hand and pulled hard on Boots's hair to keep him from jumping off the wagon.

George pulled even tighter on the reins. "Whoa!" he gasped. His voice was hoarse with fear.

Mary took a quick look behind and stared in disbelief. On the moonlit pathway, the large bear had stopped and was now nuzzling two young cubs on the trail.

"She's not coming after us," Mary yelled. "She only wanted her cubs."

It took George a while to get the horses to stop. When they had finally ground to a halt, George looked at Mary and panted, "Well, what do we do now?"

"Let's go on," urged Mary. "She has her cubs now. She won't bother us. . . . Will she?"

"I don't think so, but we should give her time to move away from that narrow spot. She'll probably take the cubs back into the woods."

"If we get to Catharine's tonight, we could start home early in the morning. Let's wait a bit and then go on."

The stars came out brightly as they sat quietly on the wagon. Boots crawled over and stuck his head between them, and Mary scratched him behind the ears.

"Mary, do you ever wonder about the future?" George asked.

"All the time, when I have time."

"Do you ever think about getting married?"

"Yes, I do, but I don't see much chance out here."

"How about if you met someone in King's Town?"

"King's Town?"

"Yeah, maybe Lucy would introduce you to someone."

"Oh, Lucy!" Mary said in an amused tone. "So who's she going to marry — you or Tobias?"

"Neither of us if we don't go to see her soon. There's all kinds of available men in King's Town."

"That's a great thought, George. Don't you think we could get away before fall? I'd like to meet some of those men. As for Lucy, she really likes both of you. I used to think she liked Tobias more — she danced more with him than anyone at Catharine's wedding — but now I'm not so sure. She didn't tell me anything when she visited us this spring. But I *do* know that she doesn't have a steady boy calling yet. So there's still hope for one of you. I just don't know which one."

"You're right, Mary. Let's not wait. Let's go in mid-July after all the hay's in and everything's weeded and tilled. There should be a little free time then before the harvest."

"Yes, that's when we went to Albany last year," Mary said brightly. Then her face fell as she thought of John and the great fun they'd had together.

George took up the reins. "Well if we're going to Bleecker's Castle tonight, we'd better get started."

"Do you think we've waited long enough?"

"I hope so . . . I'll go slow. You keep watching the edge of the woods." George turned the horses around and started walking them slowly along the trail.

Mary peered into the trees close along the edge of the trail. The moon cast a bright light ahead, but the woods were still dark and formless. If another bear came after them, they would not have much warning.

George kept a tight hold on the reins, ready to stop the horses if they were frightened again. Mary and George both knew that Duke and

Bonnie would spook easily now. Even Boots sat upright and alert on the floor of the wagon between them with his long nose in the air as if trying to find the scent again.

By the time they reached the mouth of the Trent River, two hours had passed since they had left home. Mary looked down into the beautiful valley backed by the thick woods of stately pines. She could see a figure at the open entrance of the palisade and knew it was John.

Mary waited while George led the horses into a small barnshed that John had built by the bush. After he had poured out a generous helping of oats for each horse, they walked down to the shore and George pushed the waiting canoe out into the water. Mary knelt up front ready to paddle on her right while George slid into the back seat and grabbed the other paddle. With one bound, Boots, a long, golden mass of fur, jumped lightly into the canoe between them and sat up proudly. Only his eyes moved as they headed for the opposite shore.

John walked slowly down to the water's edge and reached out to grab the bow of the canoe. "I've been worried about you," he said. "Catharine has been looking for you for a week now, and I was sure today was the day your father said you'd be coming."

"Did you figure we fell in the river?" George asked.

"Oh, I know you can take care of yourself, George. You've proved that before. But Catharine was worried. She couldn't sleep and kept sending me out to look for you."

"Well, we're here safe and sound," Mary replied.

The night was quiet now. There was hardly a ripple on the water, and the silence around them was broken only by the chirping of crickets as they walked through the stockade gate. Mary went on ahead, but when she heard the clink of the lock and chain, she turned around to see John locking the gate.

"You can never be too careful," he said. He sounded almost apologetic.

"You sure can't," George said. "We were almost caught by a bear. Just about ran over its young. Then she chased us for a mile." Mary smiled at George's flair for exaggeration.

As the travellers and John stepped into the dark front room, Catharine came out of the little bedroom with a raised candle in her hand. She was wearing a long white shift and looked thin despite her pregnancy.

"Oh, Mary. I'm so glad you've come. I've looked for you every day this week." She was crying a little.

"We've come to take you home," Mary said, putting her arms around her. Her eyes met John's stern stare from across the room and she added, "That is, until the baby comes."

"Oh no, Mary," Catharine exclaimed, standing back from her sister. "I'll not leave John until much nearer my time. And the baby isn't due for a month yet. But I'm counting on you staying with me. I'm depending on you. You won't leave me now, will you, Mary?"

Fourteen

When Mary woke up the next morning, the sun was shining brightly through the window of the kitchen sitting-room. She had slept better and longer than she had expected. As she slipped out from under the sheets on the horsehair couch, she looked towards the bedroom door. All was quiet.

Surely she could persuade her sister to go back home for a visit. Once she was there, Mother would convince her to stay.

Mary pulled her short-gown over her head and slipped into her outer petticoat. One would be enough over a shift on a hot day like this. She stuffed the inner petticoat into her overnight bag along with her mob cap. Her tangled curly hair dropped loosely around her shoulders and down her back. Rays of sunlight streaming into the room highlighted her auburn hair with streaks of deep golden red.

Mary tiptoed across to the side-table and cut off a thick slice of bread on the breadboard. Catharine must have baked the day before, for the fresh loaf bent as she cut into it. She dipped into the small crock of butter sitting beside the bread and spread it on thick. Then she searched for some of the strawberry jam she knew Mother had sent over to Catharine.

Bread in hand, Mary went outside and around behind the cabin to find George, who had slept in the shed. To her left was a full-size vegetable garden: a few of the earliest potatoes had already been dug up; the carrot tops were about six inches high, and the peas had already formed pods. "What are you doing here?" John snapped. Mary looked up and saw him standing with George.

"I was looking for George."

John laughed. "George slept in, but I just got him up. Your father's going to be mighty restless waiting for his team."

"Not half as restless as Mother waiting for Catharine," Mary said. "I think we should wake her up now and get ready."

"That won't be necessary. Look. Catharine must be getting breakfast." John was right; smoke was coming from the chimney. "I don't think Catharine wants to leave just yet," George said. "So I'll grab a bite and be on my way."

"Mother thinks it best she come now."

"I know," George said. "But I think it should be up to John what his wife does."

"Oh, you think so, do you, George?" Mary's eyes were flashing as she shook her uncombed mop of hair and turned to John. "So, are you ready to deliver the baby?"

"Me? Why on earth would you ask me that, Mary? The baby's not due for another month.

And Catharine plans to leave long before then."

"On the farm, we often help animals give birth, but you didn't grow up on a farm, did you, John?"

"Well, we did have puppies. Remember Boots? We almost lost him. He was the runt of the lot, and look at him now."

George gave John a condescending look and said, "Maybe Mary's right. I'd be happy to take Catharine now."

"I'm not stopping her. If she wants to go, that's fine with me. Let's ask her."

Catharine was squatting beside the fire, dropping bits of dough for pancakes into the iron-spider frying pan. Her cheeks were flushed now, and Mary was glad to see she still had a bit of colour. "Has George gone?" she asked, turning around towards John and Mary.

"No, I'm still here," George said, sauntering through the doorway. "How are you this morning, Catharine?"

"Better," she said and smiled up at him.

"Good. Could you get ready in a hurry to go with us?"

Catharine glanced over at John, who was looking at her intently. "Not today, George," she said. "I thought we settled that last night. I'll go later."

John gave George a defiant look. "We're so near you folks. It really won't take us long to bring Catharine any time."

George nodded.

"May I help you with breakfast?" Mary asked. She followed Catharine over to the side table.

"Just by being here, you help," Catharine said.

"I can't tell you how glad I am to have you, Mary. You may set the table if you wish."

When the breakfast was over, George left in a hurry, and John went to see him off. From the doorway, Mary watched them go through the stockade and was pleased to see that it wasn't locked. At least she wouldn't feel like a prisoner all the time. Catharine went over and sat on the couch. "Just leave the dishes for now. Come and talk a bit."

Mary sat in a large wooden chair next to her sister and studied her more intently. She could see that Catharine was tired, even though it was early morning. "Are you well, Catharine?" she asked.

"Of course I am. I'm not as energetic as I used to be because of my condition. And that's normal. . . . But I can hardly wait for the baby, Mary." Catharine seemed to have more energy now. "Come and see the cradle John made."

Catharine got up slowly and led Mary into the bedroom, and there in the far corner was a fine little wooden cradle that had been whittled out of hard maple.

"It's beautiful. I'm sure it'll last for many babies."

"You're right, it will!" Catharine gave Mary a radiant smile. "Oh, Mary. I'm so happy. If God wills, I plan to have a baby every year or so for the next ten years at least. Maybe even longer!"

Mary pulled back the dark muslin curtains from the window, and light glinted off Catharine's blonde hair as she squatted there by the cradle. She looked up at Mary and her eyes were bright with joy. Mary's concern for her sister's health left her then as she stared down at Catharine's glowing, happy face.

In the cradle was the wool shawl that Mother had sent over in the spring. Several warm flannel clouts were piled there, too, along with some belly bindings and shirts. "Mother has lots more of these waiting at home for you, Catharine. She's determined this baby will not be deprived, even though he's born in this wilderness."

"He?" Catharine turned and stared at her sister with a little smile.

"Do you want a boy or a girl?" Mary asked. She was starting to get bored looking at baby clothes.

"I'll be so happy with either, Mary." Catharine was sickeningly agreeable, as usual, but Mary decided not to comment.

"What names have you chosen?"

"John — if he's a boy. I hope he'll grow up to be just like his father."

"And what if the baby's a girl? Will she be 'Catharine'?"

"No, I want to call her Polly if she's a girl."

"Mother will like that. Now, why don't you just rest here while I clean up the dishes."

"You'll spoil me, Mary. I'm not sick, you know." But she went over to the bed, leaned back against the pillow, closed her eyes, and said, "I'll be out in a minute."

Mary took the pail of water from its stool by the door and poured its contents into a kettle to heat for washing. Then she went out to get more water. As she walked down the pathway to the stockade gate, she wondered about the shed behind the cabin. She just had to see inside it. John would not have been so secretive without a reason.

Mary thrust her head out through the opening in the stockade. There was no sign of John. He must have gone to the trading post. So she stepped back inside, put the pail down, and ran behind the house to the shed. The door opened easily, but the shed was windowless, so its interior was completely dark except for streaks of light coming through cracks between some of the logs. It took a full minute for her eyes to adjust. She was surprised to see nothing but huge piles of dried-out hay.

But maybe something was hidden under the hay. She scurried around the shed and searched under the hay on one side of the shed. There was nothing there but hay. Then she crossed over to the other side of the shed, clawed through the thick, dry hay until her hand hit something hard. She'd found a huge barrel with a plug in the top. Liquor! That's what it was. During the war years, she had seen these kegs on cargo ships coming into New York harbour for the soldiers. It was probably rum. She dug farther and found two more barrels.

Why would John have barrels and barrels of rum stored here? Then her heart sank. The answer was too obvious. John was trading rum for furs, and he was hiding the stuff from the authorities. It was illegal here, too, wasn't it?

* * * *

"Your time is only two weeks away, Catharine. If George doesn't come this morning, please let John take us back home this afternoon. I'm surprised Mother hasn't sent George before now."

"John has to take supplies to Colonel Young at East Lake today," Catharine said. "But I'll go the end of this week, no matter what." East Lake was on the opposite side of the peninsula to the south.

"You'll go today, Catharine, or I'm going on foot," Mary threatened. She certainly didn't intend to leave Catharine, but there seemed no other way to persuade her. "Since I've been here, he's been gone overnight three times," she continued. "What if you had gone into labour!"

"He knows it's not my time yet." Catharine's voice was quietly reassuring. "I'll be just fine. But, Mary, I can hardly wait to see my baby."

"Does John leave you all alone like that when I'm not here?"

"Well . . . he did make quite a few trips for his stepfather by bateau this spring."

"He what! He must have left you for a week or two, then. And you were here all alone!"

Catharine looked away from Mary's widening green eyes.

"Catharine, why didn't you come home to visit? Or we could have come for you."

"John wanted me to keep track of things at the post. And at night, I came back inside the stockade, so I was safe. Anyway, John is well liked by the Mississaugas and the few Mohawks that trade with him. There weren't any problems, Mary."

"But didn't you get bronchitis again this spring?"

"You know, Mary, it's surprising, but it didn't seem to tighten down on me the same as it usually does. Maybe being pregnant agrees with me."

"Well, John should not have left you in charge here alone."

"John works very hard, and we needed the money his stepfather pays him. He brought back many supplies. He even had to store some of them out in the shed."

"Oh, and what does he have stored there?"

"I have no idea. I never keep track. John leaves a few staples of food — bags of flour, salt, and sugar to hold over when he leaves. He says to tell the traders to come back in a week, when he gets back, and he'll have more supplies in."

Mary knew that she would have to get John on her side if she was to succeed in getting Catharine home on time. But she would have to calm down before she spoke to him. She didn't like his leaving her sister alone like that.

"Why don't you rest now, Catharine," she said. "I'm going to start weeding the garden before the day gets any hotter."

Mary hurried through the gate, and headed south to the post. She could see four Indian ponies tied up outside, but she didn't care. She needed to talk to John about Catharine and that was final.

As she approached the post, four Mississauga traders sauntered out the front door. The first three slapped their new supplies onto their horses and tied them securely. Then she saw the last man rolling a small barrel of rum away from the post.

He lashed it onto his horse and headed north with the others.

John's back was to the door as she entered. "No!" he was shouting. "One barrel, the cooking pots, and the fishing spears. That was a fair trade. And I will not sell you more rum now at any price. That's final — only one barrel of rum!"

John turned around then and saw Mary staring at him. "What are you talking about, John?" she asked.

John's face was turning red under his morning stubble. "Nothing of importance, Mary. Nothing at all."

Now was not the time to make an issue of the rum. The main point was to get Catharine home.

"John," Mary said firmly, "I've come about Catharine. She's very weak, the baby could come anytime, and I want to take her back home — now!"

"You forget, Mary, that Catharine *is* home," he said quietly, with a tinge of pride in his voice.

"Let me put it this way," Mary went on. "Unless you are prepared to deliver this baby by yourself, John, I want to go to my home with Catharine, today. She is not well."

"She's pregnant, not sick," John retorted.

Mary stared at John in disbelief. He was not showing the concern that he should. Did he truly love her sister? "Catharine has always been sickly," she said.

John walked over to the counter and stood in front of Mary. "If you don't watch, you're going to end up just like your nervous mother. And an old maid to boot!"

In an instant she swung her arm across the countertop and aimed for John's ear. But he caught her hand in midair, laughed as he held it there, then pressed it down on the countertop, still holding his hand over hers. His dancing blue eyes stared straight into Mary's. She looked down as all the old feelings she'd had for him came rushing back, and her heart thumped so hard she was afraid he'd hear it. She just could not feel this way. He was married to her sister!

"We must leave today," she said in a low voice, not daring to look straight into his eyes.

John pulled up his hand then, and his voice sounded strangely different. "I can understand your concern," he said. "It will be much better for Catharine to be with her mother and a midwife when her time comes. If George doesn't come today, I'll take you tomorrow, I promise."

"Why not today, John?" Mary persisted.

"I promised to deliver goods to the Youngs and the Weeses. I gave my word they'd have this order by now. I should have gone yesterday, but I was waiting for those traders who just left."

"Where do these customers live?

"Both families live across the bay, on the peninsula."

"Can't that wait?"

"Why? Catharine's time is at least two weeks away."

"I hope you've told John Jr. that," Mary said. John sounded so confident she was relaxing enough to joke a little. She guessed she had been acting like a Mother hen lately. It was good to hear John's merry laughter.

"Well, I can't say that I have, but I'll remember to do that, Mary." And he laughed heartily again. The last time Mary had heard him laugh like that was the summer before, when they'd gone on the raid to Albany. John, too, had changed in the past year. He had grown strangely quiet.

John looked at Mary across the countertop. "Well, Mary, do you want to come in and look at these furs I just got? They'll bring a pretty penny, I'm telling you."

"I have work to do," she said, walking stiffly towards the door.

"Well, do as you like. You always do anyway."

As Mary walked along the pathway to the cabin, she could still feel the touch of John's hand over hers. She shouldn't have struck out at him. That temper of hers was always getting her into tight corners. But then she hadn't expected him to keep her hand glued to the countertop for so long. Maybe she had been right. Maybe Catharine and John were not suited for each other after all. They were just so different. Maybe . . . But she refused to think this way anymore. It gave her a choking feeling in her throat. John was married to her sister and that was final.

Fifteen

"Don't wait up for me," John said. He slung his rifle over his left shoulder. "It'll be dark when I get back." He nodded at Mary across the room, kissed Catharine quickly at the door, and disappeared into the sunlight.

Mary watched through the east window and saw him lock the gate to the stockade. She knew where the key hung, but she could not help feeling that they were being treated like prisoners.

Oh, well, their confinement wouldn't last for long. George might come any time — most likely at dusk when the horses were no longer needed at home. They must have the hay harvested by now, so surely he would come. Now that she knew John was trading rum, she felt more nervous about staying here. Whenever rum came on the scene, brawling was not far behind. Mary remembered drunken soldiers fighting on the streets of New York City during the war.

"You are quiet this afternoon, Mary," Catharine said. "I hope you aren't worrying about me again."

"Sort of," Mary said. "I guess we should pack for tomorrow."

"I'll put my clothes and the baby's in our bag right away. And you still haven't unpacked your bags, Mary. What's in that small one? You've never even opened it."

"Oh, Mother sent those things along — just in case I had to deliver the baby." She laughed. "You know Mother."

"Yes," Catharine smiled. "Always ready for any emergency. But it'll be good just the same to be back there. I'm glad we've decided to go in the morning. I feel tired now and ready to go. . . . But by morning, I'll probably hate to leave."

There was silence between them until Mary said, "I hope you'll stay home a good long time after the baby is born."

"Well, we both know Mother won't let me out of bed for two weeks."

It was still very hot in the room, and Catharine's eyes began to close. Mary rushed out to the garden. She would pull every weed so that Catharine's garden would survive her absence. Mary flung the weeds across to a pile at the side. The sun was hot, but she enjoyed the work.

It was almost dusk when Mary went back into the kitchen. The smell of fresh dumplings filled the spotless room. Catharine had been busy, too. She was leaning over the hot hearth now and turned and smiled up at her sister. "Everything's ready for us to leave in the morning," she said.

After their meal was over, Mary put her arms around Catharine to steady her as they walked towards the bedroom.

Catharine sank heavily onto the bed and strained

to take off her short gown and petticoats. Her white shift was stretched tight across her stomach.

"Rest easy now," Mary said.

"Don't work too late. You need a good night's rest, too."

The candle Catharine had set in some bear grease by the open window was doing a wonderful job of repelling the mosquitoes. But it smelled terrible and the night was hot. Mary felt a strong urge to get outside, away from the suffocating air. She tiptoed over to the table and, reaching under it, took the gate key off the nail on the wall.

Outside, the night air was cooler, but the mosquitoes were out in swarms. Mary swatted at them as she walked down the pathway to the stockade gate. Surely it would do no harm to walk to the riverbank.

The canoe was lying on the opposite bank, waiting for George. If only he would come riding along right now. For one of the few times in her life, Mary was looking forward to seeing her stubborn brother. She strained to see up the hill on the other side of the river, but shadows were filling in the spaces in the woods. Fireflies flashed in the darkness from time to time. When she got to the river's edge and heard the water lapping and slurping against the bank, she had to use all her strength to resist jumping in for a swim. But she must not do that. Catharine might need her.

Crickets chirped around her and an owl began to hoot. Then three more hoots came at regular intervals. She thought of Albany days and the games they used to play in the apple orchard. She and George and Tobias always used to signal each other with three owl hoots, just like those ones.

"Whoo . . . whoo . . . whoo," she hooted back, just for fun. Three hoots came wafting over the water again. It must be George. No owl would answer in such regular rhythm. Thank goodness, George had come. She cupped her hands around her mouth and answered the call once more. She waited for George's answer and kept her eyes on the wooded end of the trail, expecting to see the wagon come jostling down the trail past the thick clump of cedar trees.

But no owl's call came back to her, and nothing appeared between the cedars. A deeper darkness was settling in. What if it was not George sending the signal? What if it was the Mississaugas she had seen today — or even a stranger?

She turned and walked towards the gate. She was certain that someone was out there watching her every step. So she walked as evenly as she could. If she ran, they would suspect that she knew they were there.

To her relief, she reached the gate without hearing another sound. She took one last look across the river, and glanced over to the trading post. She did not see any movement, but she could not see clearly in the darkness.

Breathlessly, she closed the gate, pushed the lock together, whipped the key out, and ran up the pathway to the cabin. Should she waken Catharine? There was no point in alarming her. But if there was danger at hand, it would be better to be prepared. She reached for John's military musket and powder horn hanging on the wall, next to the bedroom.

Musket in hand, Mary walked to the door and looked outside. Her eyes scanned the top of the stockade as far as she could see. But there was no movement. All she could hear in the darkness was the chirping of the crickets. Then she walked to the door at the back and looked over the rest of the stockade. All appeared to be well.

Three more owl hoots came through the air, and Mary was so frightened that she let the musket slip through her hand. The heavy stock hit the floor with a bang. This time the sound outside had come from the north. As Mary was trying to decide what to do now, an answering owl call came from the west. Were they surrounded?

Mary picked up the musket and laid it on the sofa. Then she bolted both cabin doors and ran into the bedroom, where Catharine was sleeping soundly.

"Catharine . . . Catharine," she said softly, touching her sister's forehead.

"What . . . ? Why? It's dark still. Why? — "

Mary reached out and took her hand. "It's around ten o'clock. John should be back soon."

"Then why did you wake me?" Catharine said as she came fully awake. "Is something wrong?"

"Probably not. But you know I've become a worrier ever since I came here."

"I know, and it's so unusual for you. You're just like a hen with chicks, Mary." She smiled over at her sister, who was now lighting a candle on the nightstand.

"Well, I thought I heard sounds. Someone may be prowling about."

"Someone? Now, we both know there's no one near these parts to prowl . . . except a few settlers like ourselves. And they're some distance away."

"And the Mississauga traders."

"The Mississaugas? I wouldn't worry about them. They're excellent neighbours. They trade at the post all the time."

"What about the Mohawks?"

"Yes, there are a few, but they come in small numbers and have never shown any resentment. No, Mary, no one will attack us."

"Well, I heard these owl sounds."

Catharine started to giggle — almost the way she used to as a girl. "Oh, Mary. You are funny. You are so brave in some ways and so foolish in others. We have nothing to fear."

Catharine sat up on the bed and smoothed down the front of her shift. "If it weren't so hot, I'd fix you a cup of tea to calm your nerves. But come and have something to eat. That'll help. There's some strawberry pie left from supper." Catharine slipped on one of her petticoats and her short-gown. Then she went in to the front room while Mary followed slowly, still straining to hear any sound of prowlers. She was beginning to feel embarrassed about her panic.

Catharine cut two huge pieces of pie, handed one to Mary, and sat on the couch to eat the other.

"Uggh!" Catharine exclaimed, jumping up. She had sat on the musket that Mary had just laid there. "Put that thing away!"

Mary took the musket off the sofa and set it against the table. "Maybe we should leave it out, just in case. Listen. . . . Can you hear anything?"

They sat in silence.

"I don't hear a thing, Mary."

"It's almost too quiet now."

Catharine laughed again. "Look. I'll prove there's no one out there." She set her pie down on the table, reached for the bolt on the front door and struggled a bit with it before she flung it back and threw the door open.

"No, Catharine!"

Mary ran over and pulled her sister back from the door just as a spear streaked through the doorway. Like a lightning bolt, it crashed to the floor in front of the girls.

Mary forced herself over to the door and bolted it shut. Catharine moved like a sleepwalker towards the couch and sat down trembling.

Mary blew out the candle, then took the loaded musket from the table, and paced like a cat towards the open window.

"Stay back, Catharine," Mary said. She peered through the window towards the stockade wall. The moon was shining now and Mary could see three figures coming over the wall. She couldn't be sure, but they looked like the men she had seen leaving John's store that afternoon. She knew they had come for more rum. Would they be content to take a few barrels and go? She thought not, for these were not the friendly people John and Catharine had described. They were now, she believed, filled with the rum they had bought that afternoon and probably ready for a fight or a party. Who knew what else?

When the first man had climbed almost completely over the stockade wall, she aimed the heavy gun just above him and fired. She was glad she had practised to be such a good shot; she didn't want to kill anyone, just frighten them away.

The man disappeared along with the others back over the stockade. Mary hoped that John would hear the shot and be warned, wherever he was. Maybe he could talk with them, but they were probably too drunk at this point. If only John had not sold them the rum. Anger began to replace her fear, and she hurried to reload the musket. Resting the butt on the floor and using the bright moonlight from the window to see, she poured a measure of powder down the barrel and seated the ball and patch into the muzzle. She quickly drove these down the long barrel with the ramrod. Hurrying, she half-cocked the hammer and filled the pan from the little priming horn.

Another man's head appeared at the top of the stockade. She cocked the musket, leaned against the window jamb, and took careful aim. She fired just above his head and he dropped from sight like a stone.

Catharine slowly rose from the couch, pushed a chair over to the fireside, got up on it and reached for the old trade musket that hung on hooks where John always left it loaded and ready. She crept over to the south window.

Mary was reloading the heavy old army musket now. She could easily reload in less than half a minute in daylight; but it was difficult to be so fast in moonlight. Before she had finished, she saw

another figure looming over the edge of the stockade. She knew she couldn't possibly be ready in
time. Then, there was a loud boom beside her and
she saw the man drop back over the side of the
stockade. That was close; he had almost been over
the top. Mary looked over her shoulder to where
the noise had come from.

"Catharine!" she screamed and ran to her sister,
who was lying on her back in the kitchen.

"The gun kicked; I didn't hold it tight enough.
Mary! Don't leave the window!"

Mary rushed back to the east window as
Catharine leaned against the south window.

While they waited, the two sisters loaded their
muskets and stood ready in the dark with every
muscle straining. They would have to stay and
watch. The invaders might still be on the other
side of the stockade, waiting for another chance.

"We'll wait here until John comes," Mary said.

"He'll come soon," Catharine said, but her
voice was trembling. Then she gasped, "But Mary,
what if they ambush John?"

"I'll fire a shot from time to time, just to warn
him, though it may stir up the attackers."

The two sisters stood with their eyes searching
the top of the stockade wall — Mary at the front
window and Catharine at the side.

Mary's cheeks were flushed red with excitement
and anger. But all colour had left Catharine's face.
In the silence, she stood motionless, white as a
ghost.

Sixteen

"Sometimes I think we should go after that bear," Tobias said, frowning. "One of these days, the girls will bump into her when they're out berry picking."

"We could go in there now and have a look." George drew the horses to a halt on the Bay Trail. He and Tobias were on their way over to Bleecker's Grove to pick up their sisters. "Shall we?" he asked eagerly.

"We could look in but stay at the edge of the woods. There's still light there. And I'd hate to think what that bear would do if she got mad at someone walking through the woods."

"Have you ever seen anyone mauled by a bear, Tobias?"

"No, I don't think so."

"I did . . . back in Albany. Don't you remember the broom seller?"

"Not really."

"Well, some hunters rescued him after he'd been mauled by a bear in the Adirondacks. He was so crippled and scarred that people came to buy his brooms just to see the sight."

"Was it really that bad, or is this another one of your stories, George?"

"You think that's bad, Tobias. Well, let me tell you, that was the lucky case. Most people don't survive a bear attack. With one stroke of the paw, their nails can rip into your skin and through the flesh — three inches deep. They say the blood just pours out."

"Where did you hear all this?"

"Remember our neighbours, the Sagers, back in Albany?"

"I'd rather forget them."

"Oh, Reuben was all right. He was our age. He couldn't help what his father and older brothers were like. Anyway, Reuben told me about the time the bear attacked a man they knew. He was just a whimpering mass of rough, red flesh when they found him. And it was a black bear — just like this one. The man didn't live long."

"Maybe we should hunt her down, George."

"I'm ready if you are." With a free hand, George reached for his musket under the seat, then jumped off the wagon. He was spoiling for a little excitement. Now that the crops all had a head start on the weeds and the hay had been cut and brought in, the days had become deadly boring. Stump pulling was monotonous hard work.

"On the other hand, I've heard they never stalk humans and only attack when startled or protecting their young."

"Well, it doesn't take much to startle them."

"You're right, George. Let's go." Tobias jumped off the wagon.

George jumped off the other side and tied the team to a low-hanging branch of a cedar tree.

"Do you think there's more than one?" Tobias asked.

George laughed. "We know there are *cubs*, Tobias. Stay back, Boots. Don't bother the horses. C'mon Boots." He slapped the leg of his breeches and the dog came up to his side and walked obediently beside him.

The three started down the Bay Trail heading west. Close by, the waters of the Bay of Quinte lapped steadily against the shore.

"Look, George! There's a bonfire on the other side of the bay."

"Probably the Weeses." John Weese, who had served with Rogers' Rangers, had been a soldier friend of their father. The family had settled there at the end of the war, three years before the Meyers had come to the area.

"I have to admit I'd rather be sitting in front of a bonfire or swimming or something than stalking a bear."

"C'mon, Tobias, you're the one who suggested this."

"I know, but it's a perfect night for a dip!"

"Oh, all right, let's go, then." In a flash they rushed down to the water, dropped their muskets, and stripped. There were reeds near the shore beside them, so they ran a few yards to the west. Tobias spurted ahead and jumped in, splashing his way through a space free of reeds, and then swam out to the deeper water in long firm strokes.

George was next, followed closely by Boots. "It

sure feels good, doesn't it?"

The three swam around in circles, keeping each other in sight. Then Tobias swam farther out into the bay. "Come back," George yelled. But Tobias did not seem to hear.

George was dressed and sitting with his arms wrapped tightly around his knees when Tobias finally stepped out of the water. "Why did you swim out so far?" George asked.

Tobias pulled on his breeches and slumped down beside his brother. "Oh, just to see if I could do it."

"Well, don't do it again!"

"C'mon, George, you know I'm a strong swimmer."

"I know, but that doesn't mean you should take risks or try to swim across the bay."

"No, Colonel Meyers, I won't, sir." Tobias grinned. They sat then looking across the bay. The bonfire was dying down, but a few fireflies came out nearby. "You're bored, aren't you, George? I bet you wish there was another war on!" Tobias turned and stared at his brother.

"Yeah, sometimes, I do," George said. "But I like farming, too. It's this clearing the land that's so frustrating. And Father never sees that we need a change from time to time."

"A change like . . . Lucy, I suppose." Tobias looked sideways at George to catch his reaction.

George stared straight ahead and said, "Not a bad idea, Tobias. And you . . . what do you want?"

"Lucy's a nice a girl, isn't she?"

"Yes. She's very high-spirited. There would never be a dull moment married to her." George couldn't hold back the enthusiasm in his voice.

"It may surprise you to know that I've thought on those same lines, George. But I don't suppose she's waiting around in King's Town for either of us to call."

"I suppose you're right." George was thinking about Henry Finkle, a fellow who had cut in on him rather too frequently at the dance the summer before. Although Tobias was his greatest rival, George felt more animosity for Finkle. No one could stay angry at Tobias for long. He was just too easygoing to fight — even over Lucy.

Tobias broke the silence. "I wonder if Father really *will* get his deed to this land. If he does, we'll have a better chance at winning our petition."

"Yes, and we'll have farms next door to each other, right near where we're sitting now."

"We'll clear the forest, plant wheat fields, and pass the land on to our descendants."

"I hope you're right, Tobias. But at this rate, I may never have any descendants. I'll be twenty-two in a couple of weeks and I don't even have a girlfriend."

"Well, you're soon going to be an uncle . . . And that reminds me. I think we should be on our way to fetch Catharine."

A booming sound broke through the lapping of the waves on the shore.

"Did you hear a shot?" George asked.

"Sure . . . John's probably out shooting a sitting duck from a tree. I hope we'll have roast duck for dinner tomorrow."

"We better be going, Tobias."

* * * *

High, white-capped waves rolled north from Lake Ontario into the inlet, called East Lake, and washed against John's small bateau. Though a sheltered spot, this inlet tucked in the southern shore of the peninsula was not as calm as the waters of the Bay of Quinte that lapped against the peninsula's northern shore and also against the mainland at the mouth of the Trent and along the Bay Trail.

"You'd best wait," Colonel Young said. "The sun will set soon. Stay over till morning." Henry Young, a Loyalist from Husack in New York State, had found this spot four years before, just after the war, and had returned a year later to build a home for his family on the west side of East Lake. Now the family were comfortably settled, but they were too remote to make the long trip to King's Town for supplies in the middle of a busy summer. So he paid John Bleecker well to bring him necessities like sugar and salt the long distance around the lake.

John looked into the choppy, steel-blue waters of Lake Ontario. "I need to get back," he said. "My wife is expecting a baby in a couple of weeks." He had planned to make this delivery sooner, but trading at the post had been brisk lately, and he hadn't wanted to lose any business. John paced the shore, looking up at the dark clouds.

The older man's face softened when he saw John's concern. "I know you're impatient to get home," he said, "but those waves can be rough even for a bateau. Better late than never!"

"I guess you're right," John said gloomily. "I'll just wait here and watch."

"You may be standing on buried treasure, you know," the Colonel said with a twinkle in his eye.

John rose to the bait. "How's that?"

"During the Seven Years' War, Colonel Bradstreet chased a French vessel in Lake Ontario. The captain sailed onto the beach, buried a barrel of gold in the sand, and set fire to his boat before he and his crew escaped on foot to Fort Frontenac."

"Didn't they come back for the gold?"

"Oh, yes, but they never could find it."

"So it might be right under us."

"Yes, it is somewhere here. One day, my boys and I'll go digging for it. Right now, we're digging for food and crops. No time to dig for gold. . . . Come on up to the house while you wait, and eat supper with us. Your wife won't be the first woman or the last one to have a baby without her husband present. In fact, I was never there when any of mine were born."

"Off to the war?"

"Daniel, Henry, Hannah, and Elizabeth were all born before the war, but I was away for one reason or another. The wife says I planned it that way, but I didn't, I swear . . . I was busy."

"And the other children?"

"Mary and Catharine were born during the war. I was home by Christmas time each winter but away fighting when the babies came. And Sarah was born after the war, when I was out scouting for a spot to settle. Men aren't much help at a time like that anyway — except for doctors. And some midwives are better'n them. Has your wife got anyone with her?"

"Her sister."

"She'll be fine, then. Most women know how to handle these matters."

"I don't know about that. Mary is . . ."

"Take it from me, it's instinctive. I let my daughters help with the birthing animals. They have the strength for the job and more patience than my sons. Now, young man, if you weren't already married, I'd be *dragging* you up to the house for a meal. You've seen what beauties my five daughters are." Henry laughed raucously at his own humour.

John smiled at the compliment, but climbed aboard his bateau and waved to the older man. "I'll not cut adrift until the squall passes."

"Be careful then, too. She's a treacherous lake at times. As unpredictable as a woman." The Colonel laughed loudly again as he turned from the sandy beach.

John sat cross-legged under the canvas covering the central area of his bateau. After half an hour of fidgeting, he scanned the sky again. The rain had stopped and the moon was beginning to shine through the clouds. He leaned over the side and pushed out from the shore with a heavy oar. He was tempted to sail straight out into the lake and cut across to his hunter's cabin at Carrying Place, on the isthmus that separated Weller's Bay and the Bay of Quinte — and just across from Bleecker's Grove. But he kept near the shoreline — the safer route. Colonel Young was right. Better late than never. It was slow rowing the bateau alone. He wished he had asked the Mississauga youth who visited his post from time to time to come with him. It would have shortened the time. The waves were not so high anymore, but he was still travelling at a slow pace.

John smiled when he thought of Catharine and home. These last nine months married to Catharine had been like a dream. When he returned, she was always waiting for him with a smile. She never complained and always made him feel like the most important person in the world. If business continued as it had with rich pelts like those he had received yesterday, he wouldn't need to depend on receiving a farm lot picked by chance out of a hat, the government's handout. He'd have the money to choose and buy his own place and pass property on to his sons.

One day, he'd build Catharine a fine house. He could see her now, a fine lady, in the doorway of a pillared mansion, welcoming the neighbours to a party. Of course, by then, they would have many neighbours, and Squire and Mrs. Bleecker would be entertaining folks from miles around. And he'd give the men a nip of his rum from the back shed.

John approached Carrying Place, where he was planning to tie the bateau and walk the short distance overland past his cabin to his waiting canoe. As he steered into shore, the moon came out full, and he heard a distant boom like the sound of musket fire.

Seventeen

"I'm not wasting my gunpowder this time, Catharine. The first one over the wall gets it!" Mary said through gritted teeth.

"No!" Catharine's voice, though trembling, was firm. "I'll not allow it. You must not hit anyone."

Mary turned from the window to her sister, whose face was so drawn she could barely recognize her now in the dim light. "Are you telling me not to shoot at all? My aim is good, but these muskets are never too exact at best . . . and in this semi-darkness, I might accidentally hit one of them."

Catharine staggered over towards Mary. "You are right. We must stop shooting except at intervals to warn John."

"I suppose, once they find the rum, they may be satisfied." Mary had not intended to mention it, but it was too late now.

"There may not be enough rum left to satisfy them," Catharine said. "John only has enough to have a nip with his friends now and again. Somehow the Mississaugas must have found out. But they'll be disappointed. Oh, Mary, I hope they won't come in here to look for more."

"You're wrong, Catharine. They'll find plenty of
the stuff out there," Mary said in a low voice. It
would probably ease Catharine's anxiety to know
that they wouldn't come to the house . . . at least
not to hunt for more rum. But Mary suspected
that they were already drunk. And who knew what
any drunk man would do? If only John had not
sold them that keg this afternoon.

Mary leaned her musket against the couch and
sat down beside her sister.

A burst of loud cheering came from the shed.
The invaders must have scaled the palisade and
gotten into the rum.

Catharine was mumbling, "Dear God, help us . . .
Dear God."

Mary was silent for a minute, then she broke
into her sister's prayer. "Those invaders are probably busy drinking the rum now, and John will be
here any minute. He said he'd be back tonight."

Suddenly, the shouts stopped and a frightening
silence enveloped everything. The sisters sat there
with their arms around each other for what
seemed a long time. Then Mary felt for the musket by her side and pulled it up onto her lap.

If any of the men came through that door, she
would shoot. She didn't care what Catharine said.
She had every right to defend her sister and herself. No council of Mississaugas would refute that.

They waited for what seemed like hours, though
Mary knew it was probably minutes. The crickets
were singing in chorus again as if all were well.

"Ohhhh!" Catharine's low cry broke the silence.

"What is it? Did you see something?" Mary rushed over to the window, her musket still in hand.

"No, Mary! It's me. I had a pain. I think it could be the labour beginning. Oh, Mary, whatever will I do?"

"It's probably false labour. That comes first, Mother says. So don't be too concerned." Mary hardly believed her own words. When Catharine had fallen on her back because of the recoiling musket, her body may have been shocked into labour. That could do it. Her sister was probably going to have the baby right here — a scary enough thought in normal circumstances.

Mary trembled as she moved closer to the window, her back to Catharine.

In a minute, Catharine said, "The pain's all gone. You were right, Mary. . . . Can you see anything out there?"

"No. Nothing." She walked back to her sister, pulled a chair up beside the couch, and rested the musket across it.

Then they heard a sound. Was it footsteps?

Mary braced the musket over the back of the chair, a few feet from the door, and crouched behind it as she took aim. She had never shot a person in her life. Would she have the nerve to do it, even to an attacker . . . and at such close range? Beads of perspiration stood out on her brow.

The door was opening.

Catharine lifted her head from her knees and saw Mary crouched there with her gun raised. "Don't shoot!" she screamed. From the other side of the door came John's loud cry. "My God, Mary. It's me! Do you hear me, Mary?"

"Yes, I hear you. C'mon in." Mary lowered the musket onto the chair and stood upright.

John stomped in. "What has been going on here?" He ran over to Catharine, who was trembling on the couch. Clutching him with both hands, Catharine began to sob violently.

When Catharine's sobs subsided a bit, he turned to Mary and said, "Tell me what on earth has happened?"

"Some men — I think they were the traders I saw at the post this afternoon — came over the stockade. They raided your shed. We tried to keep them away, but it was useless."

"Why did you even try?"

"We knew they got into the rum," Mary said viciously. "We heard their cheers."

"How long ago was that?"

"I don't know. About twenty minutes or so. It seems like hours, but it could have been a shorter time."

"They're probably long gone, and if they are, they're not apt to come back tonight. But I must go and check."

"Please, John, please don't go," Catharine begged.

"I must. I'll take my musket. And anyway, I can handle this situation." His voice was steady and confident and calmed the girls' fears.

In a few minutes, he was back. "They've gone," he said.

"Thank God!" Catharine said. "He answered our prayers." She started to get up, but sank back into the couch again, clutching her stomach. "Oh, no, it's back, the pain's back."

Mary rushed over to her sister and crouched down beside her. "Remember what Mother said about false labour pains."

"Labour pains?" John suddenly turned white.

"No. False labour pains. Mother says that false labour pains always come first, and since these are Catharine's first ones, they aren't the real ones. They have to be the false ones."

"How long will they last?"

"I forget."

"You forget!"

"Well, I'm not a midwife!"

"Stop arguing!" Catharine yelled with unexpected strength. "I'm fine now. . . . Do you think the invaders will come back?"

John crouched beside Catharine and held her hand. "I'm afraid they might. I think we should leave immediately."

"Why would they come back?" Mary asked.

"Just a hunch," John said without turning to look at Mary.

Mary knew then that the drunken men had not taken all the rum and might return for the rest.

"Our bags are already packed," she said, "and Mother will be happy to see us."

"We can't go through the woods at this time of night. We'll take the canoe across to my cabin."

"Why? Will we be any safer there, John?" Catharine asked. "They could follow us."

"They want the rum, not us, Catharine," he said. "They won't follow us."

"But John, I thought — "

"Hurry, Catharine. It's a warm night, but throw on a shawl. It was raining earlier over at East Lake." John put Catharine's right arm around his shoulders and with his other arm around her back helped her to her feet.

"I have the bags," Mary said. "Do you have blankets and things at the cabin, John?"

"Yes, I used to stay there occasionally before I was married." He helped Catharine over to the door. "Stay here while I check around the stockade."

He was back in a few minutes. "No sign of anyone. If it weren't for the missing rum keg, and those two shots I heard, I'd say you two had been having nightmares."

Mary grimaced.

For Catharine's sake, they walked slowly down the pathway to the water's edge. John held the canoe steady while Mary helped her sister to the seat in the middle and handed her the one big feather pillow she had brought. Then Mary knelt in the prow and grabbed the paddle. John sat in the stern, where he could paddle and steer.

"Are you ready yet?" Mary asked.

"Yes," John said, and in unison they paddled rapidly towards Carrying Place.

"It's a beautiful night now," Catharine said quietly. She trailed the fingers of her left hand through the water and smiled up at John, who was facing her. She still looked pale, but her voice was steady.

"Have you had any more pains?" Mary dared to ask.

"No. You were right. They're gone. Oh, Mary, what would I have done without you?"

Mary was paddling so hard that she could hardly believe any time had passed at all before the canoe reached the other shore. The shoreline was smooth and sandy, but the terrain might be more difficult farther inland. It was hidden by clumps of cedar and low-hanging willows. John jumped over the side and pulled the canoe right up on the shore.

Ten minutes later, the three refugees were safe inside John's cabin. The flickering light cast shadows over the contents of the room. Mary picked a blanket off a shelf on the far wall and threw it over the straw mattress on the one bed built into the southwest corner of the cabin. Then she plumped up the soft feather pillow she had brought.

"Do lie down, Catharine," Mary said softly.

Catharine nodded, and sat down heavily on the bed. Mary lifted her feet up onto the foot of the bed while Catharine lay back on the white pillow.

John was squatting by the fireplace in the north wall, where he had started a small fire. He looked over at Catharine and swallowed. Mary wondered if it was the fire or anger that was making his face turn so red.

Mary sat down on a straight-backed wooden chair by the fire. In a few minutes, they could both hear Catharine's heavy breathing. "She's alseep now. She's exhausted," Mary said.

"Who fired those shots?" John barked, glowering into the fire.

"We did," Mary said. "We were trying to scare them away."

"That wasn't very intelligent. Someone might have been hurt."

"Well, they threw a spear inside."

"They what?" John growled. His face flushed even darker.

"Well, Catharine looked out and it was then — "

"I just can't believe that a few unruly youths could . . . I'll report them to their chief. He'll punish them."

"And will you report that they were drunk on the rum you traded them this afternoon?" Mary shot back.

The silence hung heavy between them.

After a few minutes, John cleared his throat and said, "All the trading posts start that way, Mary. I need the capital."

"That's a lie, John Bleecker. I don't believe they all start that way," Mary hissed back. "And besides, the chiefs may not be too sympathetic. They could make their own liquor if they wanted it, but they've had sense enough not to. So I don't suppose they'll thank you for selling the stuff to their children!"

"C'mon, Mary, your own father is not above serving a nip to his friends."

"That's different. He's in control. He doesn't dole it out in volumes. Besides, Mother doesn't approve. And neither do I. So the men have their nip in the barn."

"You're getting more like your mother with every passing day."

"Thank you, John."

John snorted, stood up, and opened a window.

A pleasant breeze blew across the room. Mary knew he had only started the fire in case Catharine went into labour and they needed hot water. On the 10th of July, they certainly did not need the heat.

"I'm going out for fresh water," John said. He picked up a pail beside the door and rushed out.

Mary rummaged around the open shelves John had tacked up on the north wall looking for a kettle. She found some dirty towels and a few wooden plates and spoons that were thick with dust before her hands fell on an old tin kettle.

Mary picked up the midwife's bag and opened it on the side table. She smiled with relief when she saw the fresh linen towels and soft lye-and-fat soap. Mother's meticulous housekeeping was all right sometimes.

In a few minutes, John returned with the water. He handed the pail to her silently, then he squatted by the fire and stared at the flames.

Mary filled the kettle and hung it over the fire. Then she poured a little water into a pan, washed her hands, and shook them dry by the heat. Next, she took the scissors from the bag and put them in the kettle. When she was finished, she sat in silence near Catharine and listened to her heavy breathing. A few minutes later, John stood up and walked over to the window. Then he started to pace back and forth across the floor.

The minutes grew into hours, and it was almost two o'clock when John finally said, "Catharine's fine, Mary. I've something to attend to, but I'll be back before dawn."

Mary was furious. "No, John, you can't go!"

"The Mississaugas will not come here. There's nothing to come here for, and besides, they don't even know about this place. It's well hidden. It doesn't need a stockade."

"And what about Catharine?"

"Can't you see she's fine? Even if she did wake up in labour, what can happen in a few hours? My mother told me the first baby takes at least twenty-four hours to come. I'm not completely stupid about these matters, Mary. And after what she's been through, I doubt she'll wake up before morning."

Mary felt too tired to argue and without another word, watched him go. She was beginning to wonder if she even liked John Bleecker anymore. What kind of husband was he? What kind of brother-in-law was he? Leaving them both alone and afraid. For a few seconds, Mary sat there paralyzed by her fear and pride. Finally, her fear got the better of her pride, and she ran across the room and through the doorway.

She scurried wildly along the path between the trees, only guessing which way John had gone. But in a few minutes, she did reach the shore of the bay, where they had left the canoe.

Then she spotted him. He was already halfway across to Bleecker's Grove. She scanned the whole area closely and gave a low groan. On the opposite shore she thought she saw someone or something moving through the cedars close to the mouth of the Trent River.

Eighteen

Mary trudged reluctantly back to the cabin, and to her sister. She might wake up at any moment and find herself alone. Mary knew all too well why John had left so suddenly, and it bothered her. He was going to check on his home — and the rum. What if there were still some youths there and they were drunk? She had never known John to back away from a fight even when he was outnumbered.

"Aaaah, aah! John! Mary! . . . Help me!" Catharine screamed. Mary ran the short distance to the cabin and burst through the doorway. In the sputtering light of a candle floating in its melting base, she could see her sister sitting up in bed, bracing herself with both arms. She was in deep pain.

"Oh, Mary, the pain is much worse. It woke me up. But it's gone now." Catharine lay back on the pillow with a deep sigh.

Mary went to the fire and raked the coals, then threw a couple of pieces of kindling on the fire to bring it to life quickly. She lifted the kettle off the hob and set it on the sidetable beside Mother's bag. She poured a bit of water into the basin and washed her hands with the strong, soft soap.

"What are you doing, Mary?" Catharine asked.

"Just washing up a little. Would you like a basin of water, too?"

"Yes, I would. But I'll come over there." Slowly Catharine pushed her feet over the side of the bed and sat for a minute before she stood up to start across the room. "Oooo," she groaned, sinking weakly back onto the bed. "Mary, it's back! It's back!"

Mary put Mother's towel down and rushed over to the bed. Catharine grabbed her hand and dug her nails in so deep that Mary thought she would bleed.

When the pain had passed, Catharine sank back on the pillow again. She was silent for a minute, then said, "Where's John?"

Mary drew in her breath sharply. What would she say? Surely her sister should not have to worry about John just now. But she could not think of any excuse for him, so she said, "I think he's gone back to your place. He didn't say."

"Oh, no! He'll run into those invaders."

"They'll be long gone with their spoils or else so drunk they'll have all passed out."

"Oh, no. If John found them like that, I don't know what he would do to them. I really don't! Oh, Mary!"

Mary looked away. Catharine looked like a frightened animal. Her hand began to tighten over Mary's again. "The pain's back."

"Breathe deeply, Catharine. Mother said to breathe deeply." Catharine nodded but started to breathe out in short gasps as the pain increased. Heavy beads of perspiration gathered on her forehead. Once more Catharine tightened her grip on Mary's hand until the spasms of pain had passed, and she sank limply into the pillow again.

Mary stood up, frantically trying to remember Mother's instructions. She hurried over to the midwife's bag and looked inside. If John did not show up soon, he would hear plenty from her after the baby was born.

* * * *

Streaks of light fell onto the far corner of the bed where Catharine lay very still, her eyes closed. A fat bundle of a lamb's wool baby blanket lay next to Catharine, and in the middle of the wool was a small red face with wisps of white hair. Mary looked at her sister fearfully. Was Catharine sleeping or was she unconscious? The baby boy was silent, too — though he had screamed loudly enough right after he'd arrived. Mary had wrapped him in a piece of broadcloth and the little wool blanket and placed him beside his mother. Somehow she had managed to remember enough of Mother's instructions to make the delivery.

Catharine had lost so much blood with the afterbirth that Mary had used up all the towels to stop the bleeding. No wonder she was not waking up, even though blue jays were making a racket outside the window.

As Mary sank weakly into the chair beside Catharine, the baby began to make strange snorting noises. Mary wondered what she should do. Perhaps he was about to choke to death. Maybe he had been born with Catharine's croup. Mary jumped up and closed the windows in case the baby needed to be warmer.

Mary sat beside the bed again and gazed at the baby. The snorting noises had stopped. He wiggled a little, then opened his bird-like mouth and yelled!

"There's nothing wrong with you," Mary gasped. "Not with a cry like that!" Maybe the baby just wanted to be fed.

Mary heard footsteps outside and turned to see John coming through the door. "It's about t — " Her words caught in her throat.

John was a mess. His nose was a mass of swollen red flesh and dark clotted blood. A large bruise extended from his left eye across his lower jaw. His shirt was hanging loose from one shoulder. He looked past Mary to the bed, and with a deep intake of breath stopped and stared at Catharine, who was staring back at him. Then he fell to the floor beside her.

"Oh, Catharine," he sobbed. "I'm so sorry. Catharine . . . Catharine!"

Catharine did not move as she whispered weakly, "John. . . . You're . . . ." Her words were drowned out by a loud demanding howl from the other side of the bed. John's head shot up and he stared across his wife to the bundle beside her.

"The baby?"

Catharine gave him a weak smile. "A boy."

John lifted the bundle and looked at the little round red face with the full mouth now opening wider and howling louder. "I guess he wants something to eat, Catharine." But his wife's eyes had closed again. John turned to Mary. "Was it a difficult birth?"

"It seemed long and hard, but it wasn't nearly as long as Mother said it would be. She has lost a lot of blood, though, and she's very weak, but the baby is hungry. If only Mother were here. She'd know what to do."

"George and Tobias have gone for her, Mary," John said quietly, looking down at the baby in his arms. He had gone to sleep, too.

"Were they in on this fight, too?" Mary asked scornfully.

"They're not hurt," he said as he laid the sleeping baby down on the other side of Catharine and fell on his knees beside her again.

Mary stared at John as he took Catharine's hand in his. Her sister's eyes were shut and her face was whiter than the pillow. John's shoulders were shaking now, and Mary could see tears starting to stream down his bruised face as he said, "Catharine, oh, Catharine . . . I'm so sorry. . . . I should have been here. . . . Can you forgive me? . . . I couldn't . . . I couldn't live without you!"

Mary tiptoed to the door, walked out into the July morning, then raced towards the shore. She barely noticed the weeping willow branches as they lashed against her face. Did John think Catharine was going to die? Surely she would not die! The family could never manage without her.

Mary looked out across the water, more afraid than she had ever been in her life. She slumped down to the sandy ground and leaned against a large pine tree, her eyes still scanning the horizon across the bay.

Half an hour later, Mary opened her eyes and saw what she thought was a canoe in the distance. It was not long before she recognized George's red head gleaming in the morning sun at the front of the canoe. Then, as his strong paddling strokes brought the craft closer, she saw Tobias and — Mother!

She had never been so happy to see anyone in her life.

Nineteen

"**M**eyers' Creek is drying up," George said. "Father's not going to be able to build his mill there after all." It had been a dry summer and the crops were not doing well. Still, they would have enough, Mary knew, for they had all worked hard to carry water to the nearby garden, and the produce would fill the small dug-out space that they reached through a trap door under the kitchen.

Despite the drought, it had been a happy month since the baby's arrival, for Catharine was at home with the family. Her brothers had willingly given up their bedroom to sleep in the barn. She was still weak but improving, and John, Jr., was a contented baby. He cried only when he was hungry. The rest of the time, he lay in his cradle and smiled up at anyone who would speak to him.

"Father will be disappointed about the mill," Mary said absentmindedly. She wasn't really too worried. He would think of something. He always did.

Tonight she was especially busy. The baby was one month old today, and they were planning a little celebration for Catharine and her baby, and maybe John, who was scheduled to arrive home sometime soon from one of his many trips to King's Town. Since the baby's arrival, he had stayed over only a few times at the Meyers. Mary knew he didn't want to lose any of his trade to the competition — Singleton's trading post on the Moira River.

Mother stuck her fork into the wild turkey and said, "Ahh, Mary, it's just right." Mary lifted the heavy bird off the spit, dropped it onto a large wooden board, and set it down beside a waiting platter.

The moist dark meat fell off the bone as Mother carved it into thick slices and laid them on the platter. Mary went over to the fireplace and dropped a bit of flour in the pan of grease droppings. A few minutes later, she added water from the vegetables and whipped up a delicious-smelling light-brown gravy that she poured into a heavy wooden bowl. She plopped a large wooden spoon into the centre of the bowl and took it to the table.

Mother had allowed a jar of fresh raspberry preserves for pie filling, and Anna was whipping cream to put on the pies.

Jacob, his face red from the sun and wind, came bursting through the front door. "The bateau's come to shore," he said. "John's here!"

* * * *

"It's been a hard summer for many reasons," Father said, "but it's been a good one, too." He looked around the table at his family. They had just finished their banquet of turkey and pie and were now drinking tea.

"We are so proud to have a wonderful new addition to our family," Father continued. "He reminds me so much of my own sons at that age — the same hearty yell and the curly hair!" He smiled over at Catharine, who was sitting beside John halfway down the left side of the table.

Mary couldn't help noticing that her father ignored John completely. She wondered if they had exchanged words over his neglect of Catharine. Still, when she thought about it, Mary realized that Catharine's lot was not much different from that of many pioneer women.

John cleared his throat to say something, but Father continued. "I am leaving in the morning to go to King's Town to submit my petition for ownership of this land now that it has been surveyed. These lots are now numbers eight and nine in the first concession of Township Number Eight."

"I'm going, too," George said eagerly.

Father turned towards his son. "Yes, if you want to, George. You and Tobias may both accompany me." Father stroked his chin to hide a smile as his son grimaced slightly.

"Lucy will love seeing you both," John said.

"And how is your sister?" Mother asked.

"Oh, she's busy helping Mother and . . . ," he looked over at George, "and going to parties. King's Town is really expanding. New folks moving in all the time."

"Any special new person?" Mary asked. She knew her brothers were dying to know, but they wouldn't ask outright — at least not in front of Mother and Father.

"No. I don't think so. But then I wouldn't know. Some day, she'll probably just elope."

"You can't talk, John," George said. "That's almost what you did."

John laughed heartily. "You know, you're right, George. I guess we almost did." Everyone smiled except Father.

"I think it's my turn to go to King's Town," Jacob grumbled between bites of raspberry pie. He was eating his third piece.

Mary wanted to go, too, but she felt there was no point in saying anything. She knew she was needed here, so she wouldn't even bring up the subject.

"I will not be staying in King's Town," Father said. "I plan to travel on to Montreal, where I will present my claim to the British government for compensation." The government was no longer giving supplies to Loyalists as they had for the last three years, but they were now compensating them for their losses in the United States, since the new government there had done nothing to help those driven from their lands.

"Waaaaa," Johnnie yelled from the nearby bedroom.

Mary jumped up before Catharine. "Sit still, Catharine. I'll bring him out to you."

"I don't know what everyone would do without Mary," Catharine said, "but I think she should go to King's Town, too."

"Mary!" Father said with surprise. "Why would

she want to go? Anyway, she's needed here."

"Well, I'm going home tomorrow. So she won't be needed to help me. John has bought a cow and chickens, so we'll have milk and eggs now. And I'm getting stronger every day."

"Oh, Catharine, I really wish you could stay longer — for the company," Mother said. "And I don't think you're very strong yet."

"If Catharine thinks she's ready, she *is* ready," John said in a loud voice. Mother looked hurt.

"Thank you, though, Mother Meyers," John said in a softer voice. "I appreciate all you've done. And I'll never forget how happy I was to see you right after the baby came." John looked down as he added, "It's lonely back at the post. I was looking forward to Catharine and Johnnie coming home with me."

"Yes, it is lonely there, John, for a woman alone. Will you be home more often, now?" Father asked abruptly.

"Yes, I will. I don't plan to take any more overnight trips for a while." He gave Father a cold stare. "But, as you know, sometimes a man has to leave his family to do what he has to do."

Father grimaced a bit but went on to say, "Have you heard from the Mississaugas since that night?"

"Yes. Their chief gave me a formal apology for the attack. He says it will never happen again."

"I wonder what could have caused such an outbreak. It's the only incident I've heard of in these parts. The Mississaugas have been friendly and seem to bear no grudge for selling some of their land to the British government."

Silence hung heavy around the table. George gave Mary a knowing glance, then looked down at his teacup.

John broke the silence. "I get along fine with the Mississaugas now. Did you know that there's to be a meeting in September at Carrying Place with their chiefs and the government officials? Sir John Johnson will be there, and I've been invited." John smiled importantly and raised his eyes to Father with a glint of pride in them. Father stared back quietly, but Mary could see he was impressed.

They all knew Sir John Johnson, a Loyalist, who had led the King's Royal Regiment of New York. He had been appointed Superintendent General of Indian Affairs in British North America three years before. It was a great honour for John to be invited to this meeting. Mary was not too pleased, however. Why was John invited to the meeting when he had been causing trouble by selling liquor to the Mississaugas?

Mary took a sideways look at John, but he was still looking at Father and there was a glint in his eye. Perhaps Father had met his match in John Bleecker. Mary hoped the two would learn to agree as time went on and that they would never be pitted against each other over anything important.

Father turned back to the family. "I am also going to apply for land to build my mill," he said.

"Your mill!" George said. "There can be no mill on Meyers' Creek. It's gone dry!"

Father smiled calmly at George. "I know that, George, but I'm going to ask to buy land on the

Trent River north of John's property. There's a waterfall farther inland, a perfect place."

Mary feared John's reaction, but when she turned to look at him, he was smiling at Father. "That's an excellent idea! Our land will touch, then, and when the farmers come to have their grain ground, they'll visit my post for supplies. I wish us both success!"

"I'm glad you're with me on this," Father said, staring back at John. A hint of admiration passed between them.

"Well, I've got a few things to attend to," Father said. "Then I'm going to turn in early."

"And I'll get a list ready for you. I need quite a number of supplies for winter," Mother said.

"Make your list long. If my petition for compensation is accepted, I'll be able to buy a few extra comforts. Sir Guy Carleton, or should I say Lord Dorchester, is now Governor-in-Chief and he's getting things done faster than Haldimand did. He's already increased the size of the land grants for the 84th Regiment Royal Emigrants. So we expect he'll do the same for the rest of us." Father got up from the table and the others followed.

Mother smiled as she turned to Mary. "Come help me with this list, Mary."

Mary took a quill pen from her father's desk beside the fireplace along with a piece of rolled birchbark and went over to Mother, but she was not thinking about the supplies. She was wondering how she could persuade Father to let her go to King's Town.

Twenty

"I tell you it was the size of the large barn door," Jacob panted. He and Boots had come running up to Mary, who was sitting on a tuft of grass next to the Meyers' dock. It was the last week of August now, and two weeks ago, Father had left for King's Town with George and Tobias, and Mary had come out to watch for them tonight. She had not succeeded in convincing Father to let her go with them.

George and Tobias should have been home by now, but she knew that Father would be longer if he went on to Montreal. He would catch a ride home with John, who was scheduled to bring up a load from King's Town.

Mary stared at her brother with a knowing smile. Jacob was so bored he was always looking for excitement. Although they now had new neigbours, he was home most of the time. There were no boys his age to play with. The Vanderheydens, who had moved in just to the east not far from the Singletons, had children, but no young boys.

Mary had made no new friends either. Although Mr. Vanderheyden and one son had worked on their lot all summer to build their home and plant their crop, the rest of the family were still living in King's Town. Probably they would not come until spring now. It would be a lonely winter again.

"I tell you it's true!" Jacob said, yanking Mary's sleeve. "There's the biggest bear I have ever seen in that corn field."

Mary choked back a laugh. Jacob had obviously convinced himself that he really had seen a bear. But she doubted it. In spite of the dry weather, the corn had been good, for everyone in the family had helped to carry water to the field. It was an endless and seemingly fruitless task, but Father had insisted. In the end, it had been worth it.

"Well, what did the bear do when it saw you?" Mary asked.

"It didn't see me!" Jacob's eyes were wide. "I barely saw it when I ran. I wasn't stupid enough to stay there! I know danger when I see it."

"Yes, Jacob, I'm sure you do. Now, let's see who'll spot our bateau first."

Boots beat Jacob to the spot beside Mary. So Jacob flung himself down on his stomach on the other side of her, and with his elbows dug into the ground in front of him, he stared up at his sister. "You don't believe me, do you? I still get treated like a kid even though I'm almost grown up. It's terrible being the youngest." He grabbed a piece of marsh grass, then reached behind Mary's back and lightly tickled her neck.

Mary screamed and Boots jumped. "Stop that, Jacob!" Mary shouted. Boots joined Jacob as he rolled along the ground in laughter. Mary turned towards him with a scowl; then as she stared at his happy robust face and the grin that spread from ear to ear, she couldn't help laughing, too.

"Oh, there you are, Jacob," Leonard grumbled as he came out of the barn and started along the path towards them. "As usual, you ran off before the chores were all done. We have a number of animals to care for if you remember: two cows and four horses, to say nothing of the pigs and chickens."

"Well, I was planning to come back, but I ran into this bear. I had to tell Mary."

Mary looked up at Leonard and laughed. "It's another one of his bear tales."

Leonard, as robust as Jacob and still an inch short of six feet, sat down on the other side of Boots and wrapped his arms around his crossed legs. "He may not be exaggerating, Mary. I thought I saw it, too, early this morning. I'll be glad when Father gets back. If we're right and it is there, it could ruin our whole corn crop. And there may be more than one."

Mary was suddenly alert. "I hope not. We worked too hard this summer carrying all that water from the bay to have the crop stripped now."

"That's just what could happen. Father says a bear will often roll around in a corn field and destroy a huge portion of it with a single roll. Then it'll strip the ears and eat them. Bears have huge appetites."

"I'm not surprised, since they're so large."

"Look!" Jacob was pointing down the bay. Boots rushed out to the far end of the point and looked out at the water.

The bateau had already passed the turn where a settler named William Bell had built a store and cabin that summer.

"It's them, all right," said Jacob. "And I think they ought to know about the bear."

"Not tonight, Jacob. We'll have too much else to do."

Mary was hoping that Lucy might be aboard. It was so lonely now with Catharine and the baby gone. She strained her eyes in the dusk to see ahead. She thought she did see a white handkerchief flying over the side of the bateau. It would be just like Lucy to fly a special flag to announce her arrival.

"Hello!" It was Lucy calling from the boat.

"Hello there!" Mary yelled, jumping to her feet. Boots was waving his tail wildly now and zigzagging up and down the wooden dock that jutted fifteen feet into the bay.

George was silent as he steered the bateau towards them. Leonard and Jacob grabbed the prow and tied it to the stake.

Lucy stepped carefully across the makeshift gangplank that Tobias set down. "I'm glad you've come." Mary said as the girls gave each other a big hug, then picked up Lucy's overstuffed haversack.

"Well, it wasn't easy persuading Mother, but here I am now, and positively dying to see my new nephew."

Jacob came over and grinned at Lucy as she mussed his hair with one hand and smiled down at him. "You'll be as handsome as the other Meyers men one of these days soon. Why I — "

"Lucy, guess what we've got?" Jacob interrupted. "A bear!"

"Oh, yeah, Jacob," George growled. "I believe you, I do." Mary wondered if George was annoyed because of the bear or because he had lost out in courting Lucy.

"It may be true," Leonard said. "After I took the cows to the little meadow by the dried-up stream, I circled around the corn field and saw a few stalks down on the far northwest corner."

"Well, I can't see a bear knocking down a few and leaving. He'd do a lot of damage or none," George said.

"I don't know," Tobias said. "I think maybe we should check it out. We can't afford to lose that crop. We worked so hard to carry water for it, and with this drought, all our wheat and barley have amounted to almost nothing."

Mary was surprised to see Tobias so concerned. She knew that Father was disappointed in the crops this summer, but she didn't know it had been that bad.

"Here, Jacob, take this bag in to Mother. It's flour. She's sure going to be glad to see it." George handed a large bag to Jacob, who proudly threw it over his left shoulder and strutted towards the house.

"Here, Mary, take this one. It's got a number of the smaller items on Mother's list. It should make her happy." Mary saw George smile as he handed her a big lumpy sack of kitchen supplies. "We've got apples, too," he said. That explained George's smile. Mother's apple pie was his favourite.

Lucy and Mary headed towards the house with George and Tobias close behind.

"What are those two talking about now?" Lucy asked.

"The bear, I think," Mary said soberly. Surely they were not going to consider going after that bear tonight after travelling since sun-up. She didn't like the sound of their voices.

After the girls had gone inside, the boys spoke out a little louder. "I say we unload and go scare off the bear," Tobias said. "You know we can't afford to lose that crop. As it is, things will be tight for us this winter if Father doesn't get enough compensation money to buy extra supplies."

George stared at his brother in disbelief. The mild-mannered Tobias was the least likely person to suggest a bear hunt. But he knew his brother was right about this year's crop. "If I take the time to hunt up that miserable bear, Tobias, I'm not just going to scare her off. I'm going to kill her." George sounded tired and irritable. "We've put up with that beast ever since we came here."

"You're right, George. So let's hurry and unpack and go find her."

"Not without me," Leonard said as he came off the bateau and headed towards the house with a basketful of Mother's groceries. George and Tobias stared at Leonard, then smiled at each other. "Leonard, you can unload the bateau. We're going bear hunting."

"Now wait a minute," Leonard shouted, but it was too late. His brothers were already running for the back door of the house.

"Now, don't tell Mother," Tobias said.

"You're right," George said. "She'd worry. We'll sneak into our room, grab our muskets, and leave. If she asks, we'll tell her there's a wild turkey out back."

"I think I'll tell Mary so Mother won't worry if we have to stay away too long. We may have to wait half the night for the bear to come out."

"If you have a chance, Tobias, that's not a bad idea. Mary'll cover for us."

Once inside the back door, the brothers could not see the women anywhere and rushed into their room. Through the thin wall, they could hear voices from the girls' room. "What a beautiful gown!" Mary was saying.

"I could make you one like it if your father brings back that linen I put on my list," Mother said in a scarcely audible voice. "I ordered a bolt of light green. It will go beautifully with your hair, Mary."

"I've nowhere to go in it, anyway," Mary mumbled.

"You're coming back with me, Mary," Lucy said. "And you'll have lots of invitations to parties. In fact, I've someone special I want you to meet."

"C'mon, George," Tobias said, slinging his musket over his shoulder and taking his powder horn off its nail. George took down his own musket carefully.

As they went out the door, they could hear Mother saying, "Well, I must rustle up something for the boys to eat. Mary, could you run out to the henhouse and see if we have any eggs? I just used our last one."

Once outside, they sneaked around to the west side of the house. "We'd better wait for Mary," Tobias said.

They didn't wait long. The door swung wide open and she came running out and leaped off the stoop, missing both steps. She was well along the path to the henhouse by the time Tobias caught up to her.

"Mary," he called softly. "We've decided to go for the bear." He was shifting a little uneasily under Mary's intent stare.

"You're crazy, both of you!" Mary said. "Wait until Father comes home."

"That could be too late, Mary," George said. "We can't afford to lose this crop."

Mary stared back at them. "When is Father coming?"

"We don't know," Tobias said. "He was lucky enough to catch a bateau going to Montreal as we landed in King's Town; so we stayed to handle all the business there, and he went on. He might catch a ride back with someone else — maybe Singleton or Bell. Or he might be held up in Montreal for a month. It all depends on when he gets a chance to present his petition. Even if Father comes home tomorrow, it could be too late if the corn's all destroyed."

"Where's Boots? Aren't you taking him with you?"

George shook his head. "He may just spook the bear when we're after him. I put him in the barn."

Mary laughed. "But you know he always manages to get out somehow."

"I know, but we'll be long gone."

The boys took long firm strides towards the corn field. The moon was bright now. They passed the flickering light coming from the candle in the south window in the house and walked to the side of the wheat field.

In less than ten minutes, they had reached the corn field. They stood there for a few minutes, staring into the darkness. The stalks were a foot higher than the two of them, and the growth was thick, for no frost had hit yet. The musky smell of corn husks was heavy in the air. The moonlight cast deep shadows, and the rows were so thick that it was difficult to see anything farther then a few feet away.

"I can't smell any bear," Tobias said, breathing in deeply as they walked north along the east side of the field. "The wind's coming from the northwest. I think we'd smell her if she's around." A fresh gust of wind blew a few green and yellow maple leaves across the pathway.

They stopped at the corner of the corn field. "She's probably somewhere on the north side of the field . . . or waiting in the woods," Tobias said, looking at his brother. "Let's walk along the path between the woods and the corn field." Tobias started walking swiftly to the west.

"Wait!" George said in a low voice as he followed right behind his brother in the dry, packed wagon-wheel track. "Say, do you think Father will get the land grants registered?"

"Probably," Tobias said, "but if he doesn't this time, he'll get them next time. He never gives up."

"Well, I hope he gets my land grant. I can hardly wait to start my own place."

"With Lucy?" Tobias asked abruptly.

"Yes, I'd like that. Do you think I have a chance, Tobias?"

"Ask the lady, not me." Tobias sounded irritated.

"Well, I guess the reason I'm asking you is that . . . well . . . maybe there's an understanding between you and Lucy."

"And what if there is? I can't believe that would stop you, George."

"You're right, Tobias," George said in a determined voice. "Nothing will stop me except her marriage to someone else." Then more quietly he added, "But Tobias, I hope we can still be friends . . . no matter how this turns out."

Tobias stopped and turned around then and stared at his brother for a second. Then his brow relaxed and the firm lines around his mouth softened. A smile lit up his whole face as he gazed at his headstrong brother. "As well as my brother, you're my best friend, George," he said softly, "and you always will be. No one and nothing can change that."

Relieved, George fell silent. Yes, they were best friends, but still he was going to give his brother the fight of his life. "Best friends," George repeated. Tobias turned and walked straight along the wagon pathway.

Five minutes later, they came to the place in the middle of the pathway along the north side of the cornfield where the woods came nearest. George looked to the right, between the trees, while

Tobias checked the rows of corn to the left.

"We could cut diagonally across this end of the corn field to the west side and search there or we could go into the woods," Tobias suggested as he took his musket off his shoulder.

George shivered a little in the cold. "I don't know, Tobias. I think we should stay clear of the woods."

"But, it's almost as light as day. Anyway, I think I'd like to have a look in the corn first. I'll be right back." Tobias put his musket back on his shoulder again and took deep strides southwest into the thick corn field.

George took his musket from his shoulder and checked to see if it was ready to fire. He didn't want to be taken by surprise. Then he looked warily into the woods and listened. The night was still but the wind seemed to be shifting a little. Turning a little to the left, he looked into the corn field and noticed the shadows deepening between the rows of corn. He blinked. Was he starting to feel the fatigue of the journey? He thought not. Their days often started at dawn. But this day, he must admit, had been full . . . with Lucy along.

George smiled as he remembered Lucy's excitement at each new place they'd passed along the shore. "Why, George, there'll soon be homes all along Lake Ontario and the bay, too," she'd said. "In no time at all, it'll be just like the Hudson River, all settled and farmed." She had turned and smiled up at him then, and he was certain she would love to be the mistress of one of those estates. He would have the biggest farm around, next to Father's, of course. After all, he was the firstborn. He smiled again.

"Bang! Powff!" George jumped and stared into the thick corn stalks. Tobias must have shot his musket. Was it a warning? Or had he shot at the bear? The night seemed darker now. The moon must have gone behind a cloud. He couldn't see Tobias in the corn or the clearing by the woods. Where was he? His musket ready, George ran along the clearing between the corn field and the woods and then looked into the corn field in the place where Tobias had disappeared.

The moon was completely hidden now, and George could not see well. "Tobias," he shouted.

There was no answer. In a panic, George dived towards the gunshot he had heard. He ran diagonally between the thick stalks. He could hear only the loud beating of his own heart and the thumping of his feet on the hard dry ground.

Then George heard a low growl, and raising his head, he saw the bear. She was felling stalks on either side of her as she moved away from him down the row. Was she going for his brother?

"Tobias!" he shouted.

The bear turned, her brown nose extended as she sniffed the air, and started towards him. Then less than thirty feet away, she reared up and stood looking down on him.

George pulled his musket down and without taking time to aim, fired. In that very same second the bear dropped down on all fours and ran away through the field with the speed of a cannonball.

George stood frozen to the spot. There was no

point in chasing the bear through the corn. She would be almost impossible to find.

Where was his brother? He must have shot at the bear, too. "Tobias! Tobias!" he shouted.

There was no answer. Tobias must be somewhere near. Had he misjudged the location of the musket fire that he had heard just before his own? Perhaps Tobias had gone farther than he thought.

Then George heard Boots's low whine just ahead. "He's out again," George thought as he pushed back the sharp-leafed cornstalks and rushed to the the sound. He spotted Tobias on the ground with Boots nuzzling his thick, brown hair.

"Tobias! No, God, not Tobias!" George shouted as he dropped to the ground beside his brother. The bear must have mauled him. George drew in his breath and hesitated, afraid of what he was going to see.

Then George turned Tobias over and gasped. Tobias's eyes were as deep a blue as ever, but they stared back without expression. His shirt was stained with blood on the left side of his chest.

Tobias had been shot.

Twenty-One

A cool gust of wind blew the muslin curtains into the Meyers' kitchen sitting-room Mary shut the window. She was here alone with Leonard now, for she had finally persuaded Mother to go to bed. Lucy, too, had gone to bed, tired after her long day. Mary suspected from the silence that they were all asleep. Leonard sat at the table munching the leftover cobs of corn. Mother had boiled a whole pot full.

"I don't like it, Mary," he mumbled. "I'd go out there to help, but I might just cause trouble. They might think I was the bear and shoot at me."

Mary put her finger to her lips, not wanting to waken Mother. She opened the front door, and the two went out into the yard and looked across the wheat stubble to the corn field. Just then a cloud crossed over and covered the moon. Mary peered anxiously towards the woods but saw nothing in the darkness.

"What was that?" Mary whispered, grabbing Leonard's arm. She thought she'd heard a musket shot.

"I can't take any more of this," Leonard said.

"I'm going for my musket." He ran back into the house. In a minute, he was out again with his musket over his shoulder.

Mary grabbed his arm. "Look, if there is trouble, one of them will come for help. Anyway, it wouldn't be wise to go out there alone. You were right before. They might think you were a bear in the dark."

"Even George isn't that stupid," Leonard answered. But when he saw how flushed and restless Mary was, he stood and waited.

When they heard the second shot, Leonard pulled his arm free and ran across the wheat field towards the corn.

"Be careful, Leonard," Mary called out. "Be careful." She watched him grow smaller and finally disappear among the thick stalks of corn.

The door opened behind her. Mother was standing there in her white flannel nightgown and linen bedcap. "What is it, Mary? Did I hear a musket shot?"

"I don't know," Mary said evasively.

"Come in, Mary," Mother said. "Those boys should know better than to hunt for that bear without your father. But then I can't tell them what to do any more than I can your father. So come on in. I don't want to worry about you, too."

They sat in silence on the couch. Mother looked tired and soon closed her eyes, but Mary knew she was not sleeping. She would be praying silently. Mary said her own short prayer, and then opened her eyes to find Mother looking at her calmly. She seemed to have renewed strength.

About ten minutes later, they heard Boots's

barking and Leonard's hysterical shouting, "Help! Open up!"

Mary could not move. Mother flew to the door and opened it. Leonard and George were carrying Tobias's limp body. They brushed by and laid Tobias on the mat in front of the fireplace. Now Mary could see a bloody mess hardening on his chest. Mother grabbed a towel and followed the boys over to the mat.

Mary could hardly recognize George. His face was ashen and his eyes were glazed over. He knelt beside Tobias on the mat. "I shot him," he said. "I shot my own brother. I shot Tobias." But he wasn't speaking to any of them. He had clasped his arms around himself and was rocking back and forth.

Leonard was kneeling on the other side of Tobias. His shoulders were shaking, too, and he was sobbing.

"No!" Mary screamed. "No, he isn't . . . he isn't dead!"

Mother bent over her son and felt for his pulse. She kept her trembling hand there for some time. Finally, she lovingly laid her hand on Tobias's forehead and drew it down across his staring eyes. They closed under her gentle touch.

"What's the matter? Why is everyone here?" Yawning, Lucy emerged from the girls' bedroom door. All she could see were the bent heads of the family all squatting around something in front of the couch. When Mary looked up at her, tears were streaming down her face.

Lucy came awake with a jolt, flew around the end of the couch, and looked down. "No!" she screamed and threw herself on the floor beside Tobias. "No!" Then she turned to Mother. "Is he hurt badly?"

Mother put her arm around Lucy and said, "Yes, Lucy." Then Mother looked down at her son and quietly repeated a verse familiar to all of them.

"The Lord is my Shepherd, I shall not want. . . . "Yea though I walk through the valley of the shadow of death, I will fear no evil, for Thou art with me. Thy rod and Thy staff they comfort me. . . . And I will dwell in the house of the Lord forever."

They all stared at their brother's body, lying still as stone on the hearth. Then George stood up and ran from the room. "Go with him, Leonard," Mother said. "We know it was an accident. He mustn't blame himself."

"George shot Tobias?" Lucy said, her eyes wide.

Leonard turned back from the door and stared at her coldly. "It was an accident. George was shooting at a bear rearing on his back legs in front of him. But the bear dropped as George fired. Tobias was on the other side of the bear. As I see it, if George hadn't distracted the bear to come for him instead of Tobias, the bear would have gotten Tobias anyway." He went out after George.

Kneeling beside Mary, Lucy reached over and took Tobias's hand in hers. Her tears splashed heavily down on his chest. Mother sat on the couch and gazed at her son's face in disbelief. After a few minutes, she said, "Mary, please go and tell George and Leonard that I need them to put your brother in the bedroom."

"But Mother —"

"Lucy is with me. We'll be fine."

The moon was out again as Mary ran to the barn and opened the door. "Come inside," she shouted. "Mother needs you." There was no answer. So she waited.

"We'll be right there." It was Leonard's voice, and suddenly Mary thought how strong and steady he sounded.

Mary trudged back to the house without looking back. She could not stand to look at George's stricken face again.

Mother went to the door as George came in and took him by the arm to Father's chair.

"George, it was not your fault," she said calmly, drawing up a chair and sitting in front of him. "Tobias would have been mauled by that bear — a much worse fate — if you had not come to his rescue when you did. No one will blame you. And you must not blame yourself."

George sat bent over, staring at the floor. Mother took his hands in hers and went on. "And George, our days are in God's hands. Remember how He brought us through all those difficult times during the war when everything was against us? Well, He could have intervened now, too, if it had been His will."

George only mumbled in a voice that sounded as if it was coming from far away, "Then why didn't He?"

Mother hesitated a moment. "Now, George, your father is not here. You are the firstborn. You must take the responsibility for the family's needs, for my needs. I know I can depend on you. I must depend on you."

George lifted his head for the first time since he had come back with his brother's body and looked at his mother with a semblance of recognition.

"You and Leonard must take Tobias into our bedroom."

"To his bed?" George choked out.

"No, to mine. I don't want to disturb Jacob."

Neither Jacob nor Anna had roused in spite of the commotion. Lucy was still kneeling beside Tobias in her nightgown and nightcap. With tear-filled eyes, she looked up for a few seconds as George and Leonard approached. Then she reached over and picked a yellow leaf out of Tobias's hair. She held it between the palms of her hands as she stood up.

Slowly George and Leonard lifted their brother and took him through the open doorway into Mother and Father's bedroom. Mother threw her best quilt over the bed first, and they eased Tobias's body onto it. She pointed to the door and they went out ahead of her.

"Now, as soon as it is daylight, you must go for John. Ask him to bring Catharine and the baby here, and then go for your father."

"I'll leave now," George said.

"No, you won't, not with that bear still out there," Mother said. "You'll have a bit to eat first and then it will be light. Mary, start the porridge, please."

Mary almost gagged. She couldn't even think about eating. How could Mother even mention it? Didn't she care about Tobias the way the rest of them did?

Mary staggered a bit as she went over to the cupboard and dipped water out of a pail and put it into the kettle. Leonard had already poked the low coals into a light blaze and thrown on a couple of small pieces of hardwood. He seemed to be one step ahead in knowing what Mother would want. Mary hung the kettle over the blaze.

George was back in Father's chair with his head buried in his hands. Mary went over and put her arm around his shoulders, but there was no response apart from the trembling of his body.

* * * *

It was mid-morning when Catharine and the baby came with John. Mary opened the door and stared at her sister. In the few weeks since they had last seen Catharine, she had lost a considerable amount of weight.

"Have you been sick, Catharine?"

"Yes, my usual croup. But it's nothing. Now where's Tobias. I must see him. I must." Her voice had a plaintive sound that was not at all like Catharine.

John stepped into the room just behind Catharine and handed little Johnnie to Mary. The baby gurgled his happy baby smile at Mary as if he was old enough to remember her. She rubbed his rosy cheek with her forefinger but didn't have the heart to smile back.

Anna came over and helped Mary take off the baby's knitted blue bonnet and coat. Then Mary handed the baby to Anna so she could go into the bedroom with Catharine and Mother. Catharine stood by the bed, crying, her arms around Mother.

Suddenly Mary realized that she had not yet seen Mother cry.

The women turned as they heard the sounds of loud thumping on the stoop and the front door opening. "Well, that's a fine greeting for your father. . . . What's wrong? I can tell something has happened. What is it?"

Mother walked briskly towards the doorway. "What is it, Polly?" Father asked, looking gently at his wife.

"There has been an accident, Hans. A terrible, terrible accident. . . . A bear attacked Tobias, and George accidentally shot Tobias instead of the bear."

George was sitting in Father's chair again, with his head in his hands. Mary saw his shoulders shake a little, but he did not look up.

"Dear God, no. Is he hurt badly?"

There was an intake of breath around the room. Then Mother's quiet voice broke the silence. "He's gone, Hans." Her voice broke into a sob but no tears followed.

"No!" Father's cry filled the room. Mary stared at Father's stricken face as he leaned a little on Mother and she led him into their bedroom and closed the door.

* * * *

A sharp wind blew cool air from the bay across the slope where the family stood around Tobias's grave. John had brought the Reverend John Langhorn, who had been visiting in Adolphustown, to lead the service. A surprising number of people had come to the funeral. Even Henry Young and his wife from East Lake had come. From across the bay were the Weese family. John Weese wore his military uniform, and his new wife, Juliana, stood beside him along with two of John's children, his oldest son, John Jr., now about Leonard's age, and his second daughter, Catharine, who was Anna's age. Even Major John Howell was there in full military uniform. He had been commissioned to serve in Butlers' Rangers during the Revolutionary War and now farmed near Adolphustown. Peter Van Alstine had come with him.

The Mississauga chief and two middle-aged men from his tribe stood in their bright native dress and watched silently from the side. Mary could hardly believe how many people had learned of her brother's death in the past two days.

As the service began, the little crowd fell back from the inner circle, where the family stood with bowed heads around the grave. Mary and Lucy held each other's hands tightly. Tears streamed down Lucy's face while Mary stood staring with a great empty feeling. John stood beside Catharine with a well-wrapped Johnnie in his arms. The day was cool and the wind from the bay was brisk and damp. Next to Catharine, Leonard kept a steady hand on Jacob's trembling shoulder. Mother placed one arm around Mary's waist and her other arm was around Anna, who was sniffling into a handkerchief. The sisters and Lucy wore their best dark clothes — linen grey outer petticoats and dark brown short-gowns. It was their silent way of showing respect and love for their brother and friend.

On the other side of the grave, Father and George stood together, a little apart from the others. Father wore his military uniform — his breeches and waistcoat of white wool and his short green coat with the red lapels, collar, and cuffs. George was dressed in his brown breeches, tan linen shirt, and homespun brown short-coat. His curly red hair, blowing out in the wind, was longer than Father's now. Mary wished she could help George somehow, but he had slept in the barn since the accident and only occasionally came into the house for some food.

The minister had come a long way, but he was determined not to prolong the family's agony by delivering a long sermon. His final words rang out clearly in Mary's ears.

"I am the resurrection, and the life: he that believeth in me, though he were dead, yet shall he live: And whosoever liveth and believeth in me shall never die."

Twenty-Two

"I'll not be gone long," Father said from his chair beside the fireplace. "But I think I should go with George. I'm relieved that he's willing to work at Adolphustown. Peter Van Alstine is delighted to get the help of a strong young man and it will do George good."

Two months had passed since Tobias's funeral, and George was still sleeping in the barn.

"We'll miss him," Mother said, kneading bread on the kitchen table. "It'll be terrible with both George and Tobias gone. . . . But I agree it's for the best that he leave for a time, Hans."

"And he'll be back with us in the spring. It'll be a black winter for him, but he'll make it through. But Tobias — " Father's voice broke, and he stared at the low-burning coals in the fireplace. Silence filled the room. Mary felt like running away, but instead she kept right on peeling the potatoes at the work table, tears rolling down her face and into the potato water. The familiar, comforting sound of Mother pounding out the bread dough continued.

"So our land is registered," Father said in a

steadier voice as he watched Mother work. "Lots eight and nine of the first concession of Township Number Eight are ours now. But I still don't have my site for a waterfall."

"Nor your just compensation, either, I would say."

"No, but the 247 pounds sterling that they did allow me will help us get a new start in the spring. We'll be able to buy more seed as well as animals and tools. Still, it's far short of what we left behind. I had figured our loss at four hundred pounds, and that was a modest estimate."

"I know, Hans, I know. And nothing will ever compensate us for the loss of our son in this wild land."

Father fell silent then. If they had stayed back at Cooeyman's Landing, would his son be alive today? He would drive himself mad with such thoughts, but it was difficult not to wonder and remember.

Father was drawn back to the present by the soft sound of Catharine singing a lullaby to the baby in the girls' bedroom. She had been with them for a week this time while John took one of his trips to King's Town. It had helped a little to have Catharine and the baby there. When sorrow overcame them, the baby's laughter gave the family some relief. And the extra work gave Mother and Mary a needed distraction.

"I'm going out to gather the eggs," Mary said. It was the last week of October and unexpectedly warm today, though the days were already much shorter. Mary looked up at the bare birch and

maple trees as she took the little path to the barn.
In spite of the mellow day, a crispness was in the air.
George and Leonard were bringing in a wagon load
of freshly cut logs to chop and store in the lean-to
beside the storage shed. Mary set down her empty
basket and walked over towards her brothers.

George drove the wagon up beside the shed,
and then he jumped off the wagon and started to
unhitch the team. Leonard was already throwing
the lighter branches down beside the lean-to.
They would pile the wood into neat cords afterwards when it was all cut. George flung the reins
back over the horses' backs and untied them from
the whippletrees. George took the reins and
began to lead the horses to the stable. Mary fell
into step with him. "George, can't we talk?"

"I suppose," George mumbled. He was thinner
than he had ever been, and his shoulders were
bent.

"I just heard that you're going down to
Adolphustown."

"Yes, Mr. Van Alstine's had more settlers come
in this summer and needs help getting them ready
for winter."

"We'll miss you, George."

"I'm sorry, Mary. But I have to keep busy. And
come spring, I'll put the money I earn to good use."

"There's lots to do here."

"Leonard will take my place."

Mary had to admit that Leonard had grown up
overnight, it seemed. He had been a strength to
all of them, and now he was doing more than his
share of the work.

They walked to the stable in silence, and Mary opened the door while George separated the horses and led them into the barn. When he had finished, Mary put her hand on his arm. "No one blames you, George. And Tobias could have met a worse death from the bear if you hadn't reached him when you did." ·

"Don't, Mary. . . . Please don't. I just can't stand to . . . ." George's jaw tightened. He unbuckled Duke's collar, pulled it off, and hung it on its hook. Mary could hear him blowing his nose before he returned for the other collar.

"Will you see Lucy when you go to Adolphustown, George?"

"She lives at King's Town, not Adolphustown."

"But I know she'd like to see you. She's worried about you, George. We all are."

George looked Mary straight in the eye then. "I don't need anyone's pity."

"She cares a great deal for you, George."

"It was always Tobias that she cared for the most. She just liked to laugh with me. We were the jokers. I was more like a pal than a beau. Anyway, I'm not going to win this way, Mary. I honour my brother's memory too much for that!"

"I don't think he would mind, George. He loved you both. I just don't think he would mind seeing you together."

* * * *

After the supper dishes were all cleared away, Mary hurried outside to the clothesline to bring in the baby clothes. In a few minutes, she was back with a full basket and quickly pulled the clouts and shirts and long white nightgowns, caps, and bibs, woven in the deep overweave diaper pattern, out of the basket and set them on the table. She was starting to fold the clouts and pilches into neat piles when Catharine softly closed the bedroom door on her sleeping baby and came over to the table.

"Thank you, Mary," Catharine said. "I'm going down to the bay to look for John. He was supposed to be back today. Won't you come with me?"

"As soon as I finish my job here."

"Go ahead, Mary," Mother said. "I'll finish."

The Meyers' bateau, fastened to the dock, was bobbing up and down in the waves. The wind that had come up just since supper seemed to be growing stronger.

"He may not come tonight," Mary said. She sat down on the grass and leaned against a young birch tree.

"I know that, Mary," Catharine said in a soft voice. "I came out here because I wanted to talk with you alone."

Mary looked down at Catharine with surprise. She had no idea what Catharine was going to talk about. Tobias's death, perhaps.

"It's best that George go to Adolphustown, Mary. It will help him."

"I don't think so. He may become even more withdrawn from the family. I'm afraid he'll never be the same again."

"Oh, he'll come back!" Catharine said in a quiet

voice. "His family ties are deep. Remember during the war years, how he ran away to join us? He'll come back in the spring. Maybe not the same person, but better than he is now."

Mary sighed and looked down the bay. "You always make me feel better, Catharine. Do you think George and Lucy . . . will ever make a match of it?"

"I hope so. They care about each other, and they both cared deeply for Tobias. They could share their grief. It would help them both."

"But George doesn't see it that way, Catharine. And we both know how determined he can be."

They were silent for a while. Catharine moved off the damp ground to sit on a tall stump. She looked more like a little girl than a married woman of nineteen with a son. Looking down at Mary with blue eyes larger than ever, she said, "Mary, I've been thinking about how brief life can be. Even during the war, it didn't seem so, for we all came through fine, but now . . . with Tobias taken so suddenly, it's made me realize this. And also it's made me think about how much my family means to me. I think we're even closer now as a family. We don't often express our feelings, but maybe we should . . . Mary I want you to know how much you mean to me — how close I've always felt to you . . . and still do."

"But, Catharine, you have plenty to keep you busy. After all, with a baby and husband, you don't have much time to miss me."

"Oh, but I have Mary!" A shadow seemed to fall across Catharine's face, and Mary was reminded how thin Catharine was. Lately she'd been cough-ing far into the night.

"I haven't told anyone, not even John, but I'm going to have a baby again in the spring — early May, I think."

"How could you be expecting again? You're still nursing your baby."

"It happens to some women."

"Really? I thought that's why a lot of women let their babies nurse until they are almost two years old — to keep from getting in the family way."

"Well, I guess it *is* true with some women, but not with us Meyers women. After all, George was only ten months older than Tobias, and Mother nursed all her babies."

"Are you really sure you're expecting again?"

"No, but I think so. Still, I'll wait until I'm sure before I tell anyone else."

"But you aren't too strong, Catharine."

"Oh, Mary, I'm so happy. I love Johnnie so much and now I'll have another baby. I just can't explain how happy I am." In her excitement, Catharine began coughing uncontrollably. Finally, she took in a few gulps of bay air and began to speak. "But sometimes I do worry, Mary. Sometimes I wonder if I'll have a healthy baby this time, or . . . maybe I won't live through the birth to take care of my babies."

Mary looked down at her sister's thin face and suddenly she was afraid, too, but she could not let on to Catharine. "I don't think your fears are unusual," Mary said. "All women worry when they're in the family way." She laughed a light, self-conscious laugh. "At least that's what I've heard. And surely the second time will be easier, not harder. That's a known fact, too."

Catharine's face seemed to relax a little now, and Mary continued. "And this time we're bringing you home a month ahead even if I have to pick you up and carry you all the way!"

Catharine laughed, and the shadow lifted from her face. But she said, "Still, Mary, if anything happens, promise me you'll take care of my babies, and John, too? You will, won't you? Remember, Mary, I'll not think like George. I'll look down and smile if you take my place."

Mary's heart skipped a beat. Why had Catharine mentioned John? Did she suspect how she had once felt about him?

Mary didn't look at her sister but said, "I'll always be here for you, Catharine, to do whatever I can. You surely know that you can count on me."

Twenty-Three

The year 1788 brought the worst winter that the Meyers family could remember. All Loyalists suffered and some were calling it the "Hungry Winter." As Tobias and George had predicted the night of Tobias's death, the drought left most cellars with meagre supplies. People living in civilized areas like King's Town and the nearby townships were in the worst straits, for wild animals were scarce with so many hunters out looking for food for their families. Everywhere the animals were thin and starving.

The snow had started falling in late November, and had kept coming down all winter. By the last week of March, everyone thought the snow was disappearing for good, but that was when the worst storm of the year hit. The snow was four feet deep on the open meadow, and the banks on either side of the shovelled paths were as high as Leonard, who was now over six feet tall.

It had been a month since the Meyers had seen Catharine, and everyone was worried except Father, who assured them that John would get through to them if there was trouble. Mary remembered little Johnnie's arrival and was not so sure.

Still, John seemed to be staying closer to home. Last September 23, he had been present at the meeting between Sir John Johnson and other government officials, and the Mississauga chiefs at Carrying Place. There they had signed the Gunshot Treaty with the Mississaugas and arranged a further land purchase with them. Leonard said John was no longer selling rum to anyone.

The family had received no news from George after November when Father had brought supplies up from King's Town. He had stopped at Adolphustown to see his son. George was helping a family of late settlers build a home for the winter, working from sun-up until after dark some nights. He had little to say to Father when they met on the worksite. Afterwards, Father spoke to Peter Van Alstine. He said that George kept to himself when he wasn't working and his only companion was Boots, who trailed after him wherever he went.

Now it was the last week of March, and they had been hopeful that this dreadful winter might soon be over, but instead the worst storm of the season had hit. By noon of the third day of the storm, the wind went down, and the Meyers men — Father, Leonard, and Jacob — pulled their coats and scarves off the nails by the door and started to shovel wider paths to the barn. Mary watched from the window and wondered if summer would ever come.

"Spring is right around the corner," Mother said. "Who knows what a kind southwest wind might blow in."

Mary knew that their supplies in the cellar beneath the floor were almost gone. They must not eat the seed potatoes or the wheat and corn seed. Although Father and Leonard were hunting every day now, lately they had come home with nothing. The family wouldn't starve to death, of course, with animals in the barn. But they had already butchered one cow.

"Even in this northern land, spring must come soon," Mother said.

As if in answer, the howling wind swooped down on the cabin and shrieked into the chimney with fresh vengeance. Father went over to the fire and threw in two small pieces of hardwood. He raked the coals around the sticks and then turned to Jacob. "We need more wood, Jacob." Glumly, Jacob headed for the back door.

As he opened the door, they heard the jingle of sleigh bells. Mary rushed to the front window and looked across the field. It was John. His horses were struggling along up to their flanks in the snow.

"It's John . . . and Catharine, I think," Mary shouted. She could see a lumpy buffalo robe on the back of the sleigh, which might be hiding Catharine and Johnnie.

As John drove the team straight up to the front door, Father and Leonard rushed out. Leonard took the horses' reins while John rushed to pull back the buffalo robe. Catharine lay very still while John picked up Johnnie and handed him to Father.

At the door, Mary reached out for the plump

bundle of beaver fur. Only Johnnie's two bright blue eyes and rosy cheeks showed out from the thick coat sewed in at the bottom. She brought him inside and pulled out the long hawthorne thorns that fastened the thick coat together.

Johnnie smiled up at Mary as she unwrapped him. Once free of his binding clothes, he put both arms around her neck and gave her a big kiss on the cheek. But Mary was looking past Johnnie to his mother.

Catharine's eyes were closed and she was groaning a little as Father and John carried her inside. A sickening feeling closed in on Mary. "She's not, she's not in labour . . . yet," she mumbled as she watched. "It's at least a month too soon."

Mary handed Johnnie to Anna, but he started to scream loudly, so Mary took him back. As she walked the baby up and down in front of the fireplace, she heard John say, "Please put some water on to boil, Mother Meyers."

* * * *

The first streaks of morning light were streaming through the window of Catharine's parents' candle-lit bedroom when a loud baby's cry was heard. Out in the kitchen sitting-room Father smiled at John, who was standing in front of the fire. Apart from Mary and Mother, who were with Catharine, all the others had gone to sleep.

John jumped to his feet and headed for the bedroom door as Mother came out. "It's another little boy," she said. "He's having a little difficulty breathing, but I think he'll make it all right." She placed the newborn boy in the old cradle while Johnnie now slept on the couch. The baby was well wrapped in a warm woollen cloth and surrounded with soft lamb's wool.

Mary sat beside Catharine and looked out through the open bedroom doorway. John stared at the baby. "Was it a hard delivery?" he asked.

"No, it wasn't. But Catharine is very thin and weak, and she's still coughing. Has the cold never left her since she was here, John?"

"I'm afraid not. I wanted to bring her sooner, but she felt she should wait. When we started out this morning, she was fine. She didn't tell me the baby was coming."

"The second baby generally comes faster," Mother said. "But this is too early. It's probably due to all that coughing."

John rushed to the bedroom door. Inside the room, he knelt beside the bed and took Catharine's hand in his. "It's a boy . . . a fine boy."

"I know," Catharine said, looking up at John. "He's little George. I want to call him George."

Mother bustled back into the room. "Could you watch your new son, John? I'll wash him later. Right now, I need to attend to my daughter." Catharine had already closed her eyes and seemed to drift off to sleep.

"The afterbirth should have come by now," Mother mumbled in a worried tone.

It wasn't long before Catharine woke and moaned as the afterbirth slipped out. The bleeding would not stop. Mary and Mother tore up a whole sheet for packing, but it did not help. The sheets became drenched with the blood.

Finally Mother looked up at Mary with fear in her eyes. "Call John and your father," she said. "I've done all I can." Then she dropped on her knees beside the bed and started to pray in silence.

"Come quickly," Mary called out sharply through the doorway. She stepped back inside and stared at her sister in fear. She did not think it possible for Catharine to look paler.

John came rushing into the room, looking alarmed. Father came in, too, and stood behind his wife.

John dropped to his knees on the mat beside Catharine's bed. He took her hand in his and stared at her with fear and love. Catharine grew paler and paler until a stone-like whiteness spread over her face.

"Catharine! Catharine!" John cried. Father leaned over and felt for Catharine's pulse. Then he shook his head and stared softly at John.

Mother looked up then, too, and shook her head as she tried to find a sign of life.

"She's gone, son," Father said.

Sobbing, John lifted Catharine's head a little and wrapped his arms around her.

Father put his arms around Mother and led her to the door. Turning back, he motioned Mary from the room.

But Mary refused to leave. She knelt down at the bed beside John and stared at her sister's life-less body. With tears streaming down her face, she cried out, "No, Catharine, not you, too!"

Part Three

A New Estate

Twenty-Four

"We buried her beside Tobias," Mary said, pointing to Catharine's grave. Leonard had carved out two wooden crosses, which were surrounded by wild roses. It was a hot Sunday morning in the middle of July, but a fresh breeze blew up from the bay and across the side hill that had become the little cemetery for the area. Last night, George had come home, and after Father's Sunday morning Bible reading, he and Mary had gone for a walk.

"Did you plant the roses, Mary?"

"Yes. . . . Catharine always loved roses."

George stared at the words on the cross: "Catharine W. Meyers, the Wife of John Bleecker, and Mother of John Jr., and George."

Mary said softly, "It was Catharine who named George. It was her last wish."

Seeing George swallow in distress, Mary turned to go, but George was staring now at his brother's grave.

"This spot is one of the most beautiful pieces of land in the area," Mary said.

George nodded.

"But it's a better land where they are . . . no tears, no cold, no hunger, and no dying."

Because the trails had been filled with snow and the bay clogged with ice, no one had been able to get to George with the news about Catharine's death until after the burial.

George was still not his old self. Mary wished he would return to his irritating, teasing ways, but so far, it hadn't happened. Still, she liked this George, too, for he was more like Tobias now. He listened without laughing at her.

"Lucy told me to tell you that she has all kinds of young men lined up for you to choose from," George said, holding back a maple sapling so it wouldn't snap back at Mary. "She's hoping you'll come to visit her and Henry in their new home." George had brought back the news that Lucy had married Henry Finkle, the young man who had been calling on her for the last two years. But no one, including Lucy, had taken him seriously — until lately.

"And I'm going!" Mary smiled. "After we get through the raspberry picking and preserves, I'll go."

In early May, John had taken his young sons to King's Town so his mother and sister could care for them, and he had returned to the trading post alone. But he had not visited the Meyers family.

Mary turned towards her brother. "Will you take me to John's mother's place instead? I know I'm always welcome there. And I do want to see Catharine's babies."

George hesitated. "No, I would sooner help

Father and let Leonard go. He needs a break."

"I don't know how the family could have managed without Leonard this last year. He seemed like a boy at the start of it all, but now. . . ."

"I'm sorry, Mary. I should have stayed, but I just couldn't . . . after the accident. I'm sorry."

"It was a dreadful winter, George. I couldn't begin to tell you about the folks who came by for food. From distances, too."

The two turned towards home. Then Mary said, "So . . . did you see Lucy when you visited King's Town — before she married?" Mary asked.

George gave her a sharp sideways glance. "Yes, but I was never her beau — not after Tobias. . . . Anyway, I'm calling on someone else." George brushed back some willow branches hanging over the path, and Mary stepped ahead.

"You are? I didn't know that. Why didn't you tell me?" Mary said.

"Well, you didn't ask, and anyway, there's not much to tell."

"Who is she?"

George laughed. "Really, Mary, you're as impatient as ever!"

"Like my oldest brother! Now, tell me more." George's laughter had sounded good, so Mary decided she would keep him on this topic.

"Her name's Alida. She's a Van Alstine."

"The daughter of Father's friend."

"Yes, the only daughter. She has been keeping house for her father and two brothers since her mother died five years ago when she was only twelve."

"So do you have an understanding?"

"No. And I'm not going back until fall. I'll visit Alida then."

"Does she know how you feel? And how do you feel, George? Are you going to marry her?"

"Well, aren't you the nosey sister!" George laughed a low laugh and gave Mary a light punch in the shoulder. Then he said, "I know I would like to marry her, but I'm not so sure just how she feels about me. The family was so kind to me that I wonder if she wasn't just being like the rest of them. So I'm planning not to go back until fall, and there's no understanding between us. Maybe by then she'll be seeing someone else."

"Is she anything like Lucy?"

"No, not at all. She's quieter . . . and somehow . . . deeper. She's believes there's a purpose behind everything that happens to us."

"She's quite devout then."

"Yes. She believes that God works things together for good in the lives of people who have faith in Him."

"It sounds like you've had some serious talks."

"We did, I guess. We went to a few dances, too . . . when we could get out during the winter. Once spring came, there was no time to go anywhere. Folks are determined to have good crops this year. I spent all my time working the land and seeding."

"We've had a hard spring, too. But Leonard is as strong as Father, and Jacob is a great help now. Father is thankful for his army half-pay, though. We had eaten or given away all our seed potatoes and hand-crushed most of our seed wheat. So he had to go by bateau to Montreal to buy more."

"I know it'll be a hard winter again for some folks. Most of them ate their seed. But those who have will share with the others at Adolphustown."

"Father says you filed for your own land when you were in King's Town."

"Yes. I own the land directly west of Father's now — Lot Number Seven going straight back from the bay. They gave it to me because I was the son of a Loyalist. It's not nearly as large as Father's, but it's right next door. We'll be able to share tools and work, and we'll seed and harvest the land together."

"I thought you were going to move away from the family."

"You know, Mary, this last winter, I realized how important all of you are to me. We need to be near each other in this wilderness. We don't want forest lots between our farms. It will only make a haven for more bears and wild creatures. The more we clear the land side by side, the better off we'll be."

Mary looked down. This was definitely not the old George who wanted excitement and adventure. But this George would make a good farmer and probably a good husband and father.

"George! Mary!" Jacob was running across the garden. He had a frog in one hand and a long, dangling garter snake in the other.

"Oh, no. That's his Sunday hobby, adding to his animals in the storage shed," Mary said as she ran the few feet to the front stoop and disappeared inside the house. As the door slammed it did not drown out the sound of George's robust laughter.

* * * *

"We'll be home in time for supper, Mary," Father
said, smiling down at his daughters, who were
clearing wooden dishes from the table after the
noonday meal.

"But, Hans, if Juliana invites us for supper
there, we'll stay," Mother said. "And she will. She
always does. So don't count on us coming back
until almost dark. It's so nice to have time to visit
neighbours. We mustn't make our visits too short."

"Well, we'll have a good time anyway," Father
said, holding the door open for his wife. "I knew
John Weese long ago, so we'll have lots to talk
over. He was in Rogers' Rangers."

The voices trailed away as Mary slushed the soft
soap bar through the dishwater she was preparing.
She started piling in the dirty dishes. Since all
children of Loyalists could apply at age twenty-
one, she would get Father to help her write a
proper letter to the authorities and she would take
it to them when she went to King's Town this fall.
George was going to work his land on shares with
Father. Why shouldn't she be a part of the family
farming team? Though not in the fields, she did
do her share of the work. And here she was on
Sunday afternoon with her hands deep in soap-
suds while George sat in Father's chair and
Leonard lounged on the couch.

"I don't know why Leonard and George can't
dry these dishes," Anna said. "I wanted to go, too."

"Run! You'll catch them before they leave," Mary said. "There's time. I'll make your brothers help." Anna threw her apron over the back of a chair and was out the door in a flash.

"George, did you see that?" Leonard asked in a surprised tone.

George smiled over at his brother. "I certainly did, Leonard. And did you hear what I heard!"

Leonard smiled. "I didn't hear a thing."

"Listen, you two. There's work to be done here," Mary said cheerfully. "So just help yourselves to these tea towels."

"Not me! I'm not doing woman's work. Anyway, I have to feed the new calf."

"In the middle of the day, Leonard?" Everyone knew that even the calves had only morning and night feedings, and most of the older animals had only one feeding a day. But Leonard got up and hurried out.

George continued to sit where he was. Mary was becoming more irritated by the second. Would she remind George about the two large pieces of her fresh raspberry pie he'd had for dinner? She had even dipped the rich top off last night's milking and whipped it into cream to make a topping.

"When I finish with this water, I know where I'll dump it," Mary said, looking straight at George's curly red hair.

"Where's that?" George said.

Before Mary had a chance to answer, they heard a loud knock at the door. Mary dried her hands and untied her apron. Since it was Sunday, she was wearing a light blue overgown on top of her navy blue petticoat instead of her usual brown homepsun. She adjusted her mob cap and headed for the front door.

George reached the door first and stood face-to-face with John. The two old friends clasped their arms around each other in silence. This was the first time they had seen each other since Catharine's death.

George was the first to break the silence. "I hear there's a young man named after me."

John smiled. He was looking much better than when Mary had last seen him. "Yes, he's a fine boy. Johnnie and George are both in the wagon. And I've brought a housekeeper back with me."

Mary felt a pang of disappointment that surprised her. As she had watched John standing there so handsome and strong, some of the old feelings began to rush back. But those emotions must be quelled now. Often housekeepers became so valuable that the men they worked for ended up marrying them — especially if they couldn't afford to pay them anymore.

"We'd love to see the boys, John," Mary said eagerly, "and your housekeeper, too. She must be tired from the trip."

"We've only come from Bleecker's Castle. We came up from King's Town by bateau a week ago and Mrs. Dick stayed home to rest today."

John headed out to his wagon. First he tied the team to a low-hanging branch of a maple tree. Then he swung Johnnie down from the wagon and let him run up to the house. He was more than a year old now, and it was the first time that

Mary had seen him walking. He ran straight for Mary and screamed, "Ma-Ma!"

Mary guessed he called all women "Ma-Ma," since he didn't have a mother anymore.

John handed the baby to George, who drew back with his arms glued to his sides. "Mary here will take him," George said. "He's . . . well . . . great . . . but he's so small. I wouldn't want to hurt him or something."

"Why, George, he's not small at all," Mary said, staring down at the bundle. "He's really grown. Look at those plump little cheeks." She turned to John. "He's picked up wonderfully. Your mother has taken great care of him."

"Yes, she did, but a man's sons should be with him — and they were too much for Mother alone now that Lucy is married."

"Somehow I can't get used to the fact that Lucy's married. How is she?"

"Fine. Henry Finkle seems like a fine fellow. And he's building her a new clapboard house. They say it'll be the first of its kind in these parts."

John came over and sat beside Mary.

"How have *you* been, John?" Mary asked.

"Busy! The trading post has been busier than it's ever been. But still it's been lonely."

"Now that you have your sons, it'll be better."

George was down on all fours, giving Johnnie a ride on his back around the couch. The child's gleeful shrieks of laughter almost drowned out John's next words. "Come over to see us any time, Mary."

"Yes, I'd love to."

Mary smiled at the sleeping baby and said, "John, may I put little George in our cradle?"

John nodded. Mary slipped the baby into the little cradle that Mother had left ready. Mary was surprised by John's gentle way with his young children. Most fathers didn't notice their children much until they were a few years old and never helped take care of them. Catharine would be proud. Mary swallowed at the thought.

Mary sat on the couch, looking down at the baby, who was now sucking loudly and contentedly from a little leather pouch. Her cheeks were flushed, and her lacey white mob cap had fallen off. Her thick auburn hair curled about her face and around her shoulders. She did not notice the soft expression that gradually crept over John's face as he listened to her humming a lullaby to little George.

"Hush! the bay shore waves are rolling in,
White with foam, white with foam,
And Father toils amid the din;
But baby sleeps at home.

"Hush! the wintry winds roar hoarse
        and deep —
On they come, on they come!
Brother plays at baby's feet;
But baby sleeps at home."

As John gazed fondly at Mary, George's face darkened and he turned abruptly and walked outside.

Twenty-Five

Mary peered over the side of the wagon. The sun was shining brightly, but the August day was not hot. John's housekeeper had arrived unexpectedly on their doorstep that morning. She had left John and the children and walked all the way along the Bay Trail. "That one's a harsh taskmaster," she had said. "And I'll not go back!" So Mother had called Jacob in from his work in the garden and asked him to go get George. When he came, she asked him to hurry and take Mary and Anna over to help John before something happened to Catharine's babies. So here they were on their way to Bleecker's Castle.

Though Mary was looking forward to seeing the babies and, she must admit, John, she still had a lonely feeling as she thought of Catharine's home without Catharine.

Boots sat silently beside George with his head held high and his long nose protruding in the air as though he was watching for someone or something. George was silent as they passed the corn field, and Mary swallowed. Was the rest of her life going to be like this? Sadness and remembering?

The sun sparkled on the Trent River. It was a quiet day as they crossed over, with George rowing and Anna sitting at the far end of the punt. What would John think when he saw them?

They could hear John singing lustily inside as they opened the door to the trading post. When they entered, Mary could hardly believe her eyes. John had his back to the door and was sorting bags of supplies behind the counter. Baby George was sleeping soundly in the carrier on his back while Johnnie stacked wooden blocks in the play area about five feet square that John had penned off at the back of the room.

"Good afternoon, John," George said quietly.

John whipped around and stared. Then he flushed red. "I guess Mrs. Dick arrived safely. I never thought she would go. She demanded I take the children over here. And I did. I figured after she had a rest, she'd decide to stay at least until Sunday."

George's solemn face broke into a smile. "Well, John, you seem to be a fine nursemaid. I never knew you had such talent." John looked embarrassed. Mary knew that George really meant it as a compliment. But she could see that John was remembering the old joking George.

John threw another bag of salt on the pile he was stacking and replied quietly, "I do my best, George. That's all anyone can do."

"And you're doing a great job, John," Mary burst out, before George could say anything else. "But Anna and I would love to help. May we take them back home with us?"

"I'll manage," John said gloomily. "I want my children with me. They've been gone too long already. Little George is starting to make strange with people and he needs to see his father every day."

"A bow-wow," Johnnie screamed gleefully. Standing on his back legs, Boots was sticking his long nose over the top of the play area, and the little boy was feeling the end of the dog's rubbery nose. Then his chubby baby hand reached the soft fur, and laughing, he stroked Boots.

Mary looked at John. "I'll stay and help — that is, if you'll let me."

John gave Mary a smiling nod, then saw George frown, and said, "I guess that wouldn't do, Mary. Folks would talk. Mrs. Dick was twice my age. That made it different."

Anna smiled, "Well, then, they'll have two of us to talk about. I'm staying, too, John. And Mother approves. She wants these babies to receive the best of care."

"Well, George? The idle tongues should be satisfied, shouldn't they?" John sounded a little bitter.

"Yes, yes. That's fine. I never said it wasn't, did I? After all, I walked out of cutting oats to bring Anna and Mary here today, John. I must hurry back." He started for the door. "Are you girls coming to unload your things?"

* * * *

Mary walked along the shore of the Trent River and listened as a light wind whispered through the cedars. It was the beginning of the last week of August, but the air felt like fall. A few trees across the river had already turned yellow.

The boys were both in bed sleeping, and Anna had gone to bed early. She and Mary slept in the bedroom, with little Johnnie on a cot and the baby in a cradle beside Mary. They had been taking care of the babies for two weeks now. John had moved out to the shed, as he said it would be more fitting. Mary wondered if the rum was still there. Was he guarding it or was he just avoiding the night feedings for the baby?

Mary sat down on a huge granite stone along the grassy shore, propped her feet up on it, and hugged her knees. It was then that she saw John coming over from the trading post. Early in the week, he had gone to King's Town for supplies and had just returned today. He had been extremely busy stacking all his extra supplies, preparing for winter. People were predicting another severe winter, but there had been more rain this summer than last, and the harvest was a good one.

John slumped down on the grass beside the stone where Mary sat and said, "It's so good to have you here, Mary."

"I've loved every minute of it," she said. "They're good babies, John. Catharine would be proud of them."

"Yes, I know that," John said.

A cloud seemed to pass across the moon and the evening sky became darker. Mary shivered a little. John took off his woollen waistcoat and put it around Mary's shoulders. His hands lingered on her arms until she spoke. "I'm not cold," she said. "You'd better keep your waistcoat."

"You were shivering, Mary, and I'm fine."

They sat for a while in silence. Then John said, "Catharine kept telling me she might not make it this time, Mary. I should have listened."

"Did she ask to go home?"

"No. She refused. I tried to get her to go sooner."

"John, I don't think it would have made any difference. I don't think even a doctor could have stopped the bleeding."

"She seemed so happy. I thought her talk about dying was natural. We all know that women do die in childbirth and little can be done about it. It's the risk they take when they want to bring life into this world. Catharine never regretted having Johnnie and was so happy to be expecting another baby."

"I know that, John. She told me."

They were silent again for a few minutes.

Then Mary stood up and handed John his waistcoat. Rising, he took it from her outstretched hand. Then he stared down at her in the darkness.

"Thank you," Mary said as she stared up into his eyes. She wondered what he was thinking.

Then without warning, he leaned towards her and kissed her gently on the lips. Mary's feelings for John came rushing back, but she held back. She did not trust him. After all, he had appeared to be in love with her two years before, then married her sister.

"I'm sorry, Mary," he said. "I thought you cared about me. In fact, I always thought you cared . . . a little. . . . I loved Catharine, but I loved you, too . . . and always have. I loved you both."

"Then why didn't you ever tell me?"

"I loved her the most . . . then. We both know that she was never strong like you, Mary. She tried so hard, but she was not meant to be a pioneer's wife. But you, Mary, would be the best of partners. Marry me, Mary. I swear, I'll be a good husband. And I do love you, Mary."

"Are you sure you don't just want a good house-keeper and a good strong back to hoe your garden and care for your children?"

"No, Mary, I love you."

"You said you'd do anything to get proper care for your children," Mary burst out. "Well, don't worry, John. Anna and I will stay and care for Catharine's babies, but I'll not marry you. You'd always compare me to Catharine. She was so loving and giving and sweet. I'm not! I'm different."

"You are a loving and giving person, too, Mary. You just have a different way of showing it."

Mary turned from him and started walking back towards the stockade. John took two long strides, and placing one hand on her shoulder, he swung her around. John's shining eyes swept across her face and met Mary's cold stare. She was certain this was all a game to get a mother for his children.

A painful expression came into John's eyes. He dropped his arms and walked slowly back to the shore and slumped down on the big stone.

Mary strode up to the house without turning around, but she could still feel the sweet taste of his lips on hers.

Twenty-Six

"It's a beautiful Sunday," John said. "Let's pack up the children and go for a walk up the river. Would you like to do that, Mary?"

"I'd love to go, John. And Anna would, too, I bet."

"Then it's settled. Let's get things ready."

Just as they were hurrying inside the stockade, they heard Anna scream. "You take the kids," John said. "I'll see what's wrong." He flipped Johnnie over his head and onto the grass in front of Mary.

A few minutes later, as Mary was putting the baby down into his cradle, John came into the front room, with his arms around Anna as she limped along almost on one foot.

"Here, let me help you," Mary said as she put her arm around her sister. "What happened?"

"Oh, I just twisted my foot. I guess I've sprained it. I can't put much weight on it."

"I think you had better take it easy, Anna," Mary sighed. "And just when we were planning a picnic with the boys."

"Well, go ahead," Anna said. "I'll be fine. But I'm afraid you'll have to take both of them. I don't think I'd be much good at walking them around."

"Well, if you don't mind, Anna," John said.

"Of course, I mind. I'd love to go, but I can't and that's no reason to keep the rest of you from having a great afternoon."

"But how could we manage?" Mary wasn't thinking a picnic would be quite so much fun with two babies and without Anna to help.

"You can carry the baby in my papoose sack, and I have a carrier for Johnnie that I made out of an old bag," John said.

Mary was surprised that her sister was taking it so well. "I'll make sandwiches and leave some for you, too, Anna."

By the time Mary finished the sandwiches, John had the baby changed and in his pack, ready to go. She couldn't help liking this side of John. Mary smiled and turned around so he could fasten the baby securely on her back.

As Mary and John were going out the door with the boys, Anna limped over to them. "Have a good afternoon. I'm going to have a great time doing nothing."

Once outside the stockade wall, John turned to head north, but he waited for Mary. Mary carried the basket of food, and John carried his musket and powder horn in his left hand instead of over his shoulder. They did not want to be surprised by a bear.

They had gone only about half a mile when they reached the hills, all dotted with orange and yellow among the dark green pines. "It reminds me of Albany," John said. "These hills are not like our mountains, but it reminds me of them."

"Yes, this is a beautiful land, too, John. And there's miles and miles of it. Father and George have their own farms, and I'm applying for one of my own, too."

"So where will your land be?"

"Next to George's and Father's. That way we can share the work. I'll cook and sew and they'll bring in my crops."

John laughed. "I believe you, Mary. You'll be the only woman farmer in these parts."

"A woman can run a business just as well as a man."

"Well, not all women, but I believe that you could, Mary. It all takes time, though. Most women want to marry and have a family."

She walked along beside John, looking down and thinking. They stayed close to the river for a mile, neither one breaking the silence. Then they came out into a small clearing.

"This must be the place," John said, smiling at Mary. She put the baby down beside John. He lay sleeping, still snug in the sack, and Mary started unpacking the basket. She spread the food out on a bright red and white checked linen cloth.

When he had finished his last sandwich, John stretched out his legs and lay on his side, propping his head up with his hand. "That was a great lunch. And thank you for staying — in spite of my behaviour the other evening. I'm sorry."

John studied Mary intently as if pleading with her to believe him. She saw the serious expression in his eyes and wondered how she could have doubted his words of love.

"I'm sorry, too, John. You've always been honest with me — ever since we were young. I shouldn't have reacted that way. I'm sorry for what I said. . . . I do love you, John."

"Waaaa!" The baby beside Mary let out a loud howl.

John and Mary turned quickly to see Johnnie poking the last sandwich into his brother's closed lips. John grabbed him. "What are you trying to do?"

"Baybee eat," Johnnie said.

"John! That's his first full sentence. Did you hear that?" Mary pulled a pouch of milk out of the basket and sprinkled a few drops on her arm. It felt cold. "I think I'd better wait and warm this when we get home," she said. John smiled at her words. "Yes, I think we'd better be getting *home* now," he said. His voice was different. It had a light-hearted, happy lilt to it that Mary had not heard since that summer two years ago on the trip to Albany.

The way back seemed even longer than the way there. Both children were awake and cranky. The baby was hungry and could not be consoled with her singing. Johnnie pulled and twisted John's shoulder until he let him down to walk. He was happy then, but the ground was uneven and walking was not easy even for John and Mary. Johnnie soon stumbled and fell, and John had to lift him onto his back again. From time to time, when Mary looked up, she saw John looking at her with that same happy look in his eyes. She smiled and looked down. Would they ever reach the cabin? When the babies and Anna were asleep, John would surely ask her again to marry him. If he did, she would accept. She no longer doubted his love for her.

Hand in hand, they stepped through the gate in the stockade wall. John pulled the gate shut behind them and the lock clipped shut.

Then before starting up the path to the house, he turned and put both arms around Mary and the baby on her back. He bent his head to hers. She felt a great warmth envelop her as she met his lips with her own.

In a minute, he drew back, laughing. "We'd better get these two to bed. We need to talk."

Mary nodded. It was dusk now, and she knew that Johnnie was asleep for the night. The baby, though, still needed to be fed. Hand in hand but still looking at each other, they started up the path to the cabin.

In the growing dusk, they did not see the solemn-faced figure that stood on the front stoop, watching. When Mary turned from John to look where she was going, she gasped. Father was staring down at her.

"Pack up at once, Mary. I'm taking you and Anna home."

Twenty-Seven

"Now, Mary, I want you to think about a few things." John Meyers held the horses' reins loosely in his hands. Anna had just run into the Meyers' kitchen, and Mary sat stiffly beside her father on the wagon seat. "Catharine had a hard married life. John was gone a lot, and she kept that trading post open all by herself. With the gardening and house to keep, she worked long days." Father looked at Mary, thinking she would reply, but her lips were firmly pressed together in a defiant pout. "John Bleecker is a strong, robust fellow. He didn't really understand Catharine's delicate nature."

"Catharine was happy," Mary said. "I never heard *her* complain, and her life was no different than that of many settlers. Besides, it wasn't John who took her away from civilization and brought her to this lonely area!"

Father sighed. "Mary, it was the circumstances. You know how it all started and how impossible it was for us to stay at the farm near Albany."

"Well, I don't think you are being fair to John!"

"I'm not really blaming him. He has enough to

face right now without blame from me, but I don't want to see him put another of my daughters through the hardships that Catharine endured."

"Well, I was just caring for the children, I wasn't marrying him, at least not — "

"It isn't proper for you two girls to stay there too long. Besides, your mother can use the help. But Anna will be enough for now. I'm heading for King's Town by bateau in the morning. I thought you'd like to go with me. You could visit Lucy."

"Yes, I suppose . . . though it will be different now that she's married and living in her own home. You know, Father, I want my own farm right beside yours and George's."

"Yes, I'll make sure you get your allotment of fifty acres. And since you will turn twenty-one this month, you may apply now."

"Fifty acres? George has more than fifty acres!"

"I'll see what I can do, Mary."

"I want my land to go down to the bay."

"Well, I don't know whether I can manage that. Both my lots and George's have bay access. New families will need access to the water, too. But I'll do my best for you, Mary."

* * * *

At dusk the following day, Mary stepped out of her father's bateau and set foot on the shore at Ernesttown. She hurried ahead of her father, past a maple tree on her left and into full view of Lucy Bleecker Finkle's new home. She could hardly believe her eyes. It was a two-storey clapboard house with a gabled roof — similar to many Mary had seen in Albany. About sixty feet to the left was a large frame building. She supposed that it served as a shelter for animals, though she noticed a half-built canoe and wood shavings in the yard outside. It also had a fireplace.

"Lucy married a carpenter," Father smiled, "and he's built her a fine house — impressive for these parts with two storeys and all those windows."

Still admiring the house, Mary climbed the front verandah and lightly tapped on the door. Light from a candle flickered through the large front window.

In less than a minute, the door swung open and Lucy stood there with shining eyes. She certainly appeared to be happy. Could it have been just last summer that she had taken the yellow maple leaf from Tobias's hair and folded it into her hands?

Lucy threw both arms around Mary. "Oh, Mary, you're the last person I expected to see, but am I ever glad to see you." Then she looked up to see Father standing behind Mary. "Come in, come in," she said. "I hope you've come for a long visit."

"I plan to leave Mary a few days, Lucy. I hear you and Henry have started to take in guests."

"Yes, we have. But you folks are not paying guests. You are my best friends. Now, come in!"

The room was bright and cheerful, with a low fire in the fireplace and the smell of venison stew in the air. Mary took off her cloak and handed it to Lucy, then sat in the beautiful, hand-carved oak chair by the fireplace. Her father sat on a horse-hair couch that was much like their own.

"This inn will help bring in some extra money, but isn't your husband planning to farm? I understand that he has a good farm lot going back from the water."

"No, he's a carpenter, not a farmer. We'll not be burning good trees to clear the land as the farmers do after they build their barns and live-in shanties. We plan to use every bit of our wood for building." Lucy was busy setting a place for each of them at the square table that Mary knew had come all the way from the Albany area. Lucy's mother must have given it to her. It looked strangely familiar.

"But farmers make their own buildings and furniture. They'll have no need of a carpenter's services," Father said.

"Henry's not going to build houses. He's building canoes now and someday ships."

A smile lit up Father's face. "That's a splendid idea, Lucy. Settlers need canoes and small boats for travelling along the bay, and more and more folks are coming all the time. His business will prosper."

They were seated around the table now, eating the stew, a mixture of tangy venison with carrots and potatoes. Lucy's freshly baked buns, layered thick with salty butter, were disappearing fast.

"It's not going to be just Henry building these boats," Lucy said. "He already has two men working here and he's gone to Quebec to meet Loyalists just coming into Canada who might come back with him to learn the trade. Lots of single fellows will work for their board and the chance to learn the carpentry business. It's a valuable skill in this new country whether a person builds for himself or not."

Father looked surprised. "That's a big venture," he said. Mary knew he was thinking about the financing, but of course he wouldn't say that.

Lucy sensed Father's skepticism and said, "We are opening Finkle's Inn and Tavern next month. Our profit from the one business will help the other get started."

Father laughed again. "You always were a lively girl, Lucy. I can just see you running the inn and making it a real success."

Lucy smiled, and Mary knew that she really appreciated Father's enthusiasm. She wished Father would be a little more eager to set up his own oldest daughter in the farming business.

After supper, Father went on to King's Town, and Lucy and Mary started to catch up on news. Mary was delighted that Henry was away on business. She would have felt like a fifth wheel otherwise. She couldn't help feeling a little envious of Lucy, who was obviously happy.

"I was so surprised when I heard that you had married," Mary said. Lucy smiled as she dumped the dirty plates into a dishpan and came over to sit beside Mary on the couch by the low fire.

"Well, he's been calling on me since away back when you came through King's Town and we went to that party two years ago on your way to Albany."

"I know, but I didn't think it was serious. I was so surprised when George told me. I always thought . . . "

Lucy looked into her lap. "It wouldn't have worked out with George. We are too much alike."

"George has changed."

"I know. He is more serious now . . . more like Tobias." Lucy looked straight up at Mary and said, "Do you think he's trying to take Tobias's place in the family by being like him?"

"No, I think it's just all that's happened. It's had a sobering effect on him. Even though he was the oldest, he always had that fiery temper and was headstrong. And he's still stubborn as a mule."

Lucy laughed. "Oh, one of these days, he'll find a nice girl and she'll change all that."

"He likes Alida Van Alstine, but I can't see him marrying anyone right away. I must say, though, that I'm sorry to lose you for a sister, Lucy."

"But we're still friends, and I'm happy with Henry. Anyway, I never would have made a good farmer's wife. They're often isolated for long stretches of time, but here I am surrounded by people. As we build up the inn and tavern and our boat business, there'll be all kinds of interesting people to meet."

"You'll make the perfect hostess. I'm glad you're settled and happy, Lucy."

"Now tell me, are there any young farmers, Mary, that have caught your eye?" Mary flushed a little but did not reply. Lucy continued. "Well, I have a couple of fine carpenters that are already building boats. They went into King's Town earlier today, but they'll be back later. They have bunk beds out in the shed where they work and come in here for meals. It's all part of the deal with them."

"Lucy, I'm really not — "

"Nonsense! Of course you're interested in meeting someone. Do you know what I plan to do? As soon as Henry gets back, we'll give a party. I'll invite all kinds of people, and you can have your pick of the fellows. There are not many unmarried young women around these parts. The men will be fighting over you, Mary, even though you still have those freckles."

Mary stifled a reply. Lucy might be a married woman now, but her personality hadn't changed. She had always prided herself on speaking her mind and was as blunt as ever. Mary gathered her thoughts and came back to the main point. "What makes you think I'm interested?"

"What's changed? Have you found someone? You are a sly one. Not saying a word about him."

Mary shook her head. "Well, I do like someone, but Father doesn't approve. I guess we should wait awhile anyway."

"Wait awhile? What for? You're twenty-one years old, Mary. You're almost an old maid. Why on earth would you want to wait?"

"Not all girls marry. I may just want to be a farmer."

"Ha! That's funny. How could you clear the land and work the fields?"

"I don't have to. I'll cook, bake, clean, and scrub for my brothers so they'll have to work my land for me."

"Don't fool yourself, Mary. In a few years, they'll have wives who'll do all that for nothing and then where will you be?"

Mary was wondering if she should tell Lucy about John when there was a loud knock at the door.

Lucy flung the door wide open and stammered in amazement as she stared out. Mary jumped up and came over beside her. She, too, could hardly believe her eyes.

John was standing there with little George in a pouch tied to his chest and Johnnie in the knapsack on his back.

"Why, John, you're the last person I expected to see," Lucy exclaimed. "And you have the boys with you! Both of them!"

John stumbled into the room. Both babies were crying loudly now. Lucy exclaimed, "I'll have to send Hezekiah for Mother to help you with the babies."

"I'm sorry, Lucy, but Johnnie has the croup and George thinks he's starving, though I went ashore and fed him just three hours ago. It's been a long trip by canoe."

John sat on the edge of the couch and looked up at Mary with a smile of relief on his face. Mary wondered if John had called in at home looking for her. Did Mother tell John where she was?

"I've handled croup plenty of times, John," Mary said. "We'll manage just fine." She took the baby from John's arms and laid him on the couch. Then she took Johnnie from John's back.

"I've missed you, Mary," John said.

"You know I wanted to stay, John. I can't understand Father. Whatever are we going to do?"

Twenty-Eight

"I intend to speak to your father, Mary, when he comes back for you. I won't sneak around behind his back." John Bleecker sat in the big armchair in front of Lucy's fireplace and was looking at Mary on the couch. He had taken the children to his mother's the day before. Lucy had conveniently decided to go shopping till suppertime at Ernesttown's general store.

"But it's too soon, John. For my family's sake, I think we must wait until spring and then tell Father."

"If that's your wish, Mary, then I'll do that. Mother has found a housekeeper for me. Betty was a slave for us in Albany and fell into hard hands when our property was confiscated. My stepfather found her this summer and told Mother. She insisted he buy her back and bring her up here and free her, but Betty refuses to take her freedom and wants to work for the family."

"Isn't she too old to care for young children?"

"She's very able still and is doing just fine caring for them at Mother's. I plan to keep her on after we are married."

"I'd like that, John, and I'm so glad that the children will have better care."

"I agree that we shouldn't marry before next spring, but I would like to ask for your hand in marriage now. That way, I can call on you this winter. I don't think I could manage without seeing you often." John turned, and seeing the happy look in Mary's eyes, he sat down on the couch and put his arm around her.

"I'll want to see you too, John Bleecker," Mary said. "The time will pass quickly. Besides, by then I'll have a surprise for you. It's a business venture — not as surprising as Lucy and Henry's, but a business venture, just the same." Mary jumped up and started for the front door. Over her shoulder, she said, "That's Father. I'd know his knock anywhere. You'd better leave by the back door."

John stood and stared at the door as Mary opened it.

"Have I got great news for you!" Father said as he stepped into the large room. He took off his leather coat and handed it to Mary. When he saw his son-in-law standing in front of the fireplace, the pleasant smile left his face.

John walked over to him and extended his hand. "It's good to see you, Captain Meyers."

Mary was uneasy as she watched the lines tighten around her father's mouth. But he extended his hand and said, "How's the family, John?"

"Fine now, though Johnnie is recovering from a bad bout of croup. I have someone reliable — from Albany — caring for the children now. Do you remember Betty?"

"I certainly do. She almost raised you and Lucy, didn't she?"

John smiled. "Yes. We were sorry we couldn't take her when we fled. But Betty was seized along with all our possessions."

"I know," Father said with sadness, "but we've better times ahead. We must look to the future now." He went over and sat in the big chair in front of the fireplace.

Mary was starting to relax a little, but she kept looking at the door. If only Lucy would walk in before Father realized that she and John had been alone together.

"Now I'm glad to hear you say that, sir, for that's just what I want to talk about — the future. John stood beside the fireplace, still with his hands held tightly together behind his back. He turned from Mary and looked Father straight in the eye. "I love Mary, and we would like to be married in the spring."

Silence.

Then John drew in a deep breath and said, "With your permission, sir, I would like to start calling on Mary."

Father stared ahead with his long legs stretched out in front of him. It seemed hours before he looked up at John and said, "Well, you can't marry her, John, because Reverend Langhorn won't marry you. I have no say in the matter."

"Why not?" Mary shot back before John had a chance to answer. "Why on earth not?"

"Because," Father said calmly, "the Church of England will not allow a brother and sister to marry."

"That's bloody nonsense!" John was now glaring at Father. "We're no more brother and sister then Catharine and I were."

"In the eyes of the church, you are brother and sister. A sister-in-law and a sister are looked upon as the same."

"What a ridiculous law!" John was starting to turn red. He glared at Father. "I've never claimed to be very religious, but I do know this much. In Bible days, a man was sometimes told to marry his sister-in-law to raise up children for their land."

"You're right about one thing, John, you don't seem to know the Scripture that well. You're referring to the Old Testament days, when one man could have many wives all at the same time. Is that what you're suggesting?"

John's face turned a deep red, but he cleared his throat and spoke softly, "No. Of course, not, but I don't see why . . . "

Father crossed his legs and smiled in a most relaxed fashion. "Well, John, perhaps some poor, homeless girl may want to marry you. Though I do hope you show her how much work she'll be getting herself into and how lonely she'll be while you're taking all those business trips to King's Town, Montreal, and Albany."

"I have help now. Betty is going to stay with us. And now that business is good at the trading post, I won't have to take as many trips."

"So you say. I wonder how long this servant will last. How old is Betty now?"

John marched over to Father. He was glaring so hard that Mary was almost afraid he might hit him, but instead John walked back to Mary and said, "I'm leaving now. Mary, I'd like to say good-bye to you — alone."

Without looking at Father, Mary got up and walked to the door with John.

"And another thing, John," Father called as they left. "I think it best you don't call on us at all for the next few months. Leonard can take Mother over to see the babies, but I think it's best you and Mary stay apart for a while. I know Mary won't defy her church. So it's best this way."

Tears started to fill Mary's eyes as she and John started down the path. Then she felt John's big, strong hand close over hers. "We'll be married, Mary. That's an unfair church law. Maybe your father just invented it. We could become Methodists or Presbyterians. They don't have such a law."

"But the Church of England is the only church here."

"Oh, the others don't have buildings yet, but they have travelling ministers and meet mostly in homes. James Parrott, a farmer halfway between Ernesttown and King's Town, has converted his barn into a good-sized Methodist meeting place for the area."

"Well, we're not going to be married in a barn. And I never heard of Presbyterians."

"They were the Dutch Reformed Church back in Albany."

"Really. Let's have them."

"I'm not sure they have a minister here yet. I think just laymen. But we could be married by a Justice of the Peace. And I know just the person —

Michael Grass. He's the founder of King's Town and the Justice of the Peace there."

"Didn't he lead that survey team you worked with?"

"Yes, that's when I first met him. He was enthusiastic about this area and worked with Peter Van Alstine to bring in small groups of refugees. Most Loyalists stayed in Nova Scotia."

John looked at Mary intently. "We don't have to wait, Mary. I can trust Michael to keep my confidence. We can come down to King's Town and be married the first time your father goes off to Montreal again. In September, you'll be of legal age. So you may do what you want."

Mary swallowed. She would marry John Bleecker. She had always loved him and would marry him no matter who crossed them — even her father. They had reached the shore now, and John turned and put his arms around Mary. She looked up at John and kissed him gently on the lips.

John got into the canoe, grabbed the paddles, and began to pull away from shore.

"John!" Mary shouted. He waved, but she motioned him back.

"How will you know when Father is taking a trip to Montreal?"

"That'll be up to you, Mary. Send George over to tell me."

"He may not go. He may even agree with Father."

"Well, what about Leonard?"

"I don't want to get Leonard into trouble."

"Well, there's always your mother."

"She would never defy Father."

"I'm not sure about that. Your mother is a strong lady."

"I'll find a way."

"That's my Mary," John smiled, and paddled fast with his canoe pointed towards King's Town.

* * * *

"Well, Mary, you'll be happy to know that I have a deed for two hundred acres in your name," Father said when she returned. "The land allotments have been increased."

"Where is this land?"

"A hundred acres is just north of George's and west of mine. "The other lot is a wooded one — somewhere north. No need to bother with it just now. I had a hard time getting one property next to George and me, I can tell you. We can work our farms together." Father couldn't help wondering if the thought of her own land would help her forget John. He thought not. But he waited quietly, looking into the low fire. He knew that Mary would soon have her say.

Finally Mary could stand the silence no longer. "That church ruling is unfair!" she burst out. "So why are you suggesting that we follow it?"

"Do you really want to defy the laws of your church, Mary?"

"What church? We only see the minister for weddings and funerals, and not always for funerals. The Church of England is far away from us —

in King's Town. I hear that the Methodist Church is sending their ministers out to the people. And the Dutch Reformed Church is starting a Presbyterian branch here."

"When more settlers come and are all settled in homes, I will see that we have a church if I have to build it with my own hands," he replied. "It will not be far from my mill, and it will last for generations to come."

Mary was silent for a moment. When had unfair laws ever stopped Father from doing what he felt was right?

"But the law is not just. I am no more related to John than Catharine was. Her marriage did not make me any blood relation of John! And he's right. In the Bible, Ruth married a relative of her husband after he died."

The colour was now leaving Father's face. Mary felt a slow fear starting to rise as he spoke out in a low, growling voice. "Mary, we're leaving now. Write a note to thank Lucy for the hospitality. Also ask her to tell her brother that I don't want to see him on my property, not now and not ever! He contributed to one daughter's death and I'll not let him have a chance with another if I have to strike him down with my bare hands!"

Mary shivered. Surely he didn't believe that! He had never said anything like that before. She did not dare say a word; his face was a greyish white, and deep lines were chiselled around his mouth. She knew that he wanted to say more, but he seemed to be fighting for control.

Finally Mary bent her head into her hands, sobbing.

"There is no time for this, Mary. I'll expect you at the shore in fifteen minutes with your bag and ready to go."

As Father strode out the front door, Mary drew her handkerchief out of her inner pocket under her petticoat and blew her nose.

Then she went over to the little desk by the fireplace and began to write.

Twenty-Nine

A fresh gust of wind blew a mixture of many scarlet and yellow leaves down around Mary as she marched briskly along the pathway to the barn, with an egg basket in one hand and an empty milk bucket in the other. It was the second week of October, and although Father had talked about a trip to Montreal, he had not made definite plans. He might go tomorrow or next month, she couldn't be sure. But one thing was certain. He would go before too long. He would not wait until after winter set in. Mary hoped that Father had not said anything to anyone about John and her. She certainly had not.

George was busy in the barn with the evening milking. A six-month-old calf in the little corner pen stuck its grey, rubbery nose out towards Mary as she pushed by.

Mary jumped up onto the landing between the cows and horses, where the hens had their nests. It would be nice to have a separate henhouse as they had had back on the farm near Albany, but Father had decided the chickens would do better during the cold winter in the same barn with the other animals. Perhaps in the spring they would have the time to build a well-insulated separate house for the chickens.

Mary stuck her hand in and out of the nests. In the last one, she pushed the hen aside before taking the egg. The hen ruffled her feathers and made a great, loud clucking sound as she moved out in indignation.

"Don't rile those hens, Mary," George called out. "We need the eggs."

"Oh, they're used to me. That was Henrietta. She often makes a fuss when I take her egg."

After she had gathered all the eggs, Mary put down her round straw basket, sat on the edge of the stone landing, and waited for George to finish milking.

In a few minutes, he let the two cows outside again and came over to pour fresh milk into Mary's clean bucket. He looked at her quizzically and asked, "Well, Mary, what's the matter?"

"What makes you think something is the matter?"

"You haven't been yourself since you came back from King's Town, and I can't figure it out. Father got that farm for you. I thought you'd be overjoyed."

"Oh, I'm happy about my farm. But I was given it for being a Loyalist."

"You mean for being the daughter of a Loyalist. If it hadn't been for Father's involvement, you wouldn't have been given the land at all. Father used his influence to get you the hundred acres next to us. You might have ended up with the whole two hundred somewhere in the woods."

"I suppose," Mary mumbled.

"And you know we'll clear a few fields for you next summer. In fact, we might even find time to clear one this fall. The sooner we get the woods line back farther, the better it will be for all of us."

Mary knew he was thinking about Tobias and the bear. "I saw Lucy. She seems happy."

"I'm pleased to hear that, Mary." There was no resentment in his voice.

"What makes you say that I'm not myself these days, George? No one else around here has noticed."

"Oh, you're quieter, I guess. And you haven't been trying to boss me around as much."

"George!" Mary gave him a punch in the shoulder.

"Ow! Now you've crippled me and I won't be able to pull stumps tomorrow."

Mary laughed. George's joking had returned and was a welcome relief. Maybe he wouldn't mind helping her. He had always been one to take a dare.

"If I tell you something, will you promise not to tell?"

"Well, now, I don't know . . . this sounds like something awful."

"Well, it's not awful. But will you promise not to tell Father? And I think you'd better not tell Mother." Mary sighed and looked George solemnly in the eye. "George, I need to tell someone because I really need help, but if you won't promise, I can't tell you."

George's brow puckered into a quizzical frown. "I really don't like the sound of this, Mary, but I'll promise, since it sounds as if you need me."

"Thank you, George. I knew I could count on you." Mary threw both arms around her brother.

"Aren't you getting ahead of yourself, Mary? I haven't done anything yet."

Mary gave him a sly smile. "But, George, you've always been one for adventure and excitement."

"Adventure and excitement? Hmmm. So are we going on another raid?"

"Don't be crazy, George. It's not that. I just want you to help me elope."

George's jaw dropped. "I didn't hear what I thought I heard. You can't be serious, Mary."

"I am."

"Who is he? Did you meet someone in King's Town, Mary? That's a little too fast . . . John!" he gasped. He could see the whole picture.

"Father's forbidden me to see him," Mary said. "He says we have to give up this idea of marrying. And, George, do you know what he said about John? He accused him of being the cause of Catharine's death! He practically said that he worked her to death."

George handed her his large red-checked handkerchief. In a few minutes, Mary had stopped crying and was wiping her face. "I'm of age now," she said calmly, "and Father can't stop me from marrying John. I am going to marry him. And if you don't want to help, I'll marry him anyway. But you can't tell Father. You promised!"

George put his arm around his sister's shoulders. "I didn't say that I wouldn't help you, Mary. I know that you've always loved John. In fact, I thought John would marry you instead of

Catharine. It's too bad he didn't. Catharine was always sickly. You'll make John a good, strong wife, the kind he needs. And you're a willing worker."

"Well, don't make me sound like a horse, George. Next, you'll want to check out my teeth."

"You two will have some dandy rows, but you'll keep John in line, I warrant. You'll not let him go off and leave you whenever he wants. Actually, it'll be fun to watch."

"Oh, George!" Mary loosened her hold on him.

"But how am I supposed to help?"

"When Father goes to Montreal, John and I are going to King's Town to be married. But I need someone to tell John when that is, so he can come for me."

"I could do that for you, Mary, but what will happen to the children?"

"Betty's caring for them."

"How will you get away without Mother knowing? . . . I think it might be better if I took you over to John's for a visit after Father's gone. Mother won't suspect anything for a few days, since John has a servant now."

"And by that time, we'll be married. But George, there's something else you should know."

"What else can there be?"

"Our church won't marry us."

"Why not?"

"It's a ruling of the Church of England."

"Oh, yes. They look upon you as brother and sister. Well, you could go to the Methodist minister."

"Father thinks it's terrible to break a church ruling."

"It's an unfair law. And I'm surprised by Father's attitude. He's always been the one to stand up for what he thinks is right, regardless of what everyone else says. You know, Mary, when Father returns from Montreal, I'll have a talk with him. I'm not sure, but I think I can help. We don't always agree, but at least he'll listen. I've always appreciated that about Father."

"Well, he wasn't in any listening mood when John and I discussed our marriage."

"Well, a lot has happened in the last year, Mary. Father needs more time. Don't you think it might be better to wait awhile?"

"We were willing to wait, George! But Father wouldn't even let us see each other. If he won't let me see John here at home, I'll see him somehow."

* * * *

At dawn, two days later, Father left for Montreal to apply for more land for his mill site, since he had been refused the land just north of John's the winter before. As things had turned out between Father and John, that was just as well, Mary decided. Father had finally decided to try to buy land along the Moira River that ran into the bay. She hoped he would be successful.

An hour later, when the family were all seated for breakfast, Mary said casually, "Mother, I've been wanting to see Johnnie and Baby George for a long time. And, George, wouldn't you like to see your namesake, too? Maybe you could take me over."

"Oh, Mary, what a delightful idea," Mother said. "I think I'll go along, too, and maybe Anna and Jacob would like to go. Let's hurry and do up these dishes." Mary gave George a despairing look across the table and then lowered her eyes. It seemed that nothing ever went right for her anymore.

"I think it's a great idea," George said eagerly. "Why don't we all go? Maybe we should take a picnic basket for lunch, though. Betty must be over fifty-five now, and it'll not be easy for her adjusting back to child rearing."

Mother frowned. "You're right, George. And I don't think we should trouble her until she's been there longer. She doesn't need the grandmother there scaring her off. I might just intimidate her. Maybe I should stay away a while longer."

"Do you think it would hurt if George and I went alone?" Mary tried to keep her voice from betraying her emotion.

Mother looked at Mary's anxious face and smiled a little as she carried the wooden porridge bowls to the dishpan. Then she said, "Go ahead, dear. Anna and I will finish up these dishes."

"Good!" George said. "I'll harness up, Mary, and I won't be long." He walked out slowly, however, to show everybody that he really wasn't in any rush.

Mary hurried into her bedroom and started to stuff her clothes into a bag. She didn't want to take enough to cause suspicion, but she did want to take a few things in case she was never allowed to come back here for the rest of her clothes. She was just packing her best blue gown and striped petticoat into the bag when the bedroom door opened.

Mother came over and stared at Mary's bulging bag. "I see you're planning to stay a few days," she said. "I think that's a good idea, Mary." She sat down on the edge of the bed.

Mary felt guilty about deceiving her mother like this — especially when she was being so nice. "You know, Mary," Mother continued, "I am glad to see how you care for those children. I know Catharine would be happy, too. She was always so close to you." Mother took out a handkerchief and blew her nose. "My poor, dear Catharine and Tobias. But we can't dwell on our loss. We have to concentrate on those who are left and do the best we can for them. And that's what you are doing, Mary."

Mary was starting to feel worse by the second. Had she forgotten Catharine? After all, she was planning to marry Catharine's husband, and even the church was frowning on her. Suddenly, she broke into loud sobs.

"Mary, Mary, whatever is the matter?"

"Oh, Mother, I wasn't going to tell you, but I — "

"You don't need to apologize to me for loving John Bleecker," Mother said quietly.

Mary gasped. "Did Father tell you?"

"Father didn't need to tell me anything, Mary. I have eyes in my head, and I know my daughters. I see no reason why you can't see John Bleecker. It was your father who went for you."

Mary gasped again. "Mother!"

"Well, you'd better hurry, Mary. I hope you

have a pleasant few days with John and the babies.
Now that Betty's there, surely your father won't
get worked up if he comes home before you do."

"When are you expecting him?"

"I never know. He may run into some old army
buddies and stay for two weeks. If you add travelling time to that, you have three weeks. Or his
business may not keep him that long. He may
make it back in ten days."

Mary felt much happier now. Even though
Mother didn't suspect an elopement, she really
was not against the idea of her marrying John.
And even more important, Catharine had
approved of the idea.

Mary pulled out another bag from under her
bed. She reached down into a far corner and
tightened her hand around the little locket that
Grandma had given her three years ago. She tied
it around her neck, then pushed the black velvet
ribbon back under the scarf at her throat so
Mother could not see it. She would wear it for her
wedding — even if it was an elopement. Like
Mother, Grandma would understand.

Thirty

At sunrise the following day, a seventeen-foot birchbark canoe sped out of the mouth of the Trent River. As it emerged into the bay and turned east, the prevailing south-westerly winds brought calm waters for early October. The air was crisp, though, and hinted of colder times to come. Mary sat on the seat nearer the front and paddled on her right while John paddled and steered on the left.

Stuffed under John's seat were a large canvas and a bearskin robe. At his feet was a leather knapsack full of cornmeal, hickory nuts, and dried berries and apples, along with a little flour, salt, and sugar. The ninety-mile trip to King's Town would take about three days, and they did not want to go hungry.

After about fifteen minutes, Mary looked over at the shore on her left. They were now passing the Meyers' homestead. "Should I lie down in the canoe?" she shouted back to John.

"No. Keep paddling. They're probably too busy to notice who's out on the bay."

"That's true," Mary laughed. Her small bag of

clothes rested on the seat beside her. She was dressed in a pair of Leonard's old baggy breeches and a pair of long, thick woollen socks that she had taken from his wardrobe. He had outgrown the breeches and wouldn't mind.

Though Mary paddled with a swift, steady stroke, her mind was not on her task. She was picturing the future. She could see John by her side back at Bleecker's Castle — over meals, at the fireside, in the trading post, along the Trent River in autumn, in winter, in spring, and in summer. Then she thought of all the children she wanted. Of course, they would have a large family and would name their first girl Catharine and their first boy Tobias. She knew her sister would be happy about their plans. She looked up into the massive clouds and felt an overwhelming loneliness. Then she heard John's voice and the feeling passed with the moving clouds as suddenly as it had come. "It's a great day, Mary. With a clear sky like this we'll make wonderful time. We may be able to make it in two days if we travel most of tonight."

* * * *

They had passed the mouth of the Moira River when the clouds started to darken the horizon, and by late afternoon, when they were paddling from the Bay of Quinte into Hay Bay, the clouds had become dark and ominous. As they continued along into Hay Bay, the water became rough.

"I think we should stop, Mary," John said. "We would have to travel half the night to reach Adolphustown."

Mary swiftly lifted her paddle and started stroking the water on the opposite side as John steered the boat to shore.

Already drops of rain were making circles in the water around the canoe. The sky was becoming darker, and Mary wondered how long it would be before an avalanche of rain followed. They both bent over and paddled feverishly towards the wooded shore.

Then the rain stopped, and lightning streaked across the sky just as John steered the canoe into the reedy shoreline. A sharp crash exploded almost instantly afterwards.

Mary grabbed her bags and jumped onto the sandy shore. John handed the knapsack of food to Mary. Then he turned and pulled the canoe well up onto the beach and away from the waves.

Another streak of lightning followed, and a clap of thunder struck so loud that Mary shook a little as she watched and waited for John. "That's close," he said, "but we're safe, now that we're out of the water." Mary knew, though, that they were not completely safe since they still were under tall trees. John slung the canvas and bear robe over his right shoulder and rested his musket over his left shoulder. He motioned Mary to follow as he pushed his way through the undergrowth to a sheltered spot under a clump of young cedars.

John threw the bear robe on the ground beside the cedars while Mary moved over to his side. Then he pulled the canvas over them both. As they huddled there together, the splattering downpour reached them and beat against the canvas.

Cold air came with the rain, and Mary shivered in this make-shift shelter, though they still remained dry. When John leaned over and kissed her, she wrapped an arm around him and felt his arm go around her. Beneath the canvas on the furry bear robe, their breath warmed the air around them. Then the rain stopped as quickly as it had come, and Mary threw back the corner of the cover. "It's over," she said and crawled out from under the canvas and onto the wet ground.

John propped his musket against a cedar tree and said, "Well, it will be dark before long, and this is a sheltered spot within sight of the shore and our canoe. I think we should stay here."

"Maybe we should try to reach Adolphustown."

"I hate to think what the lake will be like. I have seen those white-capped waves roll in over eight feet high. It just isn't safe to go on, tonight." Mary shivered while John continued. "If we did make it to Adolphustown, ugly rumours might start about us travelling alone together."

"That's true. Folks do like to talk," Mary said.

John scrambled back to the trees and started to collect firewood. Before long, he had cleared a spot nearer the shore, raked the wetness away, and started a small fire.

Mary looked through the bag of food and decided to make cornmeal fritters. She placed the ingredients on a large stone nearby and put out a kettle for coffee.

Mary dropped the fritters into the small iron-spider frying pan they had packed. Then she looked at John and smiled as he stretched out before the fire. "I think we'll be able to make it to King's Town in two more days unless we have terrible weather. We might even be able to reach Ernesttown and Lucy's by tomorrow night. I'm not sure, though. It will mean a long day's travel tomorrow from sun-up, and we'll need perfect weather conditions."

As Mary did the washing up, she watched John make two beds not far from the fire, so that the fire was between them and the shadowy woods. This time, John had spread the canvas out on the damp ground and set the old bear robe down not far from it.

"You'll need that bear robe to wrap around you," he explained. "We should take turns to watch the fire. The way the wind is blowing, I doubt any bear would come upon us, but we should watch. So, Mary, you rest first."

"No, you go first. I don't seem to be sleepy."

"Are you sure?"

"Yes."

John lay down on the cold canvas and closed his eyes. Mary sat on the ground across from him, wrapped her arms around her knees, and stared straight into the flickering flames. When she glanced at John, his eyes were wide open, looking intently at her.

"You're supposed to be sleeping," she scolded. Then she noticed he was shivering a little. She grabbed the bear robe and threw it over him. "You'd better use this. And get some sleep."

"You don't want to catch cold either, Mary. There's always room for two here." He smiled and held back the edge of the robe.

"I'm fine, John." Mary sat down a few feet away and stared straight into the fire.

Then in a more serious tone, John said, "Wake me when you're tired. Remember, we must keep the fire going till morning." John closed his eyes almost instantly after that, and Mary thought he must have fallen asleep. She could hear only the steady lapping of waves along the shore. It was a peaceful sound now, as all signs of the storm were gone. The moonlight was streaking across the bay, and she could see cleared land across the hill on the other side. A light twinkled from a settler's cabin.

Mary poked at the fire; then she put another two big sticks on the glowing blaze.

"Crack!" The sound came from the woods. Was it a distant musket or a heavy animal breaking branches as it walked through the woods? Should she waken John? He had turned his back to her now and was breathing deeply. But the musket lay within his reach.

Then she shivered. The air was growing cooler, and while her face was flushed with the heat from the fire, her back was already very cold.

Thump . . . thump!

Mary dived for the bear robe.

"What is it!" John exclaimed as Mary banged into his back. "Mary, what's wrong?"

"Nothing." Mary was starting to feel a little foolish now. She pulled back and sat outside the robe on the cold, damp shore.

John turned over and went back to sleep.

Mary sat there shivering and listening for a very

long time, it seemed, and there were no more loud thumping sounds. As her fear subsided, a fresh breeze blew in from the lake, and she started to shake with the cold.

Then she turned and stared at John's still, broad shoulders just showing above the edge of the heavy bear robe. She shivered again, then softly crossed the few feet to John, and lifting the bearskin, she crawled underneath. She lay with her back against his and pulled the robe tightly around her. She still stared out across the fire to the dark woods beyond.

After a while her shivers eased up, and she began to feel warm and secure.

When Mary wakened, it was pitch dark and she was alone under the bearskin. In a panic, she sat up to see John adding a stick to the low fire. She pushed back the robe and said sleepily, "Oh, John, I'm sorry. I must have dropped off. I was cold and got under the bearskin and that's the last I can remember."

"Go back to sleep, Mary. I had a good rest. I'll watch now."

Thirty-One

"Who's there?" Lucy called out.

"It's me — John."

Lucy pushed back the bar and opened the heavy oak door. She peered out into the darkness at her brother standing there with a brown sack in his left hand and a musket over his right shoulder.

"John! You do pick the worst times to . . . ." When she saw Mary standing behind him with a small knapsack, Lucy's eyes opened as wide as an owl's and she said, "Well, come in . . . come in. Don't just stand there on the front verandah." When the three were inside and Lucy had closed the door, she said, "John, what on earth is going on?"

"We're getting married." John pushed past his sister to the couch and flopped down.

"Mary, you look terrible!" Lucy said.

Mary was cold and tired, but she couldn't help being annoyed at Lucy for her bluntness. It was hardly the way she wanted to look for her wedding. Five days had passed since they had left Bleecker's Castle, and Mary had not had one full night's sleep since then. They had run into wet and windy weather and had had to stop and wait until it passed. At night, they had built a fire and taken turns watching for wild animals. Once they thought they had smelled the heavy aroma of a bear not far from their fire, and the next morning John had seen its tracks. Lucy was probably right. She must be a sight.

"Oh, Mary, I am so sorry. I always do say the wrong thing. What I mean is that you look like you need a good bath and a rest. Come over here and get warm." Lucy led Mary to the fireplace. "Now let's see. Mary, you can sleep in the spare room upstairs, and John, there's an empty room for you down at the other end of the hall."

"Just lead me to it, Lucy," John said.

Lucy ignored him. "Now, Mary, you come with me and I'll pour you a bath in your room. John, you can bring a couple of pails of hot water and one cold to the top of the stairs and put more on to heat."

"I just want to get some sleep," John groaned as he stretched out on the couch.

"John!" Lucy exclaimed.

"Oh, all right, Lucy." John sprang up again and poked the fire to life.

* * * *

Rays of bright sunshine made Mary blink as she opened her eyes. How long had she slept? It must be late morning, she thought. She sat up on the side of the bedstead and wondered why it was so quiet. Mary pulled Lucy's white shift over her head and slipped on a white petticoat and an outer green-and-grey striped one. Then she pulled on her pale green short overgown and white mob cap with a green ribbon. She slipped into the moccasins by the bed and hurried out into the hall.

As she started down the steep stairs, she could hear Lucy saying, "Yes, I have been expecting you. And you have five children, I understand. Yes, I know my husband promised that there would be beds for all of you."

"We'll expect meals, too," said the voice of a stranger. Mary hesitated on the stairs.

"Oh, that will be impossible," Lucy said. "You see, we're having a wedding here this evening."

"A what?" the man thundered. "I understood that this was an inn and tavern and that meals were available as well as a nip of — "

"Oh, James, just think, a wedding. I'm thankful they still have enough beds for the lot of us with five children. Will you be having many guests, dear?"

"No. I don't *think* so."

"You don't think so?" the man said abruptly. "Don't you know? Sounds like a shot-gun wedding to me."

"Well, it's no shot-gun wedding, I can tell you that Mister," Mary said, bursting into the room. "It's an — " She could bite her tongue for almost giving away their plans. Turning away in embarrassment, she could feel her cheeks burning.

"What's all the fuss over?" said a pleasant male voice. Mary looked up just in time to see a tall, slim man come down the last two hall stairs and walk over to the couple seeking lodgings. She could barely remember Henry Finkle from the party three years before, but she figured this must be the man Lucy had married.

"Henry, we're wanting those rooms you promised us," the man protested.

"And you'll get them, James. I've saved two of our finest for you."

"And meals?" The man scowled so much that his bushy dark brown eyebrows almost covered his eyes.

"Harry, we're having a wedding today! It'll take all my wife's energy. But why don't you join in our celebration. One or two more at the wedding will be fine." Henry smiled at the man, who still frowned as he continued. "Now come on out to the kitchen. I'll make you breakfast myself, and we can talk over old times. I'll never forget your father-in-law at *your* wedding, even though I was just a kid then. He sure started some — "

"You're right, John." The man was speaking at half the volume of before. "Neighbours need to help each other in these times. We'll make do in our rooms. We don't want to break up your celebration any. If you just tell me where to get water . . . and maybe we could use a kettle for coffee, we'll manage fine. In fact, we'll leave our bags now and be back at dark."

Henry smiled congenially as he followed the family to the door. Mary had gone over to the fireplace and was staring into the flames. She couldn't help wondering where John had gone and what plans had been made for this evening. Was John really going to have the wedding here?

As soon as Henry had closed the door on the family, Lucy said, "Mary, it's nearly ten o'clock! Are you ready for your wedding day? I do declare, I am so excited. And who would have thought that you'd elope? Everyone expected me to elope, but instead I had the biggest wedding in these parts. It was even bigger than Catharine's."

There she went again, managing to say things that made you feel worse. Did she have to talk about weddings right now when Mary's greatest wish would have been to have a nice wedding with her whole family there?

"I'm sorry, Mary. I shouldn't be babbling on so."

"Where has John gone and what is all this talk about a wedding *here* this evening?" Mary asked. She stood up and walked back and forth in front of the fireplace. She was uneasy now that they were this close to King's Town. What if Father had stopped over on his way to Montreal and John bumped into him? Nothing, she told herself. Father would not need to know that she was here, too.

Henry came back in before Lucy had time to answer. "I'm glad you were here, Henry. That man was insistent. Now, I want you to meet my best friend from Albany days, Mary Meyers — soon to be Mary Bleecker, my sister."

Henry held out his hand to Mary. He's not nearly as handsome as Tobias or even George, Mary was thinking as she shook hands. Though he did have wavy light brown hair and friendly grey eyes with green flecks in them.

Also, he had a most welcome smile, when he said, "I believe we have met before, Mary, but you probably don't remember me."

"I do . . . but that seems like years ago."

"Lucy, where is John?" Mary asked.

The back door slammed open just then, and footsteps came across Lucy's kitchen. It must be John. But before she could run out to the kitchen, John came into the room and walked directly over to her.

"Good morning, Mary," he said with a smile, slipping an arm around her right in front of Lucy and Henry. "I have news."

"Well, what is it?" Lucy butted in.

"Michael Grass is leaving today for business in Napanee, and he will be performing a wedding ceremony there tomorrow."

"Won't he marry us?" Mary asked abruptly.

"Of course, he'll marry us," John smiled, "but we must leave now. He can wait only so long. He has promised to be at Napanee for a wedding tomorrow — that's a full day's travel. He was planning to leave when I came there, but he's waiting for us at his home in King's Town. There is no time to lose. Grab your shawl and come on."

"But John, I have a gown to put on."

"Lucy, put it in a bag for her. There may be time to put it on after we arrive there." Then John turned to Mary. "You would get the bottom of it all wet in the canoe."

"Yes, I would. I'm not thinking quite straight, I guess."

Lucy returned in a few minutes and handed the bag to John. "Mary, you do look good in my short-gown and the petticoat you're wearing now. That shade of pale green goes so well with your hair. But you sure have a pile of freckles. You've never had such a mass of them. Canoeing down here in the wind and sun must have brought them out."

Mary stared in horror at Lucy and then looked in the mirror over the fireplace. Sure enough, she had never seen herself so freckled.

John gave his sister a cold stare. "I've always loved your freckles, Mary," he said softly.

"That's true love, Mary," Lucy laughed. "Now, John, I hope you realize how disappointed I am. Do you think I could go along in the canoe with the two of you?"

"No, Lucy, you'd only hold us up."

"But, you'll be back for a wedding meal here, won't you?"

"I wish you hadn't planned anything, but I'll see, that is, yes, if all goes well. But you can't invite guests, and I hope you didn't say anything to Mother. You know Mary's father is sure to stop there."

"I'm not stupid, John."

"Well, we don't want him to find out until he has to. By then, he won't be able to have the marriage annulled."

"Don't be ridiculous, John. Mary is twenty-one now. He can't have the marriage annulled. Of course, though, it will *never* be recognized in the Church of England. You and Mary will be outcasts."

"Well, their minister seldom calls," John said.

"Anyway, Lucy, you know we went to the Dutch Reformed Church back in Albany, and that's where Mary and I'll join. I hear they're starting up a branch here and calling themselves Presbyterians."

"John and Mary, I do wish you well and please know that you are welcome to stay here for the honeymoon."

"Oh, sure, Lucy," John said. "I've made arrangements in King's Town. Now we must go. Goodbye, Henry. And thanks for the overnight accommodation!"

It was a bright sunny day and the waters were calm, so Mary and John made good time paddling. It was less than ten miles to the sheltered harbour at King's Town. Mary's mind was racing as fast as her paddle strokes as the canoe sped ahead. Would anyone recognize John and her coming into the harbour together? It was a small harbour and often not more than half a dozen canoes and a few bateaux were tied to the jetty. She and John would be noticed arriving there together, but the gossip would not last long, for they would soon be married — if they reached Michael Grass in time, that is.

"Look at that flotilla!" John's exclamation broke through Mary's thoughts. Their canoe was going into King's Town harbour now, and Mary could see there was a lot of activity.

There were a few bateaux tied to the jetty, but a number were just leaving — over twenty by her count. Mary knew that they were government bateaux, for they were twice the size of their own.

The government bateaux usually travelled together in groups of twelve so their crew members could help each other over the rapids.

Mary sighed with relief. No one would notice them now. They would be lost in the crowd. Just then she felt John steering their canoe to the jetty. "Pull her to the left, Mary," he said, and she changed the position of her paddle.

The waves were rough and choppy from all the bateaux around them, so Mary kept her eyes on the water. In a few minutes, though, they had safely reached the jetty, and John placed his paddle across the canoe to steady it as he climbed onto the jetty. Squatting there, he pulled the side of the canoe over and held out his hand to Mary.

In the moment before she took John's hand, Mary glanced up at a bateau that was passing them at great speed, causing huge waves to wash against their canoe. Mary stared straight into the eyes of her father, who was standing at the bateau's railing.

John Meyers stared at her, too, before his eyes shifted to John, and he shouted above all the noise of the splashing waves and voices in the harbour, "I'll get you for this, John Bleecker! Stop the bateau!" Father was waving his musket in the air.

They were only about twenty feet apart, and Mary knew, by her father's beet-red face and narrowed eyes, that he really meant to harm John.

In a split second John pulled her onto the jetty, and hand in hand they ran along its narrow, wooden surface. Mary heard the sound of a musket going off above them. She knew it was a warning to make them stop, but she had no intention of doing that now.

"He's acting like a maniac!" John shouted. "Musket fire is dangerous this close. He can't be sure of his aim. It could have hit you, Mary."

The small crowd scattered from the jetty while others, eager for excitement, gathered to see what was happening. Just north of the dock, Mary and John ran into the middle of a crowd and peered out between two old men, who seemed to be enjoying the sight.

"One of the government bateaux has come back," the man said.

"Is anyone getting out?" John shouted. He was wedged in the crowd, a few people back from the man.

"Yes. A tall man is climbing onto the jetty and he's waving his musket like a madman. Where are those watchmen? They never seem to be around when we need them!"

"Go, John," Mary said. "He won't hurt me, but I'm afraid for you."

John stared down into her eyes. "Oh, Mary. I can't leave you now."

"You must. Go, John." Mary reached up and kissed him quickly. "I love you," she said and gave him a push.

John turned to go and then looked back. "Meet me at Michael Grass's house."

"I'll try, John. I'll try to get there." Mary's voice was drowned out by the noise and confusion around her. Another musket shot filled the air with a booming sound and the smell of sulphur. She looked back through the crowd for John, but he had gone.

Then Mary turned to see her father coming to the end of the jetty. The crowd was starting to disperse. He was still waving his musket about and yelling that he was going to get John Bleecker.

Not knowing what to do or where to go, Mary stood still in despair. It was all over, she guessed, for now. Father would take her home. But she would find a way to leave. Sometime, somehow, she would do it.

Suddenly she felt a tap on her shoulder and looked into the dark brown eyes of a young Mohawk woman. Before Mary could utter a word, the girl wrapped a large grey blanket with red stripes over Mary's head and shoulders.

"I will help you," she said. "Come." Her soft brown eyes were so kind and sympathetic that Mary trusted her instantly. She raced behind the girl, who moved between the remaining folk with long firm strides.

Then, on the shore not far from the jetty, Mary saw a group of Mohawk women in beige leather skirts and leggings, selling woven baskets. They had not been frightened away by the musket fire. Mary saw her new friend squat down on the ground in the centre of the circle, and she motioned Mary to do the same. Instantly, Mary dropped down beside her into the empty space that suddenly appeared in the circle of women.

She dared not turn as she heard her father speak to one of the women. "Have you seen a red-headed girl and a towheaded man pass by?"

The older woman shook her head and gestured with her hands. "Don't you speak English?" Father asked.

There was a great deal of sputtering, and some words were spoken in Mohawk, but none in English.

Then Father spoke a few words in a language Mary did not know, but the women still did not seem to understand. Mary could then hear her father's disappointed "Hmmphh!"

After a few minutes, Mary turned and saw that the crowd had all gone. Father, too, had disappeared from sight. Then she smiled at the girl beside her. She was sorry that she could not thank the women properly in their own language. She began smiling and trying to act pleased.

"You are welcome to stay with us until it is safe," the young woman said.

Mary gaped at her new friend, who was speaking perfect English. "Thank you for helping me," she gasped out, still breathless from the ordeal. "I am Mary Meyers from several miles west of here, and I have come with my friend to be married in the church. My father does not want us to marry."

The Mohawk women crowded around with sympathetic stares, but continued to talk in their own language.

"My father is dead, but if he were living," the girl said, "my mother would not allow him to boss me like that."

Mary smiled. Who was this girl? Before she could ask, the girl said, "Now, this man, your father, may return. The government bateau still waits." She pointed to the jetty. "I am Margaret and I will help you. Don't be afraid. Where are you going to meet your friend?"

"At the home of Michael Grass," Mary stammered. "I've never been there." In the confusion, she had forgotten to ask John the way.

"Won't your man marry you in the church?"

"It's a long story. I have to find John now."

"I'll take you to the home of Michael Grass, but first . . . " Margaret stepped over and pushed the loose ends of Mary's hair around her face and under her mob cap. Then she wound her hair at the back into a fast pony tail and tucked it under the cap.

"Pull the blanket over your head and come, then," Margaret said. She stepped out smartly onto the road from the dock with Mary beside her.

Mary looked at her new friend more closely. She was dressed in a pale beige leather short coat and knee-length leather skirt with leather leggings. Her shining black hair was combed back from her brow and drawn into two braids that wound around the back of her head. But her skin was not dark. Another thing that Mary noticed with just a little envy was that she did not have a single freckle.

"Is it far?" Mary asked.

"No, not far. King's Town is not very big, not like Montreal. Some people call our town Cataraqui after the river."

"Yes, I know. But we've always called it King's Town. I guess it's because my father fought for the

King in the Revolutionary War. We're really from the States," Mary explained.

"Yes. Me, too. We were Loyalists."

"You were!" Mary was surprised. "That's why we were driven from our farm. Did you lose your farm too?"

"Yes. You could say that. My father ran Johnson Hall."

"Johnson Hall! You must be — "

Margaret smiled. "Yes, I had a white father and a Mohawk mother, who still helps her brother, Joseph Brant, lead the Mohawks. My mother is Molly Brant. But quick, pull your blanket down over your face. Your father is coming back."

Father was heading straight for them. She turned her back just in time while Margaret looked at the approaching figure.

"Have you seen a red-headed girl come by this way?"

Margaret answered in her own tongue, "Ya ne da wa ga non ta na te sat lo."

Thinking she did not understand his question, Father mumbled, "Thank you, Miss," and quickly passed on along the road towards the bateau.

Mary was more worried than ever. He had asked only about her and not John. He didn't seem as irritated as before and she wondered about that. Had he already fought with John, or worse?

"Come now," Margaret said calmly, "in case your father decides to return when he does not find you at the jetty." Margaret started walking so quickly that Mary broke into a run to keep up.

"Are we far now?" Mary asked again.

"Only a few hundred feet."

"That close?" Mary sighed. "If only John got there safely."

"Does your mother like John?"

"I think so."

"Then why does she not tell your father to let you marry him?"

"It wouldn't make any difference. He wouldn't listen."

"That is sad. All the Mohawks listen to my mother, and the men listen to their women. I love a white man, but I do not know if I shall marry him. I want to live like my mother. I do not want my husband to be the sole ruler of the family."

"I guess our customs are different. Most white fathers rule their wives and families."

They turned down a street then, and Margaret pointed to a large two-storey log cabin. It was the finest house on the street. A horse was already harnessed and stamping restlessly in the open shed at the side of the house.

"That's it," Margaret said and turned to go.

"Please, wait. Maybe John isn't there." Mary turned and looked fearfully towards the heavy oak door.

Margaret smiled and waited.

Mary ran up the steps to the house, but before she reached the door, it opened and John came out and embraced her.

"Oh, John," she said. "I was so afraid. I thought you and Father would kill each other!"

"I'll never lay a hand on your father, Mary, and I think his bark is worse than his bite. But he might have stopped our marriage. He could probably do that. I was afraid, too."

"I'm not so sure he wouldn't hurt you, John. He was making threats that there would be one less Bleecker around if he caught you. And you heard the musket fire."

"Musket fire only. I think it was all powder. I doubt he put any balls in his musket the way he was flailing it around that crowd on the dock." Then John smiled as he dropped his arms from around Mary and took her hand. "Come, Mary, we can't keep Michael and his wife waiting any longer."

"Oh, John, just a minute. I want you to meet someone."

Mary looked back to the road, but her new friend had gone.

"She's gone," Mary said. "I do hope we meet again."

Arm in arm, John and Mary walked into the house.

Thirty-Two

J ohn Bleecker steered the canoe gracefully
alongside the Meyers' dock on the Bay of
Quinte. Mary Meyers Bleecker jumped up
onto the wooden floor of the dock and peered
through the lengthening night shadows towards
the back door of the cabin. It had been four days
since she and John were married and they had
returned in record time. The weather had been
especially sunny.

As she and John trudged along the trail, Mary
couldn't help wondering where Father was. Had
he gone on to Montreal as planned, or was he
waiting for them at home?

"It's best this way," John said. "If he's at home,
we might just as well face him and get it over with.
He can't change things for us now."

Mary pulled her arm through John's and
together they walked slowly along the pathway
towards the house. If Father hadn't sent word
home, then they might have to tell Mother, and
Mary was not looking forward to that, for Mother
would surely scold Mary for going against
their church. Perhaps George had broken the

ice by telling Mother. Mary hoped so.

When they reached the back door, Mary hesitated. John took her hand and smiled reassuringly. "It'll be okay, Mary. You just wait and see."

But Mary didn't feel reassured. She knew how stubborn Father could be. As they stood there, Mary could hear the sounds of someone singing to a baby. She opened the back door slowly as a lullaby fell sweetly on her ears.

> "Hush! the waves are rolling in,
> White with foam, white with foam;
> Father paddles through the din:
> But baby sleeps at home."

Mary could hardly believe her eyes. There was Mother rocking baby George with a happy smile on her face while Betty was dressing little Johnnie for bed.

As Mary and John stepped quietly into the room, Mother looked up at them and smiled a calm, sweet smile. Mary and John stood there together hand in hand while Mother carried the little baby into her and Father's bedroom.

Then Johnnie, dressed for bed in his long white woollen nightshirt, turned around and saw his father and Mary. "Daddy," he screamed and came bounding across the room. John scooped him lightly up in the air and bounced him a little while the child laughed with delight.

Johnnie continued to cling to his father even when Mary reached over and said, "Hello, big fellow."

He smiled back and said, "Hello, Maywee."

"Is Father here?" Mary asked her mother when she returned.

Mother smiled happily. "No, your father has not come home yet. You won't have to see him tonight, but some day you will."

Still, Mary felt better to know that it wouldn't be now. When he saw how happy she was and how well she was taking care of Catharine's children, then maybe he would relent. Surely he would.

John was sitting in Father's large chair and bouncing Johnnie up and down on his knee. He wasn't being much help at all right now.

"Did George tell you?" Mary asked.

"After a few days, he admitted the whole story. So I insisted we go over and bring Betty and the children here. I knew it would be hard for her alone with the children."

"I'm sorry to have put you out," John interrupted.

"It was a pleasure," Mother said. She was all smiles now. "They are such delightful babies. I loved every minute of it." She smiled so sweetly at John that Mary knew she did not disapprove of the marriage. But she would not say that outright, for fear of upsetting Father even more. Mary was starting to feel a lot better already.

Then loud footsteps were heard coming up the path to the back door. Mary froze. She could see the tension in Mother's face, too. When she turned around, she was relieved to see George standing there in the doorway.

"Well, did you do it?" George asked.

"We sure did," John said. Then he stood up and

handed Johnnie to Betty. "You go to bed now, Johnnie. Be a good boy."

"Please, Daddy, won't you put me to bed?"

John smiled. "I'll only be a minute, George, and then maybe we can talk." George nodded.

"Well, Mary. I hope all went well for you," George said. Mary couldn't believe it. He walked over and gave her a big hug and a kiss on the cheek.

Then Jacob came bursting in. "You're back! You're back. I have a present for you in the barn."

"Please, no more snakes!"

"Oh no, Mary. This time it's even better," Anna said. "It's — "

"Don't spoil it, Anna. I'll show them."

Mother got up and walked over to the side cupboard. "I don't suppose you two have had a decent meal since you left."

In only a few minutes, Jacob came back with a tiny collie pup wiggling under his arm. Mary looked at the little mass of golden fur and gasped. He had a star on his forehead and four white feet just like Boots. "Wherever . . . " she stammered.

"It's from the Weeses' dog's litter. But Boots is the father. They gave me the one who was most like Boots. He's my wedding present to you." Jacob was beaming.

Mary was smiling now as she cuddled the fat little pup. "You know you're almost like Boots, but he was a scrawny little thing and you — you're so fat. . . . Oh, John, won't he be great for the boys?"

Mother and Betty brought food from the dugout cellar and in less than an hour put together a meal of pork roast, mashed potatoes, creamed carrots, baked beans, fresh home-cooked rolls, and apple pie topped with whipped cream.

When they thought the meal was all over, Anna came with a huge fruit cake with "Mary and John" etched in the maple-butter icing.

All of a sudden the tension of the last couple of weeks just flowed over Mary and tears streamed down her face. John put his arm around her and said, "Mary, whatever is the matter?"

"I'm so happy," she said. "Thank you, Mother, and Anna and Betty, for making such a beautiful meal. And thank you, George, for helping us. And Jacob, for this wonderful pup. . . . I'm going to miss you all so much."

"Well, we aren't far away," Mother said. "We'll be over to visit."

"But can I come here after Father comes back?" Mary asked.

A deep silence hung over the table.

Then Mary said something that she hadn't even told John. "Before she died, Catharine asked me to take care of the children . . . and John. I hope that one day Father will be happy to know that I am taking care of his grandchildren. I'm kind of keeping them in the family. And we all know what a family man Father is. He has always said that he hopes to grow old with all his children around him on the land."

John gave Mary a tender smile as she spoke, and he wiped his eyes as did every member of the family. They were all thinking of Catharine.

Then George broke the tension by rising from the table. "A toast to the newlyweds. May they have many, many years of happiness together."

They clinked their tea cups together, then Mother opened up the sweet apple cider and filled their glasses. Mary knew that they had rum in the basement that Father brought up for special occasions, but Mother never allowed it at the table.

"And may I be worthy of so wonderful a bride," John said seriously.

"Will you stay the night?" Mother asked, breaking into Mary's thoughts. "I hate to see you wake the children to take them home."

"Thank you, but I think it wise that we go on to the post," John said. "Your husband may come at any time, and I feel uncomfortable being under his roof. But I do hope he'll accept our marriage in time."

"I hope so, too."

It was then that Mary heard a loud thump. Were Father and Leonard unloading supplies on the dock? Mary looked around the room and saw how tense everyone was. "I'll go out and check," George said. They all got up from the table then. Mary came and stood beside John. She would throw herself in front of him, she decided, if Father came bursting in. And she would not obey if he ordered her to stay. But he wouldn't do that now that she was married, she decided. Instead, he might tell her to leave and never return. She almost choked at the thought. She had been cut off from her church. She could not stand the thought of being cut off from her family, too. And yet if she must, she must.

George came in smiling. "No one seems to be

out there. And I was thinking. I'd better take Betty and the children over tomorrow, John. It'll be safer than crowding you all into the canoe." Mary smiled. That suited her just fine. She would have another night with John all to herself.

"It's strange," John said as they walked hand in hand down the pathway to the canoe, "I could have sworn that I heard George talking to some-one."

* * * *

Moonlight also shone on two occupants of a bateau waiting just around the corner from the Meyers' landing spot. A tall man stood there, silently watching the canoe gliding gracefully out of his sight. Then with a deep sigh, he said to his son, "Leonard, we'd best be getting on home now. I told George we would be coming in right after they left."

Leonard started to row the back oars while Father took the front ones. "What's done is done, and I wish them well now. But there's no sense in forgiving them too soon. I want John Bleecker to know I am a force to be reckoned with if he doesn't treat our Mary well."

Leonard just shook his head and kept on rowing.

Historical Note

John W. Meyers (Hans Waltermyer) has been identified by a few previous sources as German rather than Dutch. *The Dictionary of Canadian Biography*, Volume 6. Toronto: University of Toronto Press, 1966, says "probably" German. *The Historical Atlas of Counties of Hastings and Prince Edward*, Toronto: H. Balden & Co., 1878, says "Capt. Myers was of Dutch descent . . . " His four sons are named and his daughters are mentioned. Many of these old atlases were financed by the families, who paid to have their family mentioned in the atlas. Whether or not John W. Meyers' grandchildren paid to have their names in the atlas, it is apparent that the wish of the family was to be known as Dutch, for most of his grandchildren were alive at the printing of this atlas. In fact, Mary died only ten years before. Since this is a family story, I chose to follow their wishes.

The events in this novel are true, although I have changed the timing slightly in order to bring some episodes closer together. All the main dates in Loyalist history, such as the depiction of the Hungry Year, are accurate, but some of the marriages, deaths, and births took place at different times. In older records, there is some conflict anyway about some of these dates;

handwritten numbers are not always easy to read and sometimes historians differ by a few years. John and Catharine, for instance, were married on October 7, 1788, two years later than in my novel, and Catharine died in 1791, three, rather than two years, after that. This slight change in timing does affect one historical event. The Reverend John Langhorn, the Rector of Bath, did perform John and Catharine's wedding ceremony, but he did not come to Ernesttown until October 1787 — a year later than Catharine's wedding in my novel. This also affected the birthdates of their two children. John and Mary's wedding took place even later — a year after the formation of Upper Canada, and Tobias died in the 1790s, not in 1787, although the circumstances of his death are historically accurate.

John Bleecker, the son of Catharine and John, was the first white child to be born at Carrying Place, and if they had not left home the night of his birth, he would have been the first white child to be born at the present site of Trenton, Ontario.

Mary and John Bleecker had five children: Catharine, Tobias (my ancestor), Gilbert, Henry, and Jane. Their first children were named for Mary's sister Catharine and her brother Tobias, who both died young. Some mention of their children's births can be found in the records of the Reverend Robert McDowall, the first Presbyterian missionary in the Bay of Quinte, who was sent by the Dutch Reformed Church in Albany in 1790. Business prospered at Bleecker's Castle and their fort eventually became an inn and ferry. Mary became an astute business woman in helping her husband run their successful endeavours. There was never another incident like the attack depicted in my story, the facts of which came from a number of old sources. John lived and traded peacefully with the Mississaugas and was the unofficial Indian agent in that area.

George W. Meyers acquired his own farm beside his father's in Sydney Township and married Alida Van Alstine. They had seven children. They named their first son for Alida's father, and their second son for Tobias. Jacob also named one of his children Tobias.

Lucy became a prominent businesswoman. After her husband died in 1808, she kept his businesses going with the help of her sons and daughters. Lucy was instrumental in bringing steamships to the area. She believed better boats could be built and brought in men who could help her sons design one. The Frontenac, built in her own shipyard, became the first steamship on the Great Lakes. The house-inn that her husband built for her was the first frame house in Upper Canada.

Mary's father, Captain John W. Meyers, became the first moderator of Sydney Township in 1790. He purchased a mill site, near the mouth of the Moira River, ten miles to the east of his farm in Sydney township. By 1790 he had built a mill and dam there, and a small community, known as Meyers' Creek, grew around it. In 1816 the town's name was changed to Belleville.

Within ten years of settling in Canada, Meyers was so prosperous that he was able to build one of the first two brick houses in Upper Canada for his family. Situated a half-mile from the mill, it was a large two-storey Georgian structure on a hill overlooking the Moira River. He called it Meyers' Castle and welcomed all who visited — from the Reverend John Strachan, Bishop of the Church of England, to farmers who came from long distances away to have their grain ground into flour or feed at Meyers' Mill. The house was demolished in 1876.

Polly died five years before her husband, and by the time of his death, in 1821, John W. Meyers owned more than three thousand acres of land and had an estate worth more than twelve thousand pounds. He left all his goods to his grand-children — "to males and females share and share alike," as he wrote in his will.

Mary's father was also one of the founding elders of St. Thomas Anglican Church at 201 Church Street in Belleville. It is one of the oldest churches in Ontario, and a plaque, dedicated to his memory, adorns its sanctuary. But the original building of brick and wood, built in 1818, has been completely replaced.

Meyers' Creek still trickles down to the west of the site of the burial ground now called Whites' Cemetery on the highway between Belleville and Trenton. There the Meyers family are buried, though the first small wooden markers have rotted into the land. Mary did not die until 1868, and her granite tombstone still stands beside the grave of her husband, John Row, in the lower southwest corner of the graveyard. John Bleecker died of pneumonia at forty-five years of age in 1807.

On July 21, 1990, the descendants of John W. Meyers, led by Captain Christopher Almey and Jane Bennett Goddard, U.E., author of the epic history *Hans Waltimeyer*, dedicated a monument to the memory of John W. Meyers, his wife and children, his Loyalist Mohawk Allies, and his released black slaves. (John W. Meyers freed his slaves long before he was legally required to do so.) Ontario Lt.-Governor Lincoln Alexander unveiled this commemorative stone honouring the grave of John W. Meyers. Captain Almey, a sixth-generation descendant of Meyers, summed up the thoughts of many in the following words: "In addition to founding Belleville and being instrumental in founding Sidney Township, Meyers helped make the area a multicultural one by freeing his slaves. We are paying tribute to a great Canadian. He was a churchman, a judge, and a humanitarian. He has contributed to what makes Ontario important — its small towns with their record for service, decency, and integrity."

This dedication testifies to the fact that Meyers lived up to his words to his family: "It's building a new nation that's the real challenge. We're here and here we'll stay, God willing. We're building for the future now — in a land we can be proud to call our home." Meyers's living legacy are his descendants, who helped to build Upper Canada and who are still proud to call this country home.